Twists of Fate

A tense Castle Ridge drama set in the 1970s and 80s

Ann Thorsson

Broad Cove Books

First edition [2025]

Print: ISBN 978-9935-25-917-2

Digital: ISBN 978-9935-25-920-2

NOTE: This book was written with the passion and pen of a genuine author. Written in British English with Derbyshire colloquialisms

NOT AI GENERATED!

Dedications

INSPIRATION

We never know when we will be seized by inspiration.
It's all around us if we care to look, or listen, or smell.
To give ourselves time to process a moment.
To watch the sky, to listen to birdsong.
To observe the world as it passes by.
The laughter of a child, the barking of a dog, the howling of the wind.
Vital details to enrich a painting, or a poem, or a paragraph in a novel.
Maybe you'll be inspired to try something new.
Who or what will inspire you today?

To Russ C – from little ideas, great novels grow.
Thanks for giving me the inspiration for
Twists of Fate!

To Pam A – from little novels, great authors grow.
Thanks for feeling inspired to study and write!
I wish you luck in both!

Meet the Author

Image: Gabriel Rutenberg Photography, Iceland

Originally from Chesterfield, England, Ann Thorsson moved to Iceland in 2000. She now lives on a farm by the sea, nestled beneath the iconic Snæfellsjökull (Snaefells-glacier), in the beautiful West Peninsula of Iceland. She shares this idyll with her Icelandic husband, their two sons, and two crazy Labra-Collies. Ann is also an artist, café owner, and forestry farmer. (See website and social media for more info).

For more information about Ann Thorsson:

@ann.thorsson.author

Facebook:

https://www.facebook.com/ann.thorsson.author/

Instagram:

https://www.instagram.com/ann.thorsson.author/

GO TO AUTHOR WEBSITE

Scan the QR code:

Other books by Ann Thorsson

Downhill: A gritty family drama set in the 1980s, in the fictional mining town of Castle Ridge, Northern England. This is no ordinary boy-meets-girl Romeo and Juliet! (pub. 2019; UK Book Publishing). Can be read as the prequel to *Dark Shadows*.

"Downhill is endearing and scary, sweet and disturbing, all at the same time.

[...]we get to love the characters and wish their lives wouldn't take certain directions. To me, only a well written and powerful book can do that."

Matt Ferraz, Author. (Five-star review)

Dark Dreams: How long can Maggie run and hide before the truth catches up with her?

A dark and disturbing tale of secrets and lies, with a supernatural twist. (pub. 2020; UK Book Publishing)

"From the beautifully crafted sentences to the simple but powerful ingredients, Thorsson turns the words into a film playing in your mind. She knows how to make the characters jump off the page!"

Lisa G Shannen, Freelance Writer and Author.

Dark Shadows: Will Elaine ever be able to lay the Castle Ridge ghosts to rest? Or will she always be followed by her dark shadows? The heart-rending and dramatic sequel to *Downhill.* (pub. 2022; UK Book Publishing)

"The author's 3rd book in her own 'spooky' style, this is a good drama that I enjoyed and had me questioning the whole way through."

Mark Fearn, "Book Mark," online reviewer and book blogger. (Five-star review)

PURCHASE LINKS:

Scan the QR code:

What is Fate?

"And fate? No one alive has ever escaped it, neither brave man nor coward,
I tell you – it's born with us the day that we are born."
(Hektor, in Homer's *The Iliad*)

The Seeds Are Sown: 1977–1979

1: Prawn Cocktail – 1977

The young waiter handed out the menu cards to the diners sitting around the table.

'Happy Mother's Day, Mrs Watkins. I hope that you have a lovely evening.'

'Thanks, Chris.' She smiled at the young lad. 'It's also my birthday, so Dennis says that I can have anything I want tonight. The Mother's Day Special menu looks fantastic, by the way – best prawn cocktail this side of the Peak!'

'Aye, I wish I had 50p for every time I've heard that – I'd be a rich young man by now,' he chuckled, then winked at her. 'Anyroad, I'll leave you folks to have a look at the menu, and pop back in a jiffy.'

Irene Watkins beamed. She felt lovely this evening. Pampered. Dennis had booked a table for the family, so she and their three boys could have a meal together without her having to do the cooking and washing up on her birthday. Plus the added bonus of it being Mother's Day – extra chocolates and flowers, as well as a bottle of her favourite Chanel No5 perfume! Yes, she felt pampered.

Murmurs of agreement from the family concurred that they were all going to have the prawn cocktail as a starter, and while the men were going to have the Chef's Special of a medium rare steak, Irene was going to have the exotic Chicken Kiev from the Mother's Day special. She noticed that Black Forest Gateau was also on the menu, but would save ordering dessert for later. Didn't want to look too greedy!

After Chris had taken their food order, he returned a short while later with a bottle of House Red and House White. And as an extra surprise, he brought Irene a complimentary bottle of chilled, sparkling Asti Spumante. The chef had insisted on sending something as bubbly as the lady herself. But then again, the chef was her cousin, and he could more than afford this fizzy gesture.

The Castle Ridge Sports Bar and Grill had been the centre of the community for many years – a place where professionals, miners, factory workers, and sports-people could mingle. Perched proudly on the same ridge as the historic Castle Ridge Castle, it was *the* place for all occasions. The function room had seen its fair share of tears, laughter, and joy, whether people were celebrating the living or the dead: Christenings, funerals, significant birthdays, engagements, or weddings. Sports teams had held many trophies aloft at the end of a successful season, and companies had honoured their staff for a job well done.

The restaurant and grill was the best in the area for a generously laden prawn cocktail, or a juicy gammon steak with pineapple, and the general bar stocked an excellent selection of well-kept beers. For those who preferred to keep things a little more exclusive, there was a private *Members Only Lounge*, for which access was gained through an annual paid subscription. And on Friday nights, there was the *Ridge Nightclub* for those who wanted to strut their stuff on the dance-floor. Such was its reputation (for good or for bad), the nightclub often had coachloads of visitors from outside the area – usually Hen or Stag Night crowds. Not only that, the Friday disco was locally renowned as "Grab-a-Granny" night – when tigers prowled the dancefloor for unsuspecting younger prey. The weekend entertainment programme usually played host to local bands, comedians, and other artists, with the occasional "big name" to pull in the crowds.

It was fair to say that most of Castle Ridge's populace had been to the club at some point in their lives.

As the owner of a reputable damp-proofing, plastering, and building company, Dennis Watkins had been encouraged to join their *Members Only* club. It was a place to keep up with local business gossip, and to scratch each other's backs with reciprocal trade (as did being a member of the local Rotary Club). Their significant others (mostly dutiful wives) were an equally important part of the fraternity, knowing when to offer support, sympathy, or a dinner party. And they all knew how to dress (or undress, depending on who you spoke to), for the occasion.

With her role as private secretary to one of the higher-ranking officials at the local NCB Area Headquarters based at Castle Ridge Colliery, Irene had also earned her place within this elite clique of members. Having started at the offices as a general typist in the typing pool, she had been to night school to learn shorthand, enabling a promotion to shorthand-typist, then ultimately as a private secretary. An achievement she was rightly proud of.

There had been a small office scandal a few years ago when she worked as a PA to one of the other officers, but her name had been cleared of any wrongdoing, and the incident had mercifully been forgotten, much to her relief.

Being part of this money circle meant the upkeep of a certain lifestyle. The Watkinses lived in an imposing, stone-built detached house located near the bottom of the steep and winding Ridge Lane, nestling below the historic ramparts of the castle. They were a four-vehicle family, having a company van and a reasonably new Rover 3500. The two oldest lads each had a car of their own, given to them as an eighteenth birthday gift from their mother.

Of their three boys, the eldest, Kenny, had recently joined his father in the damp-proofing business, Barry, or Baz as he was known to everyone, had a good job at the local colliery, and their youngest, Mick, was in his first year of sixth form at Castle Ridge Comprehensive School.

One quirk that the boys shared was their significant birthday dates, with characters to match. As a New Year's Day baby, Kenny was always an optimist and forward-looking. True to his Bonfire Night birthday, Barry had a quick and fiery temper, and Mick was the April Fool.

Mick's arrival had come as a bit of a surprise to his parents – at four years younger than Baz, they had already cleared out all the baby stuff, only to find that they needed to start again due to this unplanned pregnancy. Needless to say, Mick had been an absolute pariah for his mother's attention, sucking up every last drop of her time and energy. Yet she didn't seem to mind having unwittingly created the spoiled brat that he had become, much to the chagrin of his older brothers and father.

As a convivial way to round off their meal, Dennis ordered four Irish coffees; one for him, one for Irene, and one each for Kenny and Baz. He could see that Mick was about to start simpering for having been left out, and swiftly reminded him that he was still only sixteen, and that he'd already been sneakily permitted two glasses of wine throughout the evening. Although Dennis knew that most kids of Mick's age were already drinking underage in the local pubs, he still refused to let him have too much to drink while out as a family. And especially not on Irene's special day.

Starting to feel bored, Mick surreptitiously checked his watch, then lightly tapped it while he thought of a plausible excuse to leave. After all, he didn't want to offend his beloved mother. He knew better than to upset the one who doted on him.

'I'm gonna head off, if that's okay with you, Mam? I've got some stuff that I need to prepare for school tomorrow – got a test in Biology, and just wanna be sure that I've read the chapter.' He gave his mother one of his best smiles.

Warm, replete, and heady from the pleasant evening, Irene just smiled and nodded. 'Be sure to go straight home, love. It's dark on the lane. Would you like some money for a taxi?' She reached for her handbag.

Her youngest son came and gave her a hug and a kiss. 'Don't worry, I know my way home. I'll be fine. Thanks for a lovely evening, Mam.'

Mick gave his father and brothers a courteous nod of thanks before leaving. He was quite sure that his parents would stay for the after-dinner dance, and his brothers would head for the bar, giving him a few hours to himself.

As he walked out of the restaurant, he chided himself for not having taken the money for a taxi; a missed chance to pocket some cash. Damn!

He headed towards the shadows to find better, more profitable opportunities – he certainly wouldn't be wasting his valuable time on useless studying!

2: Light Fingers

Irene dumped her handbag and bag of shopping onto the kitchen table while she wriggled out of her thick sweater. Surely at forty-two, she was too young to be starting with hot flushes? That said, it had been an embarrassing afternoon.

Maybe she was still feeling the heat from standing at the checkout in Fine-Fare with not enough money in her purse? Luckily, there had been no one else behind her in the queue while she'd faffed about making excuses. Thank goodness she'd got her cheque book with her so that she could pay for the shopping! She sighed. It was bad enough that the checkout girl knew about her financial whoopsie, even if none of the other staff or customers had witnessed it.

But where had the five-pound note gone? She was 99% sure that there should have been enough cash in her purse. Maybe she was also starting to reach that age of forgetfulness, as well as hot flushes!

She checked the amount of water in the kettle before flicking the switch to make herself a restorative cup of tea. Her mind began to wander as she unpacked the shopping and put it away. This hadn't been the first time that something valuable had gone missing from the house. Her elegant Cartier dress watch had recently vanished, as had a pair of Dennis's gold cufflinks. Surely none of the boys would steal from them? They had no reason to. The company was doing well, and they all had a reasonable income from their respective jobs. Even Mick had a little after-school job helping out at the local butcher's, as well as a generous pocket-money allowance. Could one of the boys' friends have lifted these items from them? Or were they just simply misplaced, not put away properly after an intoxicated late-night out?

The kettle clicked off, puthering a cloud of vapour from its spout as she poured boiling water over the teabag in her china mug. Irene mused over some gossip that she'd heard – one of their neighbours had recently had their garage broken into and had a few small but valuable items stolen, and the florist in Castle Ridge town centre had had the back window jemmied open and their petty-cash tin stolen. Perhaps some light-fingered folk were on the prowl?

Maybe it was time to put up some security lighting – some of those PIR things that came on automatically? She would speak to Dennis when he came home. One should feel safe in one's home!

Irene jumped with a start, almost spilling her tea, when she heard the front door clatter open and slam closed. Scuffling sounds came from the hallway. She twisted her body position, enabling her to see through the doorway into the hall.

'Only me, Mam!'

She raised her eyebrows towards Mick, indicating that she'd observed his schoolbag-and-shoes error. He rolled his eyes in acknowledgement and corrected his "health and safety" misdemeanour. Yes, it was dangerous to dump stuff in the middle of the floor – some poor unsuspecting person could fall over it and break their neck. He'd heard the spiel a thousand times, and a thousand times he'd lazily forgotten.

Mick came into the kitchen and immediately ripped open the pack of newly purchased Jaffa Cakes. For all his otherwise uncaring faults, he took note of his mother's rosy cheeks. His brow furrowed.

'Are you okay, Mam? You look a bit flushed.'

She sighed in response, then proceeded to tell Mick all about her embarrassing moment in Fine-Fare. Oh, how she was grateful that none of Mick's shelf-stacker school friends had witnessed it! He grimaced, before clearing his throat...

'Ah, erm, that would be me... Soz, Mam. I took the money this morning – my dinner money for the week, and the rest as pocket money. I meant to leave you a note, but had to run for the bus. I'm sorry...' He pouted his bottom lip, knowing full well that she couldn't be mad with him.

'Mick! What have I told you about going in my handbag, let alone my purse! Five pounds is a lot of money to take without asking.'

'I know! I know! I'm sorry. But like I said, I was in a hurry, and you were upstairs painting your face. You forgot to leave some money for me on the table last night, presumably because you came home late from your birthday meal. So I just dipped in there...'

With the matter resolved as being her fault, Irene then shared her newly discovered knowledge about the recent local break-ins. Mick stuffed a whole Jaffa Cake into his mouth while he listened, before exploding into a greedy, spluttering mess of crumbs.

'Funny you should say that. One of my schoolmates said that his house had been broken into while they were away over the half-term break. The thief had rummaged through all their drawers and found their stash of rainy-day money. The thief had also left the mum's vibrator on top of the TV!' He burst out laughing. 'Can you imagine coming home to find that...'

Irene blanched at the thought, all flustered, before joining Mick with a fit of laughter. She made a mental note to herself to hide anything of the sort, just in case they became the unwitting victims of a burglary!

'Anyway, I'm going to have a word wi'ya dad. I think it's high time we increased the security around this place. Install some PIR lighting outside, and such like. Maybe even get a burglar alarm fitted. You never know who's prowling about these days. That's the problem with having a house that backs onto open fields. It leaves you vulnerable.'

Mick grabbed yet another Jaffa Cake, then got up and wandered to the fridge to get a drink, his interest in the burglary conversation having already waned.

'Ugh, didn't you get any fresh orange juice? You know I hate this Robinson's dilute crap.' He rummaged around in the fridge just to make a point.

'Sorry, love. That's the one thing that I forgot. Anyway, how did your Biology test go today?'

'My Biology test? What Biology test? Ohhh, *THAT* test, the one I was studying for. Some of the questions were a bit tricky, but I gave it my best shot,' he lied. 'Anyway, I might quit school at Easter...'

Irene looked at Mick, her mouth open, but lost for words.

'Quit? Why? I thought you liked school?'

'I can't see the point, to be honest. The owner of the butcher's shop is willing to give me more hours and train me in butchery. I'd rather have the money and learn a decent trade.'

'Hmmph, and there I thought we had at least one academic brain in the family... But, well, if that's what you want to do. At least it's better than being a shelf-stacker.' Irene rolled her eyes.

'My God, you can be such a snob at times, Mam,' he laughed. 'Anyway, think of the benefits. You'll get all the best cuts of meat.'

They both looked up when they heard the engine noise of a van reversing onto the driveway.

'Sounds like your dad and Kenny are home. Crikey, is that the time? I'd better get on with dinner!'

'And what is for dinner?' Mick asked.

'Shit wi'sugar on!' she teased.

Now it was Mick's turn to roll his eyes and give a cheeky grin.

'Ugh! We had that yesterday – I hate having warmed-up leftovers. Can't we have summat else?' he chuckled.

'Oh, all right then. How does breaded cod with mashed potatoes and garden peas sound?'

'Fish?' Mick pretended to gag. 'I think I prefer the first option!'

3: Grab-a-Granny!

It was the end of a long, hard-working week, and as was customary for Friday night revellers, the evening began with a pub-crawl around Castle Ridge's numerous hostelries, before winding up at the Sports Bar.

Already half drunk, Kenny, Baz, and their close circle of bachelor mates staggered into the nightclub. They were ready for some extended drinking hours, maybe a dance or two, and a grope and a kiss if they could find any willing maidens.

There was not a spare inch of space on the dancefloor when the lads arrived, as nightclub guests boogied along to ABBA's *Mamma Mia*. It mattered not one jot whether they sang the correct lyrics; everyone was there to have a good time. The younger girls were pretending to be Agnetha and Anni-Frid, singing back-to-back into imaginary microphones, while the youths bopped around the best they could.

The legendary cougars of Castle Ridge were already on the prowl, eyeing up their prey, trying to find themselves a younger stud for the night. Who looked drunk enough and gullible enough to buy them their next drink? Or maybe walk them home?

ABBA eased into the Bee Gees, keeping the floor alive with *You Should Be Dancin'*. The group of male friends looked for a viable spot at the bar to grab the barmaid's attention and get in a round of beers. As well as a packed dancefloor, there was not an empty seat to be had; it was standing room only. There appeared to be at least two Hen Night crowds of lively ladies, plus a company outing, which would account for the slew of coaches out in the car park.

The DJ announced that Elton John and Kiki Dee were next, so everyone had to grab a partner and sing along with *Don't Go Breakin' My Heart*. Then he would do his *Rock 30* session, giving headbangers the chance to listen to half an hour of quality rock music, while the disco queens rested and refilled their glasses. The dance crowd complied with the DJ's wishes, singing along as loudly and tunelessly as possible, killing all hope of a reasonable conversation. It had reached that point in the evening when people just shouted into each other's ears or gave up and spoke in some kind of drunken sign language.

Kenny spotted a couple of Castle Ridge's most notorious older ladies starting to work their way up the bar, clearly asking the younger, unsuspecting lads to buy them a drink. As if by some coordinated exodus, the wisest ones left the bar area to go for a piss or go to the cigarette machine in the foyer, while others turned their backs and huddled in close so that the cougars couldn't get in. He nudged his brother.

'Time for a piss and a smoke, Bazza. Lilo-Lil and Blossom are on the prowl. Quick, shift yer arse...'

Barry didn't need telling twice. He had once been cornered by these two and still bore the mental scars. He laughed and shuddered at the memory.

'On my way, bruv. Let's go...'

After grabbing a smoke and a fresh pint from the lower bar area, the brothers noticed that some of the disco crowd had moved out for a while. This meant that the DJ was now doing his *Rock-30* session. Time for them to head back upstairs and listen to some proper music and not that disco shite!

While AC/DC growled through *Dirty Deeds*, Kenny and Baz found a safe place to nod their heads along to the music without spilling their beer. The rest of their group was on the dancefloor, imitating Angus Young. Barry crushed out his cigarette, then nudged his brother to get his attention.

'Have you seen those two birds over there?' he shouted into Kenny's ear.

Kenny tried to follow the direction in which his brother was nodding, towards the upper seating area.

'Don't make it obvious that you're looking, you twat! Those two lasses over there.'

'Do you mean the one with the hair?'

Baz rolled his eyes. 'Yes, the one with the hair. And the other one – the one who looks like Purdey.'

'Who's Purdey?'

Kenny's innocence with the opposite sex was beginning to frustrate Barry – there was no wonder he'd made it to twenty-two without having a steady girlfriend. Motorsport and football were his only loves.

'Fuck me, Ken, don't you ever watch normal telly! Purdey from the New Avengers. You know, Joanna Lumley, the actress.'

The penny suddenly dropped with Kenny.

'Ah, now I see which two girls you mean. The one with the Charlie's Angels hair – the blonde one, and the other one. Yeah, with the Purdey hair, if that's what it's called. What about them?'

'They're looking at us. Purdey's waving at me! Fuck me, I think we've cracked it tonight, Kenny. The lass with the Farrah Fawcett hair is looking right at you. Wave back...'

Kenny took a swig of his beer, then grinned shyly, giving a thumbs-up towards the two girls. The girls giggled at each other, before returning the thumbs-up to Kenny and Baz. The Friday night ice had been broken.

'They're waving for us to go over to them, Baz. What should we do?'

Baz looked at his older brother in disbelief.

'Did you seriously just ask me that, you divvy! We go over to them. And if they seem like nice lasses, we buy them a drink and walk them home later.'

The DJ announced the next record as the opening riffs to *The Boys Are Back in Town* kicked in.

'Ready?'

'Yep. Ready...'

4: Double Date

For years, Claire had listened to numerous stories and gossip from her Uncle Ted about the larger-than-life happenings connected to the Sports Bar and Friday nightclub. Both she and her best friend, Sally-Ann, had tried to get in on a few occasions, piling on make-up and perfume to make themselves appear older. But there was no getting past the doorman, for the doorman was none other than Claire's Uncle Ted. He'd made the girls wait until they were of legal age before letting them into the hallowed ground of Castle Ridge's Sports Bar and Grill. And finally, here they were, at the Friday night disco in a belated coming-of-age celebration!

As Friday night novices, the previous two weekends had ended in disaster. Having consumed too much beer too early in the evening meant that they never made it to the nightclub. The girls had vowed not to make the same mistake tonight. Instead, they had sensibly opted to have just one drink in the pub to get into the spirit of things, before heading up to the nightclub with the other patrons.

Oh, to now have the sacred General Membership card!

The Sports Bar was already busy when the girls arrived. The smell of gammon and pineapple lingered in the air from the now-closed restaurant area, and the noise levels were on the rise, fuelled by people talking extra loudly over the clatter of the slot machines and glasses. Shrieks of raucous laughter could be heard from the hen-party crowds as they geared up to give the brides-to-be a good send-off before the big day. Disco music punctuated the cacophony every time someone opened the door to the upper-floor dance area.

The girls stood for a moment, soaking up the atmosphere, allowing the pulse of the music to envelop them. Each beat drummed a heightened sense of excitement and anticipation into their bellies. Claire rolled on a slick of lip gloss, while Sally-Ann teased her fingers through her blonde tresses, fluffing out the curls. She also added a slick of her favourite cherry-flavoured lip gloss.

Claire linked her arm through her best friend's.

'Okay, then – here goes!'

'Wait! I'm nervous. Do I look okay?' Sally-Ann shook her hair and pouted, then did a twirl, showing off her slender figure in the body-hugging jumpsuit. Her legs went on forever, accentuated by the high-heeled wedges.

Claire laughed. 'If you don't crack it tonight, Sal, I'll eat me handbag!'

The door to the disco area opened, allowing the strains of Leo Sayer to escape momentarily. Claire began to sing along with the song and led her friend in the direction of the disco.

'"You make me feel like dancin', gonna dance the night away..."'

Sally-Ann joined in and began jiggling around to the song.

'Ooh, I love Leo Sayer and his cute curls! Okay, I'm ready!' she declared.

Now armed with half a pint of lager and lime each, the two best friends found a couple of empty seats by the edge of the dancefloor, first carefully checking that they were not already taken before they sat down. Claire's Uncle Ted had warned them that fights often broke out over the smallest of things, usually fuelled by alcohol and hormones, so they chose to err on the side of caution for their first night.

One by one, all their favourite songs came on, tempting them to join the energetic throng of dancers: *Disco Inferno, Mamma Mia, Play That Funky Music, Dancing Queen*. The DJ certainly knew how to work the crowd and keep them on their feet, regardless of whether it was disco, duets, or rock anthems. Next up was a sing-along to Elton John and Kiki Dee.

Sally-Ann winced as her shoes began to rub on her heels and make the soles of her feet ache.

'I need to take a break – shall we sit down for a while?'

Claire nodded her agreement. 'Deffo. My feet are killing me! Let's grab a fresh drink first, though. I'm dying of thirst.'

Just as the girls were preparing to take their dance break, the DJ announced that the next half an hour would be dedicated to the rockers of Castle Ridge, causing an en masse exodus of the disco fans. Claire and Sally-Ann joined the exodus for a much-needed breather and to find some cooler air.Once they had replenished their glasses in the lower bar area, the girls returned to the upper floor to watch the headbangers and scout for male talent. Having lost their previous spot by the edge of the dancefloor to other patrons, they found a new place to sit on the elevated seating area. But at least this area was a little cooler, rather than being near the swampy, sweaty heat of the testosterone-laden headbangers. Plus, it gave them a better overview of the club.

'This is the best night ever,' laughed Claire. 'I'm so glad we finally got our membership.'

'Me, too. It's great, isn't it! Have you seen any familiar faces?' asked Sally-Ann.

'Nah. Just a few lasses from the factory.' Claire scanned the crowd. 'Most of the blokes in here seem a lot older than us. There are a couple of cute guys over there, though.' She nodded in the direction of Kenny and Baz near the bar. Her hair flopped over her eyes, so she swept it back into place with a practised hand.

'Do you mean the one with the long, curly hair? The one that looks like that guitarist in Queen – Brian whatshisname?'

'It's May. Brian May. I think you've got a thing for curly-haired guys! Anyway, yes, him. And the other one that's with him. I prefer him.'

'I wonder if his curls are natural, or permed!' laughed Sally-Ann. 'I can't imagine a bloke sitting in a hairdresser's with a head full of perming rods!'

Claire joined in with her friend's laughter, trying to envisage tough-looking guys in the local Silver Scissors hairdressing salon.

'You'll have to ask him,' she teased. 'Let's wave to them. See what happens...'

Claire gave the two guys a coy wave and a smile. Having grabbed their attention, Sally-Ann also gave them a little wave. She fluffed her hair and tossed it around. The girls nudged each other, then grinned at the boys, gesturing for them to come over. The guys nudged each other, then grinned at the girls, giving them a thumbs-up.

Feeling buoyed by the next song on the turntable, the two lads, Kenny and Baz, headed in the direction of Claire and Sally-Ann.

Thin Lizzy had hit the nail on the head – the boys were most definitely back in town!

After introducing themselves, the two brothers and the two best friends seamlessly formed an attraction: Kenny with Sally-Ann, and Baz with Claire. Fuelled by hormones, adrenaline, and a few more beers, the rest of the evening flew by in *getting-to-know-you* conversations, punctuated with laughter; in particular, the amount of hair shared between Kenny and Sally-Ann. They also discovered that Kenny's long curls were natural, not permed. Baz's luscious shoulder-length waves were also natural, whereas Sally-Ann and Claire were slaves to hairspray, Carmen rollers, and curling tongs for their hairstyles.

Kenny was particularly happy to learn that, despite her glamorous look, his new girlfriend was a motorsport fan like himself, particularly Formula One; she was a big fan of James Hunt. It was rare to find a modern lass that was into cars, but her father and older brothers were mechanics and steel fabricators, who also raced banger-cars at High Edge Raceway, near Buxton. Being a petrol-head was obviously in her genes. The age gap of four years – he being twenty-two and she newly eighteen – didn't seem to bother him either. If she liked cars and understood the workings of an engine, that was good enough for him.

Claire and Barry also discovered they had much in common, particularly the love of tough cop shows like *The Sweeney!*, and horror films – the scarier the better. She'd managed to get in at the cinema, slightly underage, to see the new *Sweeney!* film in January, and had just watched *The Exorcist* on video. Superb! And yes, she was a fan of *The New Avengers*, hence the Purdey hairstyle. The only difference they could find was that he was part of a large family, whereas Claire was an only child, and her mum was a divorcee with no intentions of *ever* remarrying.

Before they knew it, the DJ was putting the last song of the evening onto the turntable – the ubiquitous smoochy track which usually got couples paired up for the walk or taxi ride home.

The newly-matched foursome appropriately joined the throng for the last dance.

'Can we walk you two ladies home?' asked Baz, as he snuggled into Claire's neck. His hands slipped down towards her backside, prompting her to push them back up to her waist with a giggle.

'Hey, I'm not that easy, you cheeky bugger! Walk us home? It's a long way – we live down on the estate. And it's bloody cold. We usually just get a taxi if we've missed the last bus, with that Ripper guy still being on the loose.'

Baz looked at Claire, wide-eyed.

'The estate? Yep, that's quite a walk. You're right, we should just put you ladies into a taxi, then. Keep you safe.'

'So where do you guys live?' she asked.

'We live just down t'road, at the bottom end of Ridge Lane, near the old swimming baths.'

'Ridge Lane! You posh gits, they're all big houses!' Claire pictured her mum's modest Council house and suddenly felt a little lowly in the arms of her new boyfriend. Though she lived in a well-maintained brick semi with neat gardens on one of the better streets, it still carried the stigma of being a Council house, at least by some of Castle Ridge's more well-off residents. It wouldn't be the first time that she'd seen people look down their noses or make her feel inferior once she'd given her address. Yet you couldn't wish for a better community of folk.

'Posh? Nah, we're not that posh,' defended Baz. 'Just a hard-working family. What we've got is all bought and paid for wi'honest money, as me dad always says.'

The lights automatically came on as the last song ended, blinding all the couples on the dancefloor. It signalled that the evening was over and it was time to go home.

Embarrassed that their smoochy kissing was suddenly lit up, Kenny and Sally-Ann looked around and laughed, trying to hide their newfound passion behind copious amounts of hair.

Claire and Baz joined them in their laughter, teasing them about their kissy moment. Feeling inspired, Baz pulled Claire towards him for a kiss.

'Shit! No, not here! Not with the lights on...' squeaked Claire.

Baz looked a little crestfallen.

'My Uncle Ted is the doorman here,' she clarified with a laugh. 'I'm pretty sure that if he catches me kissing someone, he'll be straight on the phone to me mam! Wait 'til we get outside. There'll be plenty of time for a snog while we wait for the taxi!'

'Your Uncle Ted's the doorman? Wow, that man's a legend! But not to be messed with. Okay, I can wait for that kiss!' he laughed.

5: The Mystery of the Vanishing Old Spice

'Mmmm, this is bloody good bacon, Mam! Can I have a couple more rashers?' Kenny licked his lips, then lifted his plate towards his mother so that she could serve him some more.

Irene generously set three extra rashers onto Kenny's plate. 'Would you like an egg as well? There are plenty.'

'Oh, go on then. And maybe another sausage...' Kenny set the replenished plate before him, before covering everything in a dollop of HP sauce.

'I get the bacon straight from the local farm shop rather than the butcher's where Mick helps out. Extra-thick cut, that's what I always ask for. You should see the farmer's fingers, they're as fat as his sausages,' she laughed, wiggling her slender secretarial fingers.

The Saturday morning bacon-brunch had been a staple family gathering in the Watkins household as soon as the lads had become old enough to hold a sausage. Maybe they couldn't always get together for a Sunday roast, but the mixed-grill Saturday brunch was never missed. It was the one meal where they could catch up with the week's happenings and spend some quality time together before heading off for their weekend leisure plans.

'I saw that Town won their game the other night against Chester. Are you going to Saltergate to watch them this afternoon, Ken?' asked Dennis.

Kenny shook his head.

'Nah, they're playing away at Bury today. Anyway, I'm doing some other stuff later. By the way, can we borrow the Rover tomorrow, Dad? Baz and I fancy having a run over to Thoresby Market.'

Dennis looked at them quizzically.

'And what's wrong with using your own cars, pray tell?' he asked.

'Erm, the Cortina's just failed its MOT...' Kenny proffered, by way of explanation.

'And my Escort's, erm, well...' Barry couldn't think of a reasonable excuse quickly enough before the penny suddenly dropped with their father as to why they wanted to borrow the Rover.

Dennis grinned, unable to resist a bit of teasing.

'Since when have you two been interested in open-air markets? Going to buy a set of cheap saucepans, are we?'

A pale pink blush rose in Kenny's cheeks while he quickly thought of a plausible answer.

'No, not saucepans. But we've heard about the food-wagon that sells hot roast-pork butties with stuffing and apple sauce, haven't we, Baz?' He nudged his brother for support.

'Aye, they have crackin' roast-pork cobs. Everybody goes for 'em,' Baz concurred.

'Oooh, can I come with you?' asked Irene, excited at the prospect of a drive out to browse the market and do some shopping. 'We could do with a new set of towels for the main bathroom. And perhaps some new pans!' she laughed.

Kenny and Baz looked at each other, wide-eyed, while they thought of a credible excuse to deflect their mother from joining them. However, their father witnessed their secretive glance, confirming his suspicions.

'Ahh, that would explain why most of my Old Spice has disappeared. You two buggers have been doing a Henry Cooper, and splashing it all over!' He mimicked Henry Cooper's voice and actions from the TV advert.

Dennis's family crumpled with laughter at his aftershave faux pas. Baz had to slap Kenny on his back because he almost choked on a piece of sausage.

'What? What's so funny?' blurted Dennis, innocent as to why the joke was on him.

'It's Brut 33, Dad. Henry Cooper splashes Brut 33 all over, not Old Spice. Old Spice is the one with the surfer and classical music,' corrected Baz.

Dennis put on his crumpled thinking face while he tried to mind-picture the two aftershave adverts.

'Oh yeah, you're right! Anyway, keep your thieving hands off my aftershave and buy your own. Maybe they sell it at the market?' he laughed. 'In fact, here...' He rummaged in his pocket for his wallet, then threw two pounds onto the table. 'Buy a bottle each and leave mine alone.' He paused for a moment, then withdrew the two pounds and swapped them for a five-pound note. 'And get some perfume for your young ladies while you're at it.' He grinned and winked at his two oldest boys.

Irene almost choked on her mouthful of tea, as she sprayed it from her mouth in shock. She mopped her chin and nose with her napkin.

'Girlfriends! You two have got girlfriends? How did this go unnoticed under my radar? When are you going to bring them home so that we can meet them?'

Baz groaned in mock-teasing.

'Oh, gawd! Hide the photograph albums! Mother wants to meet our girlfriends.'

Irene poured herself another cuppa, then straightened up in her chair, ready to start the interrogation.

'Okay – I'm waiting... I want to know all the who, what, where, and when.'

'Hey, I've not finished eating,' laughed Kenny. 'You can fill her in with all the details, bruv.' He pointed his fork, loaded with sausage, at Baz.

'Okay... We met them about six or seven weeks ago, at the end of March. Just after your birthday, in fact. We met them at the night-club the following Friday. Except, well, these lasses are both only just eighteen...' He paused and waited, knowing how his mother would react.'

'Eighteen! That's a bit young, isn't it? I mean, you two are at least three or four years older,' exclaimed Irene.

'They're mature, sensible lasses, Mam, not giggling girls. Anyway, they're best friends, Claire and Sally-Ann. Claire's mine, and Sally-Ann's seeing our Ken. They both live over on the estate, and they've both got good jobs. They work at the local hosiery factory.'

Irene opened her mouth to comment, but was surreptitiously kicked under the table by her husband. She nodded graciously and endeavoured to be positive.

'That's nice. I bet they get all their nightwear and lingerie at a good price.'

'Oh, aye, they do. All kinds of things, not just undies. Fred Perry polo shirts, Pringle sweaters, and stuff. You'll have to give me your size, Mam.'

Irene could tell that Baz was being genuine about the offer – it was clear that these two girls had made quite an impact on her lads. Maybe it was time to put faces to their names? She took a bold chance...

'Well, maybe we should meet your lovely young ladies? Why don't you invite them over for Sunday lunch? Obviously not tomorrow if you're planning to go to Thoresby Market for a hot pork cob. And not next Sunday, as we're all supposed to be going to my mother's for lunch. It's her birthday next weekend, don't forget.'

A chorus of groans echoed around the dining table.

'Oh, no, not lunch at Granny Taylor's. Her meat is always so greasy,' complained Mick, finally managing to get a word in edgeways.

'Michael! Don't be so ungrateful. There are starving kids in...'

'Yeah, yeah, I know. There are starving kids in Africa who would be grateful for it. I've heard it all before. So, stick it in an envelope and post it to them.'

Kenny whacked him lightly around the back of the head, more in jest than punishment.

'Don't you take that tone with mi'mam, you little shit.'

Barry also took up the defence of his mother. 'Yeah, Mick, don't be so ungrateful. But yes, I agree,' he laughed. 'Her meat's bloody awful. Crackin' Yorkshire puds, though...'

Irene flared her nostrils and rolled her eyes in an "I'm waiting to speak" gesture.

'So, that's two weeks on Sunday. It's the 22nd, I think. I'll mark it on the calendar so that we don't forget. Make sure to let the girls know, won't you? – Sunday 22nd May,' she repeated.

Kenny used the opportunity to tease his mother.

'Hmm, well, let me check my diary, I might not be available. I could be in Monaco that weekend.' He pulled a little pocket diary out of his denim shirt pocket and flicked through to that particular date.

Baz gawped at his brother, open-mouthed.

'You have a diary! I thought only office-bods kept a diary!'

'Of course I have a diary, you dick-head. For when Dad and I go to price up jobs and book them in. Anyway, the 22nd is Monaco...'

The lightbulb came on in Baz's mind.

'He means it's Grand Prix weekend, Mam – the Monaco Grand Prix. It's on his bucket list of races to go to. Monaco and Silverstone. Dream on, Kenny, you'll never go to Monaco...'

Kenny scowled at his brother.

'Maybe one day, bruv, maybe one day. Anyway, until then, I'll just have to watch the highlights on telly.' Kenny took out the little pencil that sat in the spine of the diary and made a note about the girls coming for lunch that day, and closed it with a snap before popping it back into his pocket. 'Okay, they're booked in,' he laughed.

Irene cleared her throat loudly, waiting once again to be noticed.

'Ahem! But going back to your original question, yes, you can borrow our car tomorrow. *And* be sure to pick up another bottle of Old Spice for your dad, as well!'

Peeved by yet another put-down by his older brothers, Mick retreated into himself and sought solace in the darkest corners of his mind. As usual, the table conversation had turned to something that he wasn't interested in. It was always motorsport or cricket. Or football. Or Dad and Kenny's business. So boring! No matter what he did or what he said, he always managed to find a way to irritate Kenny and Baz. Being of a similar age, they had a much closer bond, and he felt it.

He was the odd one out.

The afterthought.

The surprise.

The unplanned addition to the cosy little family.

He needed to belong. But being the youngest – the baby of the family – that at least made winning his mother's affection easier.

Easier to play the victim.

Easier to claim the win.

The older brothers had each other. They spoke the same brotherly language; they had that *connection*. He was always too young or too small to join in their games. So he had to find another way to get noticed.

To belong.

Instigating fights – that was a good tactic – either by hiding something of theirs, which usually caused a fracas between Kenny and Mick, or by using tears if a game didn't go his way when he was playing with them. Yes, it was easy to play for his mother's affection and his father's attention.

Sometimes the attention wasn't always so positive; sometimes his father saw through the ruse and figured out that it was Mick who had caused the rumpus, resulting in a slap on the backside. But he mostly got away with it.

And now his brothers have girlfriends!

Yet one more thing to turn the spotlight away from him. He could already sense that his mother's attention had shifted – she would have a new audience to play to.

Bitches!

His neurons sparked in overdrive, flooding his mind with jealousy. The jealousy inched its way through every fibre of his being, causing a tight feeling in his chest.

Mick rubbed his chin, deep in thought, oblivious to the rest of his family chatting around the table. Hmmm, so his brothers were going to borrow Dad's car tomorrow and take their girls out for the day, eh?

He laughed inside his head – a malicious laugh that brought with it the formation of a malicious plan. Nothing dangerous – no, that wouldn't be wise.

But just a little something to irritate their day.

6: Grease Monkey

Kenny snapped the lid closed on the Turtle Wax tin and threw a polishing rag to Baz. As a part of the deal for borrowing the Rover, Dennis had bargained with the boys for a wash, wax, and vacuum. After all, if they were taking their girls out, then the car had to look smart. Seemed like a fair deal.

After hosing off the car (Rule No. 1 – always hose down the car *BEFORE* soaping and washing – that way, the paintwork doesn't get scratched...), the boys went through the rest of the cleaning ritual as taught by their father. Step 2: Wash the car with warm, soapy water and a sponge, rinse well, dry off with a clean chamois, before Step 3: cleaning the windows (inside and out), Step 4: waxing, and Step 5: vacuuming. If a special occasion demanded that little bit extra, then putting on some bumper-black and polishing the wheel rims was the piéce-de-resistance.

As kids, they had always puzzled over the meaning of using "elbow grease", but it was something their father had used for many cleaning tasks, especially the car. Yet they never seemed to stock it in Halfords; it was something that you had to make for yourself. The old man's wash-and-wax method was time-consuming, but if there were two things that he was a stickler for, it was clean shoes and a clean car.

Like a spectre lurking in the shadows, Mick watched his older brothers from the sanctuary of his bedroom. Dennis had tried to persuade him to help with the promise of extra pocket money, but he declined. In his mind, there were more exciting ways of making money than manual work. Besides, it was Kenny and Baz who needed the car later this morning, so why would he want to be a part of the task?

Out of the corner of his eye, Kenny caught sight of Mick half-hiding behind his bedroom curtains, spying on them. He turned the hose pipe towards the bedroom window and blasted the glass, laughing as he did so. Mick jumped backwards in an auto-reflex, almost losing his balance. He returned to his position at the window, this time more visible, and gave the two-fingered "fuck you!" gesture to Kenny. His older brother returned the gesture before spraying the window again, mouthing the word "wanker!". To Kenny, this was all a bit of brotherly fun and teasing, but to Mick, in his mind, it signalled yet another put-down. He sighed heavily, then grinned.

He knew that he would have the last laugh today. It had been tricky sneaking out yesterday evening to put his plan into place; the recently fitted PIR light had clicked on, causing his mother to peer out into the darkness – her silhouette backlit by the kitchen light. But he held his place in the shadows until the light clicked off again. It was a practised art, and one he was getting good at.

The adrenaline rush of anticipation coursed through his veins. He couldn't wait to hear all about their day out.

'Is it my imagination, or does something feel a bit off with the car? Something doesn't feel right.' Sally-Ann's brow furrowed as she looked across at Kenny.

'Hmm, yeah, I can feel it, too. A bit of a vibration. The steering's pulling over to your side, to the passenger side. We ought to pull over and take a look, just to be on the safe side.'

'If I remember rightly, there's a lay-by just up ahead, at the side of Cuckney Woods.' Sally-Ann pointed to the road sign further along the road.

Kenny slowly manoeuvred the Rover into the lay-by and rolled it to a stop. Before he'd even pulled on the handbrake, Sally-Ann was already opening her door so that she could hop out and take a look. Kenny, Baz, and Claire joined her.

'I think this could be the problem. Look.' She pointed towards the front passenger side tyre. 'It's going flat.'

Kenny came to her side, and couldn't resist the age-old corny joke.

'Yeah, but it's only going flat at the bottom. Ouch! What was that for?' he laughed, as Sally-Ann playfully whacked him on the arm. 'Okay, I deserved that...'

'So what are we going to do?' asked Claire.

Sally-Ann scowled at her friend, then smirked in amusement. She began rolling up her sleeves.

'Do you have a foot-pump or spare tyre in the boot?' she asked the brothers.

Kenny nodded. 'I think the foot-pump's in the garage at home, but knowing my dad, we'll have a spare tyre.'

'Great. Can you open the boot for me, Kenny, and get the spare out? Come and help, too, Baz. I'll need the jack and stuff. You do have a jack, don't you?'

Baz shrugged. 'Erm, probably...'

'Oh, for fuck's sake, you two! Don't you know anything about cars!' she teased, grabbing hold of the wheel-brace and twirling it around like a Majorette as she strode towards the slowly deflating tyre. 'There's no point even asking you if you have a torque wrench,' she laughed.

After swapping the damaged tyre for the spare, Sally-Ann partially tightened the wheel nuts before letting the car down on the jack. She dusted off her hands, ready to finish the job with the final tightening up.

Kenny looked at her, amazed at her skills. He could feel another corny joke coming on.

'I can see that you don't need any help with tightening nuts, Sal,' he smirked.

She mock-glared at him, a wry smile playing at the corners of her mouth.

'Cheeky git,' she laughed, poking the wheel brace towards his crotch in mock threat. 'That will have to suffice for now, and I'll check the nuts again before we leave the market and head for home. Not quite as fast as a Formula One pit crew on a wheel-change, but faster than you two hopeless cases. You really should learn the basics, you know,' she teased.

'Have you thought about being a mechanic instead of a machinist?' asked Baz, in all seriousness.

'I have. But I also enjoy sewing. Working at the hosiery factory during the daytime, then helping my dad and brothers in the garage and at race-meets gives me the best of both worlds.' She held her dirty hands aloft and grimaced. 'Isn't there a pub nearby? Maybe I can pop in and wash my hands?'

'Aye, the Greendale Oak isn't too far from here.' Kenny checked his watch. 'But it's only twenty past eleven. They don't open until twelve on Sundays.'

'Shit! I don't suppose you have any Wet-Wipes in the car, do you?' she asked.

'I'm pretty sure that we have some of those,' chuckled Baz, reaching inside the Rover to the glove box. 'Our mam never leaves home without her "just in case" supplies in the car.'

Sally-Ann began wiping her hands clean while Kenny inspected the damaged tyre.

'Here's the problem, look...' He pointed to a nail embedded in the rubber. 'It looks like one of the nails from the job that we've just cleared. I'm pretty sure that I'd swept the driveway clean after emptying the rubbish from the van and into the mini-skip. Maybe I missed a few?' Kenny began rolling the squidgy, semi-deflated tyre towards the back of the car, ready to load it into the boot.

Baz shook his head and shrugged.

'Yeah, maybe. You and Dad are normally pretty thorough at making sure that the driveway's clean. Anyway, three cheers for Sal! Brilliant job, you saved the day.' He started to applaud Sally-Ann, joined by Claire and Kenny.

'Aye, grand job, my love,' concurred Kenny. 'It's great having a petrol-head for a girlfriend. Being part of your dad's banger-car service crew has certainly paid off! But, erm...it looks like we need to get you some new clothes...' He nodded towards her beige slacks and cream-coloured blouse, now covered in road dirt and tyre streaks.

Sally-Ann grinned.

'Oh, boy – am I gonna make you pay for this, Kenneth Watkins! I hope your wallet's feeling loaded, 'cause it's going to be empty by the time I've finished spending your money. Let's head for Thoresby Market, shall we!'

Kenny began walking towards the driver's side of the car.

'Just so long as you leave me enough to buy a bottle of Old Spice for mi'dad!' he laughed.

7: Yorkshire Puds and Arctic Roll

The two best friends strolled side by side through the Estate, before crossing over the main road of Colliery Hill. A shortcut path led across the beautiful grassy fields under the escarpment of Castle Ridge Castle, towards the back of the houses where the brothers lived. A neutral and natural no-man's-land.

The sweet smell of the grass filled the air; a swaying blanket of every shade of green, interspersed with a colourful palette of golden buttercups, white dog-daisies, blue forget-me-nots, and purple clover. The May breeze was warm and gentle – it was a *good-to-be-alive* kind of day.

Today was the day for venturing over to the other side of the main road, away from the crumbling estate and over to the well-maintained detached houses. The invitation to go for a meal had materialised – Sally-Ann and Claire would finally get to meet Mr and Mrs Watkins and see where the boys lived. But even this seemingly innocent invitation had started a great debate – were they going for Sunday dinner, or Sunday lunch?

The girls had teasingly argued for hours with Kenny and Baz. They had been brought up with the knowledge that their meals consisted of breakfast, dinner, and tea. If it was connected to the beverage *tea*, then it was referred to as a *cup of tea*. No confusion. Simple.

However, the boys' family had breakfast, lunch, and dinner, and if they had tea, then it was simply a beverage, not a meal. Apart from afternoon tea, which was usually coffee and cake. Simple. They counter-argued that dinner was an evening meal. Not lunch. How could two sides of the same town have a very different take on how or what you ate? At least they all agreed that supper was a late evening snack, before bed.

So, the girls were going for Sunday dinner/lunch, and they knew it was going to consist of roast beef and Yorkshire puds. And they had been reliably informed that Mrs Watkins made the best Yorkshire puds this side of Yorkshire. Which was strange, because Sally-Ann's nanna also said that she made the best, as did Claire's mum...

Two figures loomed towards Sally-Ann and Claire as they made their way through the tall grass. The figures waved, causing the girls to sigh with relief. Much was in the news these days about the serial killer up in Yorkshire who had so far evaded capture. And Castle Ridge was only just over the border, in North-East Derbyshire. Women were constantly being advised not to go out alone, or walk in dark streets or open spaces. Not that it was dark – it was a beautiful sunny day, but all the same, it was a place where some perv could stalk you in the long grass, and take you down without anyone noticing.

The girls looked at each other with wide eyes as their boyfriends neared. It was clear to see that both Kenny and Baz had made an effort to groom themselves for the occasion, wearing smart flares and shirts.

Claire whispered under her breath to Sally-Ann.

'Aren't you glad we dressed up a bit? Wow, look at them in their Sunday best!'

Sally-Ann concurred with a nod.

'I know! It took me ages to do my hair this morning. The bloody Carmen rollers got stuck. Shit! I bet their mam and dad are wearing their Sunday best, too. Dressed head-to-toe in M&S, I shouldn't wonder,' she giggled.

'Do you think this culotte-suit will be okay?' Claire blurted, with a hint of panic in her voice.

'You look lovely, Claire. The rust colour really suits you, and looks great with your highlights. I haven't seen it before – is it new?'

'Yes – ordered specially for today!' She sneezed lightly, irritated by the pollen.

'Bless you! Is it from one of the catalogues?'

'Yeah, from Littlewoods. The woman next door is an Agent, so we always get our stuff from her catalogue. Saves a lot of hassle if we need to send owt back.'

'Aye, true. My mam has just started as an Agent wi'Kays. They've got some nice stuff in there, if you want to take a look.' Sally-Ann pulled a stalk of long grass and tickled it under Claire's nose, trying to make her sneeze again. 'Anyway, it's only their parents, not the bloody Queen that we're going to meet.'

'Feels like the same thing! Have you heard how they talk about their mam? Like she's royalty, or summat.' Still struck by her moment of panic, Claire added, 'Do you think we should have brought some flowers for Mrs Watkins?'

Sally-Ann laughed and grasped the moment to tease her friend. 'We'll probably need to curtsey and doff our caps to them as well, with them being posh folk. I hope you practised...'

A wide-eyed and open-mouthed Claire stopped dead in her tracks.

'Seriously?'

'No! Of course I'm not serious, you daft cow! For fuck's sake, stop panicking, will you! I'm sure they're nice, down-to-earth people. Anyway, shush, or the lads will hear you,' she chided.

After the warm and welcoming introductions between parents and girlfriends, Irene directed everyone into the Lounge area of the Lounge/Diner, as she called it.

It was a long room, running from front to back, separated in the middle by sliding glass-panelled doors. To one end, closest to the kitchen, was the dining area, featuring a large, oval, highly-polished dining table, with eight smart high-backed chairs and a matching wall unit for all the Sunday-best crockery and cutlery. Sliding patio doors led out onto a paved patio area and the rear garden. The bay-windowed Lounge area looked equally smart and comfortable, with a sumptuous brown velour three-piece suite, fancy tiled-top coffee table, and a smart-looking TV unit. And in the corner was the piéce-de-resistance – the recently built and well-stocked bar area.

Sally-Ann found herself unconsciously stroking the flock wallpaper on the chimney breast.

'Mi'mam would love some of this wallpaper,' she commented. 'She keeps hinting to mi'dad to redecorate, but it falls on deaf ears. We've had the same hideous lime green patterned stuff since 1971. It gives mi'mother nightmares!'

'It's lovely, isn't it!' Irene felt a moment of pride that someone had noticed her new wallpaper. 'We've just had the Lounge area re-done with this lovely stone fireplace and living-flame gas fire. And Dennis has always wanted a bar, so we had that put in at the same time. Plus the flock wallpaper and new fitted carpet – Axminster, of course. The curtains should be here next week. I'm having some of those heavy velvet drapes made to measure from Hillary's, with a top frilly valance, and side-ties.' She used her fingers to air-draw the design just to add a bit of drama and to be clear that the girls understood what she meant.

Kenny sensed that his mother was about to recount the story of the recent hassle that she'd had with Co-op Furnishings because the delivery lad had dropped and damaged the wall lights. He quickly interjected and deflected her with a question about lunch, thereby sparing the girls from all the gory details. It was a tale that he'd heard too often, and he highly doubted that Sally-Ann and Claire would be interested in it.

The homely smell of roast potatoes and Yorkshire puddings began to pervade the air. Irene looked at her watch and made a mental calculation, jiggling her head as she did so.

'Lunch should be ready in about five minutes. Dennis, love, can you go and start carving the meat while I strain the veg? It should be well-rested by now – the meat, I mean, not the veg!' She laughed lightly at her own joke. 'Kenny, would you be an angel and grab a six-pack of Fosters out of the beer chiller and put it on the dining table?' She started waving her hands around again, like an air hostess giving in-flight instructions. 'Baz, can you pop upstairs and get our Mick down for lunch? Right then, almost ready. I hope that you girls are hungry! Do go and sit down.' Irene gestured towards the dining table.

Once all the pleasantries of introducing Mick to the girls had concluded, the family and the two girlfriends relaxed into chatting and eating, until all that remained were a few lonely sprouts and a dozen empty beer cans.

Questions about home life, work, and interests were asked and answered as they all got to know each other better, and as is typical on such occasions, Dennis and Irene managed to find a few embarrassing stories to share about the boys. Then, like well-trained robots, the boys all passed their plates towards Irene, ready to be carried into the kitchen. Claire and Sally-Ann followed suit with their plates.

Suddenly feeling the urge to be helpful, Sally-Ann began stacking the serving bowls together and offered to help Irene carry the dirty dishes into the kitchen, leaving Claire alone with the males of the household. A prickle ran up her arms and caused goosebumps as she caught a glimpse of young Mick's eyes staring at her from under his long fringe. She fidgeted with her hands while frantically trying to avoid his gaze. He was a good-looking young lad, as were all the brothers, but there was something about the way he was looking at her that made her feel uncomfortable. Maybe it was the colour of his eyes – hazel green, like his mother's, whereas Kenny and Baz had grey-blue eyes like their father. His hair was more like his mother's, too; an earthy chestnut colour, fine and straight. Much lighter than his brothers' naturally curly/wavy, dark hair. She remembered Baz saying that Mick was the spoiled baby of the family – the *Mummy's Boy*. It made sense, seeing as how he was the spitting image of his mother. Breaking the silence with some conversation seemed the best option.

'Well, that was a lovely dinner, erm, I mean lunch...' she rolled her eyes at Baz with a wry grin. 'Your mum is a great cook!'

'Aye, she's not too bad,' laughed Baz, as he patted his dad's rounded belly, indicating that Dennis had fared well on her meals over the years.

His dad elbowed him playfully. 'Cheeky young bugger! Wait until you're my age, and Claire has fed you up. You can't beat a good home-cooked meal...'

The conversation was interrupted by Irene and Sally-Ann returning from the kitchen with some dessert bowls and an Arctic Roll on a serving platter.

Claire burst out laughing when she saw the still round and firm Arctic Roll, causing Irene to furrow her brow questioningly.

'My mam once bought one of those frozen Arctic Rolls from Farmfoods. But because it was frozen, she thought that you had to defrost it before serving...'

With the family now howling with laughter at the vision of the limp, thawed-out Arctic Roll, Irene looked around at her happy family and smiled – the Sunday lunch/dinner had been a success. The girls had her seal of approval, even though they were factory lasses from the Estate. They certainly had daughter-in-law potential.

She made a mental note to herself to invite both of their mothers to her next Tupperware or Oriflame party to show off her flock wallpaper. Plus, the new wall lights might have arrived by then!

8: Reflections

Much to the embarrassment of Kenny and Baz, and to the amusement of Sally-Ann and Claire, the photograph albums did come out after Sunday lunch/dinner. Even Mick didn't escape a small amount of teasing.

Irene proudly showed off every photograph from Day One: of being swaddled in the standard crocheted white blanket, bare-arsed on a sheepskin rug, first ice-cream, first day at Infants' School (in shorts!), donkey riding on Mablethorpe beach, and family holidays abroad in Benidorm and Jersey.

'Ooh, that looks exotic,' exclaimed Sally-Ann, pointing to a photograph of them lounging under the shade of some palm trees. 'Looks a bit sunnier than Skeggy!' she laughed.

'I think that's in Benidorm. Have you ever been abroad?' She directed her question openly to both girls.

Sally-Ann shook her head.

'Nah, not with the size of our family. I've got three feral older brothers, so trying to get through an airport with them would have been a nightmare! I'm sure we would have ended up losing one of them en route. It was usually a Butlins all-inclusive for us. Safest bet!'

'Same here,' said Claire. 'I don't think I'll ever get mi'mam on a plane. I struggle getting her into a car! She doesn't travel very well. The number 82 bus is about her limit.' She shook her head at the vision of her mother trying to use any kind of transport.

'Well, I must confess, it takes a couple of Cinzanos to make me feel relaxed about getting onto an aeroplane,' chuckled Irene. Her cheeks flushed slightly, having divulged her secret to successful flying.

As the photo albums continued to reveal other captured family moments, the girls giggled at the boys sitting on Santa's knee at John Lewis's in Sheffield, looking smart in their Christmas suits, and faces smeared with chocolate at Easter. It certainly passed an amusing few hours for Irene, Claire, and Sally-Ann, even if it meant the Watkins boys had to suffer through the pictorial onslaught.

'Aww, look at this one of little Mick in the paddling pool,' cooed Claire. 'You can see how the boys look like you two. Kenny and Baz have their dad's features, whereas Mick looks a lot like you, Mrs Watkins.'

'Oh, please call me Irene. Mrs Watkins makes me sound so old!' she chuckled, addressing both of the girls. 'But yes, Mick seems to take after my side, that's for sure.'

'You are old, Mam,' teased Baz.

Claire suddenly shuddered involuntarily as she sensed Mick's eyes boring into her. She refrained from looking up and turned to the next page in the album, hoping to find another photograph to comment on. Why did he keep looking at her? She had inadvertently caught his gaze a few times throughout the afternoon and had to look away.

As Claire got to the last page, Irene stood up, as though mission accomplished.

'Well, I think it's time to put the kettle on. Would anyone like a cup of tea and a slice of cake? Or maybe a biscuit, if you'd prefer?' she offered.

Having had quite enough of his mother's entertainment, Kenny interjected.

'Thanks, Mam, but I think we'll pass.' He scowled towards Baz and the girls, then nodded towards the door, as if to say, "Let's get out of here before she starts on another album…".

Baz took the hint and stood up, causing a domino effect for the girls to join them.

'Aye, I think we'll be heading off now,' agreed Baz.

'Oh! You're all going? That's a shame. Well, it was lovely to meet you both, and you're welcome here anytime,' gushed Irene, extending her hand to shake with the girls.

Like a beetle stuck on its back, Dennis huffed, puffed, and wriggled out of the comfy armchair to extend a handshake, nodding at Mick to remember his manners and do the same.

As Mick reached towards Claire's hand, she felt strangely uncomfortable and retreated from the shake as quickly yet as politely as possible.

'Will you be back for something to eat later?' asked Irene.

Kenny shook his head as they headed towards the hallway to get their shoes.

'Nah. We're just going to have a steady walk down to the ponds, then go over to Sal's. The Grand Prix highlights from Monaco are on telly tonight, so it'll be late when I get back. You don't need to wait up.'

'And what about you, Barry?' she asked.

'Same for me. We're going for a walk with them. We'll probably grab something from the chippy later to take back to Claire's. See you tonight.'

'And thanks for inviting us over. It was really nice.' Sally-Ann smiled at Irene.

'My pleasure. It was lovely to meet you both.' Irene gave them a little wave as they all headed out of the front door.

She moved over to the bay window in the Lounge and watched as the two young couples walked off together down the hill in the direction of the ponds and nature trail. An overwhelming feeling of "empty nest syndrome" suddenly gripped her, even though the boys hadn't yet left home. She couldn't deny that Claire and Sally-Ann were great girls, and they had certainly charmed her sons.

Surely wedding bells were just a matter of time...

As the foursome strolled around the fishing ponds and nature trail, conversation and laughter came naturally and easily. Once all the nervousness had been swept away, the girls conceded that it had been a pleasant afternoon of getting to know Kenny and Barry's family and vice versa.

After recalling the conversation that she and Barry had had on the night they met, Claire couldn't resist a moment of teasing.

'Hey, I thought you said your family and your house weren't posh?'

'Did I say that?' He crumpled his eyebrows in puzzlement.

'Yes, you did! But if you're not posh, how come your house has three telephones! I counted. One in the kitchen, one in the hallway by the stairs, and one on the upstairs landing!' One by one, she raised three fingers as a visual counter. 'Yes, I'd call that posh. We have one in the hallway, and we have to run like the clappers from wherever we are in the house so that we don't miss the call.'

'Ah, that's why you're sometimes breathless when you answer!' he laughed.

Sally-Ann joined in.

'Yes, I noticed the three telephones, too! And before you ask, we've only got one.'

Kenny pulled her towards him, gently kissing her as he teased.

'Oh, come here, my poor one-telephone Cinderella!'

He kissed her again, then took her by the hand as they continued on their walk, taking the lead ahead of Claire and Barry.

Claire took the opportunity to slow their pace and fall a short way behind. She had something to ask Baz without the other two hearing, so she lowered her voice as she spoke.

'I hope that you don't think this is a strange question, Baz, but is there something "wrong" with your Mick?' She did air quotes as she mentioned the word *wrong*. 'You know, like he's not all there in the head.' She tapped her temple a couple of times with her index finger to emphasise her meaning.

Baz gave her a quizzical look.

'How do you mean *wrong?* Like he's simple, or something?'

'Yeah. Sorry, I don't know how to explain it. He just kept staring at me, and it made me feel a bit uncomfortable. Don't misunderstand me – I don't mean to speak ill of anyone.'

'Hey, no worries. He sometimes does that with new people. He can be a bit weird until he gets to know folk better. He was probably overwhelmed by your beauty,' he laughed, giving her a gentle shove.

Claire shoved him back, then gave him a gentle slap on the arm.

'Aww, you charmer! Okay, well, I'll try not to worry. Just don't leave me alone with him.'

'Bloody 'ell, Claire, he's only a kid, not some psycho killer!' defended Baz. 'But okay, at least until you get to know him better.'

Claire felt a wave of relief trickle through her veins. Yet strangely, she didn't feel convinced that Mick was as innocent as he portrayed.

9: Shadow Puppet

At one with the shadows, the silhouetted figure of Mick crept stealthily along the edge of the wall line, expertly moving so as not to tread on any potential noise traps. With a practised art, he carefully swung his backpack over the wall before quietly scrambling over to make his escape. Despite having checked out the back of the newsagent's shop for accessibility, as well as the likelihood of rich pickings, he had very little to show for his efforts.

Working in the local butcher's shop full-time since quitting school at Easter had given him a new kind of kudos. And this kudos meant that he could pop into any of the other shops for a chat during his lunch break without the owners realising that they were being scoped as a potential target. Their loose talk and casual security were his golden egg.

That said, the best he could manage from tonight's haul was a measly few quid from the petty-cash tin and a backpack full of cigarettes, cigars, and rolling tobacco. Unfortunately for him, the day's takings must have been put into the night-safe box at the NatWest. But in all fairness, tobacco products were still currency of sorts, and the money from the tin was his bonus. But would a bagful of smokes be enough to pacify his source as a trade-off for some gear? Maybe he should keep them for himself, for his private sales? After all, there was always someone desperate enough to buy cheap ciggies, no questions asked.

With the decision made to give up on this particular parade of shops, he headed for his hiding place behind the old swimming baths to offload his paltry stash. The ramshackle shed on the abandoned allotment gardens served as a great hideout. No one had been there in years. It was like Sleeping Beauty's castle, hidden among the overgrown brambles and weeds. Plus, the location was just about visible from the upstairs windows of their house, so he could keep a covert eye on the place. Close enough to be conveniently monitored, yet far enough away not to draw attention to his nocturnal comings and goings.

The urge to find richer pickings became too much for Mick to resist. As this was not only the start of an extended Spring Bank Holiday weekend, but also the Silver Jubilee celebrations, most of the shops had been well-stocked in preparation for the occasion. People were in the mood to spend, spend, spend, whether it was for an excess of food, booze, or decorations for all the street parties that would be taking place.

Rather than taking a long walk back up the hill to break into another Castle Ridge shop, he decided to turn right, towards the little suburb of Castle Vale.

The goldmine of the mini-mart on Main Street beckoned.

The in-and-out of the break-in had been much easier than anticipated. Judging by the amount of laughter, tuneless singing, and music thumping overhead, a Friday night party was in full swing in the flat above the shop premises. The perfect cover for any of his inadvertent noise.

A quick scan of the shelves showed the bottles of spirits to be the easiest pickings, so he quickly loaded his backpack with a couple of bottles of Johnny Walker whisky, a couple of Beefeater Gin, and a bottle of Cognac. Heavy to carry, but worth the effort for resale. He also stuffed a few chocolate bars into his pockets.

As he skulked along the rough gravel access road at the back of the shops, the sound of a car turning into the lane caused him to step further back into the shadows and wait until it had driven past. However, the car pulled up and stopped close to where he was hiding, then turned off the engine and lights, although no one got out. From his concealed vantage point, he could see that the car windows were beginning to steam up. Mick blushed as he realised what was going on inside the car.

The chill of the night air made him shiver. Without wishing to be stuck there for hours or being caught with a bagful of stolen gear, he calculated that his only escape route was over the top of some disused outbuildings. By standing on an old dustbin, stepping onto a window ledge, then walking across the flat, rickety corrugated-iron roof, he could make it over. Not ideal when loaded down with bottles of booze, but he didn't have a choice without disturbing the shaggers in the car.

Once onto the flat roof, he quickly but cautiously made his way along the edge to try and find a place where he could safely jump down and get away. However, he hadn't calculated for the rusty old roof being unable to take both his weight and that of the bag. His foot slipped as one of the panels buckled, causing him to lose his balance. As he slid towards the edge, his survival instincts kicked in, and he grabbed for the guttering to slow down his fall. The last thing that he wanted to do was land on his back, particularly as it had a bagful of glass strapped to it. But as he grabbed the length of decayed guttering, it snapped and pulled away, not only cutting his hand but causing him to fall awkwardly, clattering as he landed.

Alerted by his dogs barking at the suspicious night noise, the lights came on in one of the terraced houses opposite. Mick froze, hoping that the owner wouldn't let them out to investigate – judging by the deep, snarling bark, the dogs sounded ready for action. The back door opened, followed by a cursory sweep of a torch beam.

'Who's there? Piss off, or I'll let the dogs out...'

Somewhere by the dustbins, two cats howled, then began fighting, causing the householder to curse at his dogs for the false alarm.

Relieved that the cats had been a welcome diversion to his noise, Mick waited for things to settle down before making a move. He sighed and adjusted his legs to get a little more comfortable.

The pain in his hand began to throb, and he realised that it was badly cut and bleeding. He stuck it inside his jacket, under his armpit, to try and stem the flow.

Though he was just a small cog in a very crooked wheel – a puppet to those in the chain above him – this had not been the easiest night for filching some gear. Yet it had been strangely worth it for the multiple adrenaline rushes.

It was a win-win situation.

But, for now, it was time to call it quits, offload his gear, and sneak home to bed.

Irene tightened the cord of her dressing gown as she stood in the curve of the bay window. There was nothing she enjoyed more than watching the morning slowly come to life. What would the new day bring?

Abruptly jarred from her absent thoughts, she craned her neck to follow the direction of a police car as it flew down the hill with its blue lights flashing.

'Ooh, did you see that?' she commented to no one in particular.

'Did you say something, love?' shouted Dennis from the kitchen.

With nothing else to see, Irene wandered through to join her husband and began pouring herself a cup of tea.

'A police car just went flying down the road in the direction of the Vale. I wonder what's happened?'

'I didn't hear anything.'

'Hmm, there were no sirens, just the blue lights.'

'Maybe it's just getting ready to close the road for the Silver Jubilee carnival parade. That's today, isn't it?' Dennis topped up his mug of tea, then took a slurp.

'Yes, I think so. But why would a police car need to go? And why so early? I would have thought that the local council or the highways would have to deal with that. Something's happened, you mark my words.'

A noise behind her caused her to look up as Mick entered the kitchen.

'Morning, love. You're up early for a national holiday – didn't you sleep well?' Irene suddenly took note of the bandage around his hand. 'Oh my goodness, what have you done? Did you cut yourself?'

Mick waved his injured hand and rolled his eyes, teasing his mother.

'No shit, Sherlock!' he laughed. 'Yes, I've got a bit of a cut. But it's nothing to worry about, it's not too deep or anything.'

But, of course, this was not enough information for Irene, who began to probe deeper.

'But when did you do that? I don't remember seeing you with a bandage yesterday. Or did I? I'm not sure now...'

'Yes, I did it yesterday, just before I came home from work,' he lied. 'I caught it on the bacon slicer when I was cleaning the blade at the end of the day.'

'You did it at work! I hope you cleaned the wound properly. Did you put it into the accident report book? In fact, shouldn't you be able to claim compensation for an injury at work?'

Her incessant questioning was beginning to irritate not only Mick but also his father.

'Oh, for goodness' sake, woman! Leave the lad alone. We all get cuts and bruises at work. I cut myself all the time,' defended Dennis. 'I'm pretty sure you must get paper cuts at the office, but don't report them or try to claim compensation...'

Mick sniggered at his dad's wit and sarcasm. 'That's right – it was just an accident, Mam. It was my fault; I wasn't watching what I was doing. Just leave it, will you!' he snapped.

'There's no need to take that tone with me, Michael. I was just showing concern, that's all.' She tightened her robe belt again. 'Are you going to the parade down in the Vale today?' she asked. But before he'd even had a chance to reply, Irene had moved on to her next topic. 'Oh, yes, talking of the Vale, I saw a police car go in that direction just a short while ago. I wonder what's happened.'

'The Vale? Police car? Erm, no, I won't be going to the parade today.'

His heart fluttered a little at the mention of the district in which he'd been light-fingered the night before. 'I think I'll just take it easy today, rest my hand, and perhaps watch some of the Jubilee celebrations on telly. Or maybe have a walk up to the garden party at Lodge Gardens. I dunno yet.' It was time to change the subject. 'Are we having the usual bacon fry-up for breakfast? It is Saturday, after all.'

'Ooh, that sounds like a good idea,' agreed Dennis.

Irene rolled her eyes and tutted as she headed to the fridge to get out the ingredients for a mixed-grill breakfast.

'Food – that's all you men think about. Well, that and you-know-what. I suppose you want sausage and eggs, too?'

'Did someone say "sausage and eggs"?' yawned Barry, as he joined them in the kitchen for breakfast. 'Put some in for me, too. Thanks, Mam, you're the best.'

Irene grinned, then did her best exaggerated bow and curtsy to the men in her life.

'Yes, my Lords, your humble servant hears and obeys! I suppose I'd better cook a bit extra. The smell of bacon frying is bound to wake Kenny.'

'Better than any alarm clock,' laughed Baz. 'And put t'kettle on while you're at it...'

10: Not All Are Celebrating

With the Silver Jubilee Celebrations in full swing, the mood of the nation was one of patriotic carefree abandon. Street parties were being held the length and breadth of the country; every lamp-post, house, and shop was adorned with red, white, and blue bunting, and pictures of Her Majesty were hung in nearly every window. Not since the Queen's Coronation in 1953 had the country had something so significant to celebrate.

With sandwiches to make and tables to prepare for their street party, a band of four little estate warriors had been ushered out of the way by their mothers. The oldest was put in charge, and they were instructed to go to the local play area and come back later in the afternoon. By which time, there would be enough sausage rolls, ham sandwiches, cheese-on-sticks, pop, and crisps to feed the estate, let alone their street. It was a deal the gang of four couldn't resist.

After an hour of playing in the local park, the boys longed for something a little more exciting. The grassland under the ramparts of Castle Ridge Castle was always a great place for an adventure. It meant crossing the busy main road from the estate to get there, but as promised, the oldest boy took care of his little sibling and their two friends and made sure that they crossed safely. He was very proud of having learned the Green Cross Code.

The large open expanse of long grass made the ideal playground for a child's fertile imagination. As the sun was shining and the morning already warm, they became bush-rangers, swishing and thwacking their way through the long grass, alert for lions stalking them, and wary of surprise attacks by elephants and giraffes. As they neared the back of the old allotments, the intrepid leader of the rangers urged his men to hide while he made sure the coast was clear. They were entering into tribal territory...

Once they had been given the signal that it was safe, the four boys clambered over the rickety allotment fence and searched for apple trees and rhubarb. They needed sustenance, and it was still ages before they knew they would be allowed home.

Spying the old shed, one of the lads gave the signal to move forward with caution – there could be natives lurking, protecting their Chief in his hut.

With the door now smashed open, the four boys stopped dead in their tracks, in awe of the treasures that lay before them. Bars of chocolate, cigarettes, and bottles of some kind of drink. They were hungry and thirsty after their jungle adventure. It was time to put this game on pause and start a new one – now they were explorers who had found a hidden cache of priceless riches...

The boys greedily tore into the Twix and KitKat, feasting like they hadn't eaten for a week. Chocolate became smeared around their mouths and across their hands. The oldest of the four explored the bottles and tried to read the labels. He liked the look of one with a Beefeater on it – the picture somehow looked appropriate for the occasion. He was thirsty and he needed a drink of water.

After taking a big gulp, he coughed and gagged. What was this stuff? A sudden rush of warmth ran through his veins, and he giggled. It was Fire Water! Though he didn't like the taste, he liked the tingly feeling that followed. He urged the others to have a go, passing a different bottle over for them to try. It looked like cold tea.

Seeing that his little brother was nervous, he reassured him that it was just giggle water and nothing to worry about. The other two boys, who were now also starting to feel the effects of the contents, began chanting.

"Drink it! Drink it!"

Not wanting to appear a weakling in his older brother's eyes, he cautiously began chugging the golden liquid. Although the other boys had told him that it was cold tea, it certainly didn't smell or taste like it. He desperately wanted to stop and to spit it out, but he also badly wanted to be one of the big boys.

"Drink it! Drink it!"

To be one of the gang.

"Drink it! Drink it!"

To make his older brother proud.

The other three boys, now clearly drunk, decided that it must be time to go home to the street party. Seeing that the little one was lying on the floor, they assumed him to be asleep, so carefully covered him over with some old potato sacks, as though tucking him into bed. They wobbled and giggled, and did their best "Shshsh!" not to wake the sleeping baby.

Feeling the pager vibrate in his pocket, Mick sighed and reluctantly pulled it out. He hated being at the beck and call of the goons.

Need gear. Usual place. Six pm.

Mick rolled his eyes. Having promised his mother that he would join the family for today's party at the local Miners' Welfare, he began racking his brains for a plausible excuse. This was going to be a tough one.

His thoughts were interrupted by the wailing screams of the emergency services close by.

Very close by.

Bitten by the curiosity bug, he slipped off his bed and almost crashed into his equally curious parents as he exited the bedroom.

'What's going on?' he asked, as they shoved past him to go into their bedroom.

'Not sure,' replied Irene, with a tinge of excitement in her voice, 'but an ambulance and police car have just turned into the lane at the side of the swimming baths. The one that leads to the old allotments.'

They all positioned themselves so they could see out of the big bedroom window, which overlooked the vast expanse of abandoned gardens and the Castle parkland. The flashing blue lights could just be seen through the overgrown trees and hedging.

'Open the window,' urged Irene. 'Maybe we can hear what's going on.'

A sudden realisation hit Mick in the stomach like a ton of bricks. He tried to keep his thoughts calm and rational. Maybe an old tramp had been found while someone was out walking their dog? Perhaps a dog walker had fallen and injured themselves, and the dog had made it back home and alerted others, like Lassie the Wonder-dog?

He could only hope.

With the patient now onboard, the ambulance set the sirens going again and backed out of the lane, screaming off at speed in the direction of the hospital. A definite sign of an emergency. Meanwhile, the police car remained, shortly joined by another. Whatever was happening appeared to be very serious, prompting Irene to go and make three mugs of tea and bring a packet of biscuits.

Muffled shouting could be heard as the police officers started spreading out and combing the area very close to where Mick's stash was hidden, in the old shed.

The knot that he had in his stomach was beginning to loosen and affect his bowels. He almost spilt his mug of tea as he tried to take a mouthful.

This did not look good.

His mind began racing. Was there anything in the shed that could lead back to him? Definitely not fingerprints, as he had always worn gloves. A shoe print in the mud, maybe? He furtively checked his back pocket for his wallet, just to make sure that he hadn't dropped it in the shed. A small sigh of relief passed through his mind. It was there. He put his mug of tea onto the windowsill.

'Back in a jiffy. My stomach doesn't feel right. Must be something I ate this morning at breakfast.' He tried not to overdramatise his need to escape for a moment.

Once in the locked sanctuary of the bathroom, Mick took out his pager. As fear-induced adrenaline coursed through his veins, he struggled to make his fingers work as he keyed in a message to the goons.

Stash compromised. Need Plan B.

The pager vibrated as a reply quickly came back.

Plan B. Cash. £100

His heart hammered in his chest. How the fuck was he supposed to find £100 quid by six o'clock tonight! He looked at his watch; three-thirty. His parents were planning to leave at four. That would give him a couple of hours to get the money and make the payoff.

Will do my best

YOU HAVE NO CHOICE. BE THERE!

Mick racked his brains for a solution. He had to come up with one – FAST!

His only option was a daylight burglary. It was risky, but as it was Bank Holiday Monday, and not only that, the Jubilee celebrations, all shops were closed, and everyone was out partying. All he needed to figure out was who and where his cash-cow victim would be.

A light tap came on the bathroom door.

'Are you okay, Mick? You've been in there a while,' asked his mother, with a tinge of concern in her voice.

'I seem to have got a dose of the shits, Mam. I don't think I'm going to make it to the party down at the Welfare. You two go on without me.'

'Oh.' His mother sounded disappointed. 'Well, if you're sure.'

'Yeah, I'm sure. Send my apologies to the others.' He flushed the toilet, then ran the tap for sound effects. He added in some retching noises for good measure.

Hearing his mother's voice gave him the lightbulb moment that he needed. Now he knew where he could find some ready cash! He just needed to figure out the best way to break into the NCB offices. Or even better, 'borrowing' his mother's office keys and staging a break-in.

As soon as Mick heard his parents' car pull onto the driveway later that evening, he lay out prone on the sofa and put a cold, damp face cloth onto his forehead, ready to continue his charade of feeling ill.

That said, after the exertion of searching for his mother's office keys, which she had mercifully left on her nightstand and not in her handbag, doing a literal daylight robbery, and then meeting with the goons, all in the space of a couple of hours, he was feeling quite drained. But lady-luck had been on his side, and he had managed to find enough cash in the office drawers to pacify the overlords. He only wished that the police would piss off so that he could go and check on his hidden assets.

'Hi, love. How are you feeling? Does your tummy still hurt?' fussed Irene.

Dennis snorted and scoffed, not quite believing his son's convenient illness. 'For God's sake, woman, he's a young man, not a five-year-old!'

'I've just had a quiet evening on the sofa watching the telly. I've still got a bit of a belly-ache, but nothing like it was,' he lied. 'By the way, the police stopped by earlier, doing a few house-to-house inquiries in the neighbourhood. Wondering if people had seen or heard any unusual activity, particularly at night – any strange comings and goings? But like I told them, we would have reported anything unusual straight away. We don't want any dodgy people coming into our neighbourhood.'

'Too right! But we've found out what all the police activity was about this afternoon. And it's not nice, let me tell you...' Irene sat down in the nearby armchair, ready to recite all that she had heard, while Dennis went and put the kettle on.

Mick began wiping his face with the cool cloth, unsure that he wanted to find out – it sounded serious. Yet his curiosity burned. He had to know.

'Sally-Ann got a phone call this evening while we were at the Welfare. It turns out that two of her brother's kids and two other boys got into some kind of trouble in one of the old sheds out back. I wish the Council would pull the damned things down if they're not going to rejuvenate the allotments. They're just a magnet for tramps to sleep in. Anyway, like I said, the boys were playing in one of the sheds and found a load of booze and stuff. The kids didn't know any better and drank some of it.'

Mick could feel the heat rising in his face, and gave it a wipe with the face cloth. And now his stomach was genuinely starting to feel uneasy.

'Is that why there was an ambulance? And why did the police end up getting involved? ' he asked, eager to know more.

'Well, three of the boys went back to their homes – there was going to be a street party on the estate – but they left the littlest one behind because he was fast asleep. Thank goodness Sally-Ann's sister-in-law realised that her oldest boy was drunk and made the connection. You can imagine the panic she was in! She got in touch with the other two mums, and their boys had given the same story. They'd also been drinking.'

'So what happened next?'

'Once they had managed to puzzle together the location of where the boys had been playing, the emergency services were called and directed to where the shed was. It turns out that the poor little mite is in some kind of alcohol-induced coma. They're not sure if he'll make it, and if he does, whether it will leave him brain-damaged or not. He's only six, bless him.' She wiped a tear away in her mother's sympathy.

'That does not sound good,' Dennis interjected, as he brought in the tray of tea.

'I know! Can you imagine if it were one of our boys at that age? Heaven forbid... Anyway, the police did a thorough sweep of the area, as we saw, and the place has been cordoned off as a crime scene. The police also seem to think that the booze and cigarettes are connected to recent burglaries in the area. Remember the mini-mart down in Castle Vale that was done over the other evening? And the newsagents up in the Market Place. They think there must be some organised gang operating in the area. God help us if there's some kind of crime wave happening!' She shuddered quite visibly at the thought.

'Well, I hope the police catch the bastards that are responsible, and throw the book at them. If that little boy dies...' Dennis shook his head, his shoulders heavy with sadness. 'And right on our own doorstep.'

'I tell you what,' said Irene, concern at the heart of her voice, 'I'm just glad the boys didn't try lighting any cigarettes or try to make a fire. Four drunken kids playing with matches in a shed – the consequences don't bear thinking about. I agree with you, Den – the sooner the police get to the bottom of this and find out who's responsible, the better it will be for everyone involved.'

'Anyway, where's our Kenny and Baz? Didn't they come home with you?' asked Mick, curious to know where his brothers were.

'Kenny took Sally-Ann straight down to the hospital to be with her family after she got the phone call about her nephew. And Barry's gone to stay at Claire's for the night.' Irene yawned as she picked up her cup of tea. It had been a strangely stressful day.

'Well, I certainly hope that the police get the culprits before the Clarke brothers get hold of them. They're threatening to tear 'em limb from limb. And rightly so,' snarled Dennis. 'I'm tempted to give them a hand.'

Mick had heard enough. His conscience was starting to get the better of him. Yes, it was shitty for the kid and Sally-Ann's family, but it was also shitty for him.

He was back to square one. He needed to find a new hiding place, and one that was a lot more secure than the rickety old shed if he was to avoid any more close calls. There was no way he could go back to the allotments. And he wasn't out of the woods yet, depending on the police investigations and the recovery of Sally-Ann's nephew.

His survival instincts told him that this could turn into a major setback with far-reaching consequences if he wasn't careful.

Only time and luck would tell.

11: A Not So Jubilant Day

Immersed in the pomp and pageantry of watching the Queen's procession in the Gold State Coach, neither Irene nor Dennis could be drawn away from the television by the ringing of the telephone. It was too much of a momentous and historical occasion to miss out on something so spectacular. It was a nation united in acknowledging their Queen's commitment to duty.

With a roll of his eyes, Mick jumped up from his sprawled-out position on the sofa to go and answer the telephone in the hallway. He could see by the involved look on his parents' faces that they wouldn't want to miss a word of the commentary, so he made sure to close the lounge-area door behind him.

He came back into the room just a short while later, his face ashen. Without peeling her eyes away from the television screen, Irene managed a half-interested, 'Who was it?'

'It was Sally-Ann. She was calling to let us know that her little nephew didn't make it.' Mick felt a genuine moment of sadness and remorse as he spoke.

Both Irene and Dennis looked at him, their eyes and mouths wide with shock, speechless. Once she had found her voice, Irene ventured to ask for more information, if he had any.

Mick nodded and continued. 'Apparently, he never regained consciousness and had a chain of back-to-back seizures. This caused his core temperature to rise to a dangerous level, and he went into cardiac arrest. There was nothing they could do.'

Irene burst into tears, prompting Dennis to hold her in his arms.

'Oh, the poor little mite,' she wailed. 'He didn't deserve this. It's the old ones who should go first, not the babies. He was only six!'

Mick returned to the sofa, an internal nervous wreck. Through all his cocky bravado and his addiction to night prowling and wheeling and dealing, Sally-Ann's phone call had given him a reality check. Yesterday, he only felt remorse for himself – remorse that his stash had been compromised. Today, he realised that his actions were having genuine, tragic consequences. He chewed on his nails, biting them down to the fingertips.

Dennis's voice brought him back to the moment.

'Well, I hope the Police manage to find out who did it. But these gangs are good at covering their tracks. In and out, and not a trace of evidence anywhere.'

'I don't know what the world's coming to,' sniffed Irene, wiping her eyes. 'There seems to be less and less moral code. Organised gangs and inner city poverty. Drug addicts desperate for money. No wonder crime is on the rise.' She took a deep breath to compose herself. 'Well, I'm sure the Clarke family will have a lot of local support. Even though we didn't know the little boy, he still somehow feels like family. I wonder if there's something we can do to help?'

'Talking of family,' interjected Mick, 'Sally-Ann said that our Kenny won't be home until later this evening. He's spending the day with the Clarkes, given the circumstances.'

'Aye, he's a good lad, our Kenny,' Irene concurred. 'The Clarkes'll need all the support they can get at the moment.'

She looked at the television, her eyes wistful with the joyous celebrations taking place, not just in London, but countrywide and across the Commonwealth. All these people coming together for one incredible lady.

'I bet the Queen doesn't have these kinds of problems within her family,' she sighed.

Although he was 99% sure that he was in the clear, Mick realised that if the Clarkes *EVER* found out the stolen goods were his, then his life wouldn't be worth living. They would publicly crucify him.

Not only that, but his mother would be back at work tomorrow and discover that the NCB offices had been broken into and a large quantity of petty cash stolen. In his mind's eye, he retraced his steps to make sure that he'd covered his tracks there, too. He'd done just enough "damage" to make it look like a cash-desperate thief or opportunist kids rather than some kind of gang crime. He didn't want to give his mother too much of a shock.

Maybe it was time to ease back a little. At least until this episode had blown over.

12: Hiding in Plain Sight

Beep, beep, beep, beep.

Beep, beep, beep, beep.

Mick turned off his alarm clock. As he lay quietly, he could faintly hear the radio-alarm burst into life in his parents' bedroom, followed by the muffled sounds of someone speaking and moving around.

07:30. Time to start another day.

He tucked his hands behind his head and let his mind wander, pondering what the day would have in store, not just for him, but for the residents of Castle Ridge. Most people would be heading back to work today after the extended Bank Holiday weekend for the Queen's Silver Jubilee. At least it would be a short working week; today was Wednesday, so half-day closing for the smaller shops in Castle Ridge. He would get the afternoon to himself.

A pang of guilt ripped through him as he thought of the Clarke family and the loss they were having to deal with. A loss that was essentially his fault. He'd felt cocky and brave as he'd made his way in and out of the shops and offices with his rich pickings, and felt a great sense of accomplishment as he stashed away his loot. A sigh escaped. As to what followed, well... He could never have envisaged that events would unfold the way they had over the weekend.

A light rap came on his bedroom door, followed by his mother's voice.

'Are you awake, Mick? It's time to get up for work.'

'Yeah, yeah, I'm awake. I'll be down in a mo'. Just getting dressed,' he lied, still lying prone in bed.

'Okie dokie, don't be long. I'll put the kettle on.'

Mick then heard his father's voice on the landing, as he too made his way downstairs for breakfast.

His mind drifted towards his mother, and he closed his eyes, feeling slightly remorseful. He knew what she and her colleagues would have to face when they got to work. It seemed like such a good idea at the time. He'd been to the Area Offices before with Irene, so he knew the layout. Easy pickings.

But had he done enough to cover his tracks at all these places?

He looked at the alarm clock. Shit! He'd better get a move on.

As he quickly dressed, he mentally backtracked over all the places he'd been over the weekend. He'd worn gloves, so no fingerprints. And he was pretty sure that he'd left no other incriminating evidence at the scenes.

Holy shit! Security cameras! Did any of the places have security cameras?

'Tea's made, and I've put some toast in for you. Chop, chop, Michael!' shouted Irene, her tone sharp.

'Just going to the bathroom, then I'll be down…' he replied, his heart now pounding over this new problem.

After double-checking that he'd put the all-important pager into his pocket, he headed for the bathroom, thereby giving himself a little more thinking time before heading downstairs.

Mick mind-scanned all the scenes. There were definitely no cameras in the newsagents, that much he was sure of. Nor were there any at his mother's office building – he'd done a cursory scan before heading in, particularly with it being daylight. As for the little mini-mart? He couldn't be sure…

Shit! Shit! Shit!

He flushed the toilet, then washed his hands and face.

'MICHAEL!'

'*COMING!* I'm just cleaning my teeth!'

He was bound to hear all kinds of gossip from the locals when they came into the butcher's shop today. Stories of the tragedy. Stories of the different burglaries. What was the local community coming to? There must be gangs operating!

Without any shadow of a doubt, he knew that his mother would make a drama out of the burglary at the Coal Board offices. But at least he'd made it look like someone had been searching for cash, and only desk drawers had been damaged and left open. And even though he'd quietly gone in with her keys, he'd made it look like a forced entry through a window.

Now all he had to do was hide in plain sight until the hysteria and commotion had blown over.

Having changed into his shorts once he'd arrived home, Mick stretched out on the sun lounger with an ice-cold Lilt in his hand. The afternoon sun was high in the sky, and a heat haze shimmered over the back garden. This summer was starting to feel almost as hot as last summer's record-breaking heatwave. Even the bees seemed too lazy to bumble about their duty today.

As predicted, his morning had been filled with local gossip, with the customers recounting their shock and horror of the Jubilee weekend atrocities in Castle Ridge. Normally such a sleepy little mining town! What were things coming to! He'd nodded and sympathised as he'd listened to each story. On the plus side, and much to his relief, he heard that the owners of the Castle Vale mini-mart were so sick of being broken into that their insurance company was *insisting* that they put up security cameras. He was in the clear!

Mick was also mindful that his mother was likely to come home from work maxed out on outrage and stress because of the office burglary. So to cover his guilt, and to smooth her tension, he had thoughtfully brought home a couple of family packs of different barbecue meats, together with some fresh burger baps from the bakery over the road. He would offer to grill, seeing as the family had been working all day, and he had only worked a half-shift. He smiled at his conniving genius.

Since quitting school at Easter, he had to admit that he was enjoying having money in his pocket. The pay at the butcher's wasn't too bad as a starter wage – more than his mates were getting as shelf-stackers in Fine-Fare, plus there was the promise of proper training. Maybe not his first choice as a career, but the hours were good, and the work was not too heavy. Plus, it gave him a good insight into who was going away and when; their loose talk was his gain. This additional cash bonus had inadvertently come his way via the market stall when the goons had introduced themselves. And here he was, already knee-deep in shit for them.

But the buzz! Oh, the buzz he got with the "night-work".

However, lazing on the sun lounger wasn't resolving his immediate problem – the allotment shed. Could he risk taking a look?

Of course he could!

The public walk-path that ran adjacent to the old swimming baths, then led towards the allotments and the open fields under the Castle, had now been reopened by the police. Dog walkers and strollers had already started using the path, particularly with the weather being so good.

After exchanging a few courteous nods and words with those he passed, he waited until the coast was clear so that he could hop over the rickety fence to get a closer look at the shed that he'd used as a hideout. Unfortunately for him, both the door and the window had been boarded over and nailed shut, so access was impossible. A piece of *Police – Do Not Cross* tape hung limply from the door handle, the only reminder of the tragic event from the preceding days. All the weeds and overgrown self-seeded plants had been squashed flat from where the police had been conducting their detailed sweep of the area.

Mick sighed. Without doubt, he would have to find somewhere new to hide his cache, and it would have to be somewhere relatively close, particularly as he wouldn't be getting his "birthday car" until his eighteenth, next April. All that he took had to be carried in a backpack. He wandered back towards the fence, carefully negotiating his way through a patch of hollyhocks and stinging nettles, mindful that he was wearing shorts.

He looked at his watch; he still had an hour or so before his mother would be home from work.

Bingo! The watch had given him a sudden burst of inspiration. Perhaps he could construct a false bottom in the base of his built-in wardrobe? After all, he had access to the tools and materials. It would be easy to disguise, and the perfect solution to his much-needed hiding place without having to make any kind of detour on the way back from his nocturnal activities. He could hide everything in plain sight. Sure, it would mean taking only jewellery and cash, but this kind of stuff was always popular for trading.

It was a win-win.

Relieved that he'd managed to come up with such a genius idea, he headed home to start putting his plan into action.

Oh, yeah, and he also needed to find the charcoal for the barbecue!

13: Five Minutes of Fame

Following all the trauma and shock that the Clarke family had recently endured, Kenny could see that Sally-Ann was starting to spiral downwards with her mood. Her energy levels were at rock bottom.

As the only daughter, she'd automatically taken on the motherly role of trying to take care of her parents and her brother's family while they grieved, though she was also grieving. He needed to get her away from home for a day or two. Do something special – something which would make a new memory, and be a dream come true for them both. And he knew just the place to do it – the British Grand Prix, at Silverstone!

Having wandered around for a while to find a good spot in which to soak up the action, Kenny and Sally-Ann finally settled for a place at Copse Corner. That way, they could watch the cars exiting the pit lane to rejoin the race, as well as get a long view over the start-finish straight looking one way, and the other straight towards the curve at Maggotts. Sally-Ann had flatly refused to stand near Maggotts, the sheer name of it sending shivers down her spine.

Television helicopters hovered overhead, recording all the action, so that it could be edited together with trackside footage for the evening's sporting news highlights.

The rising heat of the July afternoon caused a shimmering, rippling haze over the Silverstone track, adding to the mystique of this special day.

Local boy, James Hunt, in his No. 1 McLaren-Ford, had claimed Pole Position for the start of the race, alongside fellow Brit, John Watson, in his No. 7 Brabham. There could not have been a better line-up for the British Grand Prix – two Brits at the front of the start grid!

The excitement among the crowd of one hundred thousand spectators was tangible. Would Hunt go on to claim the win, as compensation *and* revenge for having been controversially disqualified last year at Brands Hatch? Or would Watson continue his winning streak? Who would take the chequered flag victory after sixty-eight laps?

Only time would tell.

After being waved off by the green flag, clutch problems for Hunt gave him a poor start from the line, immediately setting him back into fourth place and putting Watson into the lead. As the race settled into an exciting but complex rhythm for the twenty-six competitors, the crowds were entertained with daring overtaking, high-speed crashes, engine problems, and retirements. Their enthusiastic cheers were drowned out by the howling, powerful engines of the Formula One cars as they sped by; the fans either chanting for their favourite driver or collectively gasping at a brave but risky manoeuvre.

Little by little, Hunt clawed his way back up the field. By lap fifty, he had taken the lead, sending the crowd wild. Watson's Brabham began suffering fuel problems, putting him out of the race by lap sixty-one. It was down to James Hunt to save the day, not just for the spectators, but for himself – taking the coveted win on home soil would be claiming the Holy Grail of motorsport.

Just a few laps to go!

Sally-Ann clutched hold of Kenny's arm in nervous anticipation of the final result.

'I honestly can't believe we're here! This is just amazing. Look, I've got goosebumps, I'm so excited,' she gushed.

A grinning Kenny hugged his girlfriend, almost pulling her over, and kissed her on the cheek.

'I know, it's crazy, isn't it. Here at Silverstone to watch the British Grand Prix – a dream come true! It's very noisy though,' he laughed, covering his ears as a gaggle of cars sped by. 'Certainly worth going deaf for!'

'What?' shouted Sally-Ann, trying to be heard over the noise.

Kenny shook his head and wafted his hand to prove his point.

Lap by lap, Hunt eased his way towards the waving chequered flag – the victory was his! The crowd erupted into a sea of waving arms and cheering; caps flew into the air. The local boy, Sally-Ann's motorsport hero, had taken the win!

'He did it!' whooped Sally-Ann. 'He did it!'

Kenny picked her up around the waist and spun her around, both cheering and laughing in their elation of the moment.

All around them, people began shoving their way forward, trying to catch a glimpse of the winning car, followed by second-place Niki Lauda in his Ferrari, and the third-place Lotus-Ford of Gunnar Nilsson, as they crossed the line a good eighteen seconds later. A clear and well-deserved win for James Hunt.

A sudden surge of emotion tore through Kenny as he gazed at Sally-Ann. He realised just how lucky he was to find a girl who shared his passion for cars and motorsport.

There was only one thing he could do.

He bent down on one knee and took her by the hand.

'Will you marry me, Sally-Ann?'

She looked at his grinning face as he knelt down before her, her face turning to one of wide-eyed and open-mouthed surprise.

Kenny continued his proposal. 'I mean, I know that we haven't been seeing each other very long, but, well. I just want to be with you, Sal. I want to marry you.'

'You're being deadly serious, aren't you?'

'Deadly serious,' he replied.

A squeal of delight came from Sally-Ann.

'Of course I'll marry you, Ken. Yes! Yes!' she gushed.

One or two of the crowd around them witnessed their act of love and began applauding and cheering them, causing them both to flush with shyness. And unbeknown to Sally-Ann and Ken, their proposal had been captured on film by a local news reporter who was there to cover the race event. The journalist sauntered over to congratulate them and to ask if they would be willing to be interviewed on camera. Here was an unexpected scoop!

The "Grand Prix Proposal" made a heartwarming addition to the sensational news of James Hunt's successful race win at the Silverstone circuit, in the local Towcester news round-ups.

As word spread North about their story, both the *Derbyshire Times* and the *Castle Ridge Weekly* made sure to include news articles about their betrothal, together with some photographs of the happy couple.

Not one to miss out on a marketing opportunity, Ms Barbara Bryant, from *Sparkles*, the long-established jewellers in Castle Ridge, also made sure to get her picture taken with Kenny and Sally-Ann, having generously donated a simple but pretty diamond solitaire engagement ring. Even the research team from Silverstone raceway had managed to track them down, so that they could send them a congratulatory bouquet of flowers.

For the next few weeks, Kenny and Sally-Ann basked in the afterglow. They were regularly stopped in the streets of Castle Ridge to have their hands shaken by well-wishers and to have a look at the ring. Both sets of parents were also getting their own five minutes of fame once people realised who they were. It was the perfect way to lift the spirits of the Clarke family and those closest to them after the recent tragedy.

It also led to the burning question – when would be the big day?

For Kenny and Sally-Ann, there could only be one date – the Bank Holiday weekend of 29th April the following year. And the reason for this date? They would be able to take their honeymoon the weekend afterwards, at the Monaco Grand Prix.

The perfect way to start married life!

14: Hot Wheels - 1978

'Happy birthday, Sally-Ann, my love. I hope that you'll have a lovely day!'

Irene gave Sally-Ann a genuinely warm hug before handing her a little bouquet of freesias and a gift-wrapped box.

'Oh, that's so sweet of you, thank you, Irene.' She sniffed the freesias and did her best not to sneeze at the heady, floral fragrance, then tore the wrapping paper off the gift box.

'Oh, Estée Lauder Youth Dew!' Sally-Ann did her best to make her smile appear genuinely delighted.

Irene beamed with pride at the notion that she'd done something right for the young lass.

'The lady at the perfume counter in Boots said that all the young girls are wearing it at the moment. That's why it's called Youth Dew – for the youth of today.'

Sally-Ann nodded along with her. 'I didn't realise that...' she said, doing her best to stifle a giggle. She could envisage the lady on the fragrance counter in Boots stifling a giggle, too, when she made the sale, seeing as how Youth Dew is renowned as an "old-lady's perfume". But it's the thought that counts, as they say.

'Look what I got from your mum and dad, Kenny – some flowers and perfume...' She held up her gifts for her fiancé to see.

A wry grin played across his lips as he seized the opportunity to do a bit of teasing.

'Well, I hope it smells better than your usual fragrance of motor oil!' He laughed heartily at his own joke. 'Hey, talking of motor oil, have you decided what car you're getting our Mick for his 18th? That's coming up soon, isn't it, Mam?'

Irene rolled her eyes, 'It is indeed, and no, I haven't decided on anything. Mick did mention something about a Lotus Esprit...'

Sally-Ann almost choked on her coffee, needing a pat on the back from Kenny. She shook her head.

'Well, for one, that'll be too expensive to buy, and for two, he'll never be able to afford the insurance on something like that. Not as a new driver!'

Feeling irked by his brother's suggestion for such a flash car, Kenny couldn't help but add his two penn'orth.

'Yeah, c'mon, Mam! If a bog-standard Cortina and Escort were good enough for me and our Barry when we were eighteen, then our Mick can have a regular car, same as us.' Kenny burst out laughing. 'In fact, you should get him an Allegro – I'd love to see his face when he gets that on his birthday morning!'

'Oh, you are mean, Kenneth!' Irene play-slapped him at the suggestion.

'What about a Morris Marina? Or a Vauxhall Viva?' suggested Sally-Ann. 'They're all reasonably priced, sensible first cars.'

Irene shook her head. 'I don't think Mick would want to do "sensible". That isn't his style.'

'Hmmff! Beggars shouldn't be choosers, the spoiled git...' tagged on Kenny.

'Does he have a full driving licence?' Sally-Ann asked. 'That certainly helps where insurance is concerned.'

'Yes, he passed his test months ago, and he drives the little delivery van at work. He upgraded from the shop's bicycle, as he says. His grandparents clubbed together last year and paid for all his lessons, same as they did for the other two when they were seventeen.'

'Hmmm, okay...' After a brief moment of thought, Sally-Ann snapped her fingers together. 'I've got it! What about a Ford Capri? They look quite flashy, but they're not over the top on insurance, especially if you just get the basic 1300 model. I can get mi'dad or mi'brothers to ask around. They know plenty of blokes at the raceway. Plus, I think we've got a few copies of *What Car?* magazine at home. I'll take a look.'

'Oh, would you, love? That would be most helpful.' Irene breathed a sigh of relief. 'Thank goodness you know a bit about cars!'

'You're welcome. I'm pretty sure mi'dad'll appreciate the diversion away from mi'mam and all the wedding plans,' she laughed.

True to her promise, Sally-Ann helped to locate the ideal birthday car for Mick, just in time for his big day. Although he knew his wish for a Lotus Esprit was a bit of a pipe-dream, Mick was more than delighted to receive the keys to an old but gleaming Mk1 Ford Capri 1.3 in red, with black vinyl roof, chrome bumpers and Cibie front spotlights. A classic beauty. The Capri had been the pride and joy of its previous owner, who sadly needed to replace it with a pram and a family car.

And now Mick was the lucky new owner!

15: Raise Your Glasses!

A roar of laughter, cheers, and applause rang around the room as the father of the bride gave his speech. Mr Clarke was a larger-than-life character who, with his deep booming voice, knew how to command an audience. His eyes twinkled as he spoke of the love that he had for his daughter, and the pride he had felt as he had escorted her down the aisle to give her away. But in typical Clarke style, he couldn't resist rounding off the moment with a touch of humour.

'Mind you, it wasn't so much giving her away as paying to get rid of her!' he joked. 'Both my cheque book and bank account are truly grateful that I only have one daughter and three sons, and not the other way around. At least some other bugger got to pay for all this when the lads got married.' He gestured around the room at all the decorations and food, while the wedding party and guests spluttered in fits of laughter.

'I'll second that!' grinned Dennis, raising his glass towards Mr Clarke in acknowledgment.

As the laughter died down, Mr Clarke lifted his glass of champagne, this being the one alcoholic drink which he would allow himself for tonight.

'So, I now ask you all to join with me and my dear lady wife in toasting the bride and groom. May they have a long and happy marriage, blessed with loads of kids. To Sally-Ann and Kenny!'

A chorus of *'To Sally-Ann and Kenny!'* filled the room, followed by the raising of glasses and three cheers of *'Hip-Hip, Hooray!'*

The happy couple kissed and clinked their glasses together to toast each other.

Once the room had quieted, Kenny stood up to make his speech; first, thanking his new father-in-law for his rhetoric, then thanking the guests for sharing in their special day. But mostly, he directed his speech towards Sally-Ann and the deep love that he had for the amazing woman who had agreed to share her life with him; for that, he was deeply grateful. And not to be outdone by Sally-Ann's dad on the wedding-speech jokes, he also threw in a witty comment.

'After all, it isn't every day that you find a wife who can do an oil change and service on your car!'

Sally-Ann elbowed him playfully and gave him a coy smile, as everyone laughed along with his teasing.

He smiled back at her, then raised his glass.

'To Sally-Ann, to married life, and all the smiles, storms, and whatever comes our way. I love you, lass. Cheers!'

Their guests echoed his sentiments with *'Hear, hear'* and *'Cheers'*, before he handed over proceedings to Baz, as his best man.

As a way of winding-up his brother, Baz grinned at Kenny before reaching inside his jacket for his speech paper. When he flipped it out, it was about six feet long – six pages of A4 paper, sticky-taped together, causing a round of laughter from their guests.

'Well, Kenneth,' he began. 'The downside with choosing your brother to be your best man is that your brother knows all your secrets...' He paused for effect before thumbing his way over all the sheets of paper, occasionally looking up at his brother, then sucking in his breath in jest. 'Hmm, perhaps I'd better not tell people about that... Or that...' He wriggled his eyebrows for effect. 'And most definitely not that!' He screwed up the sheets of paper and threw the ball over his shoulder before proceeding to give a heartfelt speech directed towards his older brother and new sister-in-law.

Claire looked up at Baz and smiled. As chief bridesmaid, she was having a fantastic day supporting her best friend on her journey into married life and being part of the celebrations. It was the most magical of days, and just what the families needed to brush away the grey cloud that had been hanging over them all.

While he was giving his speech, Claire gave herself a mental reminder to pace herself, particularly on the drinking. She was, after all, still quite young and inexperienced. Since the tragic loss of Sally-Ann's little nephew from alcohol poisoning, the families had become more mindful of excesses. A three-course meal of prawn cocktail, carvery main course, and sherry trifle for dessert, including wine would follow the speeches. Then a disco and mid-evening buffet would round off a full day of celebrating, eating, and drinking.

Hearing her name mentioned brought Claire back to the present moment, as Barry gave her a toast of thanks for looking after Sally-Ann, and making sure that she got to the church on time. Also, for looking after the little flower girls, two of Sally-Ann's young nieces. Claire beamed and smiled, looking around at the other guests.

She caught sight of Mick looking at her, grinning. Goosebumps ran up the length of her arms as his eyes caught hers. She tried not to read anything into it – many of the guests were looking her way as Baz gave praise to her efforts. But the look felt wrong. It felt invasive. Claire pulled her eyes away from his, then refocused on Baz and his speech.

'And so that just leaves me to say congratulations to the new Mr and Mrs Watkins. I'm well proud of you, bruv! So, if you two lovebirds would like to go over to the cake table and cut the cake. Ladies and gents, if you would raise your glasses with me in a toast, then get your cameras ready for the cake-cutting. To Kenneth and Sally-Ann – Cheers!'

'CHEERS!'

A flurry of activity followed as the bride and groom moved over to the cake table, ready to cut the wedding cake and be photographed for this most momentous of occasions.

Except some prankster had put a 17mm open-ended spanner onto the table instead of the cake knife...

With the function room now cleared and prepared for the evening's disco and buffet, the guests began reconvening. An air of anticipation filled the room, and the general chatter dissipated as the DJ stepped up to the microphone to invite Kenny and Sally-Ann onto the dancefloor to lead off the dancing.

What song would they choose as "their song"?

Kenny bowed towards Sally-Ann, as she curtsied and took his hand to the opening chords of Eric Clapton's *Wonderful Tonight.* A round of applause and whistles accompanied them as they kissed before holding each other for the first dance. After a short while, Baz led Claire onto the dancefloor to join the bride and groom, together with both sets of parents, in their co-celebration of love.

Towards the end of the song, the DJ lowered the sound so that he could interject with a little bit of commentary, giving an overview of the evening's itinerary. He then whipped up the crowd to join the happy couples on the dancefloor by playing a slew of Bee Gees tracks. A bottle of champagne was on offer as a prize for the best John Travolta of the evening!

Baz flopped down into one of the chairs so that he could take a welcoming swig of his cold beer. He loosened his tie to open his collar, then proceeded to open a few more buttons and fan himself. Claire came and sat beside him, laughing. One by one, others sat down, exhausted from their best efforts to win the Bee Gees dance-off, until only a few Travolta wannabees were left. Encouraged by the DJ, the crowd clapped along with *You Should Be Dancin'*, and depending on how much or how loudly they clapped for the dancers, determined who stayed and who was eliminated. Much to everyone's jollity, and calls from the sidelines of "fix!", the remaining two dancers were Kenny and Sally-Ann's dad. As the track ended, Mr Clarke was declared the winner, prompting him to rip open his shirt in victory, causing gasps of laughter.

Irene turned to Dennis, her mouth open in mock shock.

'Oooh, thank goodness it wasn't you that won!' she snorted, almost spilling her drink. 'He's got quite the hairy chest, hasn't he?'

Dennis rolled his eyes in fun.

'Let's hope the DJ doesn't start playing strip-tease music,' he laughed, 'or we might be seeing a lot more of Sally-Ann's dad!'

Mr Clarke graciously accepted his prize to much applause, only to generously donate it to the table where many of Kenny and Sally-Ann's friends were sitting.

'Aww, what a lovely gesture. They're such a lovely family, aren't they, Dennis?'

'Aye, our Kenny's done well for himself, that's for sure.' He looked across at Baz and Claire, who also seemed to be having a great deal of fun as they headed back to the dancefloor after their breather. 'I wouldn't be surprised if they don't get married soon, either. They both seem very happy together.'

Feeling all warm and fuzzy, Irene smiled, then raised her glass towards her husband.

'That's just what I was thinking. Well, cheers, my love. Oooh, it's ABBA!' She grabbed his hand to drag him towards the dancefloor. 'C'mon, come and dance with me to *Mamma Mia*!'.

'Do I have a choice...?' he laughed.

Seeing what kind of geometric design she could make, Claire toyed with the little pile of cocktail sticks on her plate. If there was one thing she could never resist, it was cold buffet food. She mentally tried to count how many sausage rolls she'd had, and gave up. The tally of cocktail sticks told her that she'd eaten eight pieces of cheese and pineapple.

Claire remembered having had two slices of cheesecake. How many drinks had she had? She had done her best to be mindful of her limits. While her brain refused to function, her belly felt queasy with excess. She also felt hot and faint.

She nudged Barry.

'I'm just going outside to get a bit of fresh air. I won't be long.'

'Aye, okay. Do you want my jacket to put around your shoulders?' he offered.

'Nah, I'll be fine. I'm feeling too hot, a bit faint.' She carefully stood up, using the table edge as a lever, while she composed her balance, before heading outside.

The evening air felt cool on her skin as she sat down at one of the wooden picnic benches in the beer garden. A rush of goosebumps ran up the length of her arms, causing her to shiver. Perhaps it might have been wise to take Baz's jacket. She closed her eyes, only for the darkness to start spinning. Keeping them open and trying to breathe calmly seemed to have the best effect. She focused ahead on one of the trees while trying not to think about all the food and alcohol she had consumed.

So much for pacing yourself, you idiot! she chided herself.

'Are you okay, Claire? I saw you come outside, and just wanted to make sure that you're okay.'

Mick's voice behind her caused her to jump, with a half-scream.

'Mick! Jeez, you frightened the living daylights out of me! Don't creep up on people like that...'

'Sorry, I didn't mean to make you jump.'

Feeling bold from the effects of a little too much alcohol, he came and sat beside her. Although most of the Clarkes and Watkins clans seemed to be pacing themselves this evening, his nervousness around Sally-Ann's older brothers was making him a little too liberal at the free bar. They were big lads, and the thought of them tearing him limb from limb if they ever found out he was ultimately responsible for the little one's death made him anxious.

Ever since Barry had brought Claire home and introduced her to the family, Mick had always had a soft spot for her. There was something about her that was so natural; so down-to-earth. He often found himself unconsciously staring at her, sometimes locking eyes. But he guessed by the way she tore her eyes away from his that she didn't feel the same. Claire only had eyes for Baz. He had once managed to steal one of the T-shirts that she'd left at the house. It smelled sweet. It smelled of her. The thought of her sweet smell ignited something within.

A fire in his belly.

A stirring in his loins.

A longing.

A primal urge...

'You're so pretty, Claire – can I ask you something?' He squashed up close.

Uncomfortably close.

She tried to wriggle away from him, but he sidled along with her, keeping the gap between them to a minimum.

Mick looked at her and smiled, his eyes glassy from alcohol, his grin childlike. He pressed himself closer to her body and reached his hand over hers to try and hold it.

'Aww, c'mon, Claire. Don't be like that.' He thrust his head towards hers. 'Could you do me a favour? Could you let me have a kiss? Just one kiss, please? It's all I ask. I just want to feel what our Baz feels...'

Claire locked eyes with him and hesitated. His breath smelled sweet, yet heady with booze. However, the look and hesitation were just enough for Mick, in his virgin innocence, to misread the signals.

Catching her off guard, he cautiously moved in on his brother's girlfriend.

16: A Shocking Discovery

Claire eased her little Renault 5 slowly along Haddon Hall Road towards the turning point at the bottom, before pulling up in front of Kenny and Sally-Ann's house. She and Baz had volunteered to keep an eye on the place every other day while the newlyweds were away on their honeymoon.

'Are you okay?' asked Baz. 'You've been really quiet this week. A bit distant.'

She reached over to the back footwell for her handbag without really catching his eye.

'Yeah, okay, I guess. Probably just this shitty weather, coupled with the fact that the honeymooners are living it up in sunny Monaco. I bet they're having the time of their lives.'

'Pff, you can say that again! Just think, they're getting to spend two nights in a fancy hotel in Monaco over the race weekend – in the honeymoon suite – as a gift from the Silverstone people.' He rolled his eyes in jest. 'Unfuckingbelievable! That's living it up, eh!'

'Jammy sods! And here we are in old, grey Castle Vale.'

Both she and Baz pulled up their hoods before getting out of the car, protection against the early May drizzle. She sighed and took a moment to look at the bay-fronted terrace. Sally-Ann and Kenny had certainly dropped onto a great deal with finding this little house in the Vale suburb of Castle Ridge. It was near the end of a quiet road backing onto allotments, and the estate agent's details were not lying when they said it was "deceptively spacious" – all the rooms were of generous proportions. In the short time they'd owned it, the house had been transformed by Kenny's building skills and Sally-Ann's vision for making it into a cosy nest.

Baz fumbled in his coat pocket for the keys to the house before unlocking the front door. A draught of wind rushed through the house, slamming the kitchen door closed with the movement of air. Claire jumped and screamed at the unexpected *BANG!*

'That's weird. I hope the daft sods didn't leave a window open. I told them to make sure everything was closed up before they left,' said Barry, a little surprised at the feeling of a draught coming from somewhere. He closed the front door and went further into the long hallway towards the kitchen. Cold air blew around the kitchen door as he opened it.

'Oh, fuck! The back door's wide open. Stay back, Claire, it looks like it's been jemmied.'

'What do you mean? Like it's been broken into?' she asked. 'Shit, do you think someone could still be in the house?'

They both stood still to listen.

'I can't hear anything,' said Baz. Stay here and don't touch anything while I have a look at the back door, and take a look around.'

After a cursory sweep of the whole house, Barry came down the stairs, then nodded towards the sitting room door, which was slightly ajar. He eased it open with his shoulder to make sure that he didn't touch the handle.

'Oh no... Come and look at this, Claire. But don't touch anything.'

The room was littered with wedding presents, mostly the larger ones – gifts that couldn't easily be lifted or moved.

Claire sucked in her breath when she saw the devastation.

'Oh, Christ Almighty! They've been burgled! Do you think they've taken much?'

Baz shook his head.

'It's hard to say. But I can't see the video recorder that Mum and Dad got for them. Or the silver tankards from Gran. Bastards!'

'What should we do?'

'There's only one thing we can do. I'll go and call the police. You wait here.'

Barry vanished into the hallway to use the telephone and call for assistance.

Claire's heart sank as she looked around the room. Kenny and Sally-Ann were two of the nicest people she knew. Hard-working, honest, fun-loving. They didn't deserve to start married life this way. She sighed, her eyes welling with tears.

'I managed to get through to the main cop shop in Chesterfield, and they'll relay the call-out to the local constabulary. They told us to just wait here until they arrive, and not touch anything. Hey, don't cry. Come here...'

'Sorry... This is just so shitty!' Claire wiped under her eyes. 'How could someone do this? The thief must have known when they would be away. Somebody must have heard them talking about it.'

'Yeah, that's what I think, too. Someone could've overheard them in the pub, or wherever. But then again, the Derbo Times and the local rag both did a little write-up about the wedding as a follow-up to their Silverstone proposal. Any of the local criminals could've read the article and used the opportunity to break in.' He shrugged at the sad reality of the situation.

'Aye, that's true. But then again, there's been such a spate of break-ins recently – especially houses which back onto open land like these do. It must be somebody with local knowledge.' Claire paused for a moment, lost in her thoughts. 'Do you think we should try and call them in Monaco?'

'What – and spoil their honeymoon? Besides, I've no idea which hotels they're staying in. No, it's best to wait until they come home. But in the meantime, we'll make sure everything is clean and secured before they get back, once the police have finished dusting the place. I just hope that they manage to catch the bastards who did this.'

Baz looked towards the bay window as a panda car pulled up behind Claire's car. 'They're here now. I'll go and let them in.'

17: Back to Reality

Upon seeing her best friend waiting by the railings at the National Express coach terminal in Chesterfield, Sally-Ann stood up out of her seat and waved, trying to catch Claire's attention.

'I don't think she's seen me.'

Kenny pulled her gently back into her seat and nuzzled his nose to hers before giving her a soft kiss. He inhaled her scent. Despite having sat on a coach for the past six hours on the way back from Heathrow, she still smelled of sunshine, Ambre Solaire and happiness. Her skin glowed with a golden tan, and her hair was sun-kissed with natural highlights. He felt a stirring in his loins, so chose to look out of the window at the grey weather to kill the feeling. After an unforgettable week of sun, sea, sand, sex, and Formula One in and around Monaco, normality was rearing its ugly head.

'Well, here we are, Mrs Watkins. Back to reality.' He sighed and kissed her once more. 'It looks like our Baz has come with her. I hope there'll be enough room for the four of us and luggage in that little car of hers,' he chuckled.

'God, they both look so glum! Has the weather been that bad while we've been away?' She shook her head and rolled her eyes. 'Ugh, I can't believe we'll be back at work tomorrow. At least it will only be for a couple of days until the weekend.'

'Aye, that's the good thing about Wednesday-to-Wednesday holidays. Two short working weeks on either side!'

The coach pulled to a stop close to where Barry and Claire were waiting. Baz sighed, his face a mask of seriousness, knowing what news they were about to deliver. After much discussion, they had concluded that it was best to tell them straight away rather than on the journey home. He took hold of Claire's hand and kissed it.

'Here we go...'

Sally-Ann and Kenny were some of the last people to get off, by which time the driver had unloaded their suitcase from the belly of the coach. They had wisely purchased a suitcase on wheels, knowing that there would be a lot of dragging and walking to do between all the destinations.

With a light step, Sally-Ann hurried towards Claire to give her a hug, while Kenny trundled slowly behind with the baggage, grateful that they, or rather she, had chosen to travel light. He joined the trio and gave Claire and his brother a genuine hug of gratitude, being happy to see them.

After the cursory round of hugs and welcoming small-talk, Barry and Claire shot each other a glance. Barry cleared his throat for the upcoming and uncomfortable task.

'We're so sorry to be the bearer of bad news, but I'm afraid that your house was broken into while you were away...'

Both Sally-Ann and Kenny blinked in shock, their mouths falling open but unable to speak.

'What? Broken into. A burglary, you mean?' asked Kenny.

'Yeah, soz bruv. We found it on Friday evening when we went to check on the house. The back door had been jemmied open.'

Kenny's face turned to one of pure thunder, while Sally-Ann began to cry. He put his arm around his wife and pulled her close to try and soothe her.

'Bastards! Was anything damaged? Anything taken?'

Baz shook his head.

'The back door lock and frame were slightly damaged. We assume that some of your wedding presents were stolen – mostly the small stuff, at a guess. Stuff they could easily carry away. We're not 100% sure what was nicked, so the police said that you'll have to make an assessment and let them know. Also, because of the insurance.'

'Aye, I suppose we'll have to inform the insurance company, and do battle with them for compensation.' Kenny sighed. If there was one thing that he hated dealing with, it was insurance companies.

Claire reached into her handbag to get a pack of tissues for Sally-Ann, then gently pulled her out of Kenny's arms and into her own.

'Luckily, nothing was trashed or broken. It looks like whoever did it was straight in and out as fast as poss,' Barry continued. 'The only real mess was after the police came to dust the place for fingerprints.'

'Did the police find owt? Any clues? Any fingerprints?' asked Kenny.

'Not a thing. The place was clean,' replied Baz. 'They didn't find any fingerprints or footprints. They questioned the neighbours, but no one seemed to have heard anything or seen anyone hanging around. I think they even did a sweep of the allotments at the back to see if the burglars had stashed anything to collect later.'

Claire endeavoured to sound positive and help soften the blow for Kenny and Sally-Ann. After having such a memorable wedding day and dream honeymoon, this was the last thing that anyone wanted them to come home to.

'Your dad has fixed the back door and touched up the paintwork. He's also fitted some bolts and changed the locks on both doors, so we'll give you the new keys. Both families pulled together to help with the cleaning and stuff. Even Mick pushed the vacuum cleaner around.'

'My God, I would have loved to have seen that,' chuckled Ken. 'Did someone have to plug it in for him and show him how to operate it?'

It was the lighter moment that Sally-Ann needed to overcome the shocking news. She laughed lightly at the vision of her young brother-in-law attempting to do housework, then blew her nose on a dry tissue, the tears having now subsided.

'Well, I suppose we'd better go home and take a look. I just hope that it still feels like home...'

18: Happy Fathers' Day

'Oh, it's so nice to have all the family together today,' mused Irene, as she shook the tablecloth open, ready to put it onto the dining table. 'Mick, can you go and get eight dinner plates and the canteen of cutlery? Thanks, love.'

Mick's brow furrowed as he mentally calculated the number of guests to be seated.

'Eight? Don't you mean seven? Us three, plus the four love-birds.'

'Eight. I've invited your nanna as well. She doesn't get out much, and this will be the first big family gathering since Kenny and Sal got back from their honeymoon. I just thought it would be nice to get everyone together, with it being Father's Day.'

'Great, so Nanna and me will be the odd couple,' he laughed. 'The oldest and the youngest. Put her at the top of the table away from everyone, though. She farts all the time, and her false teeth clack together when she's talking or eating.'

Irene pulled a face and gave a hearty laugh at the way Mick had described her mother.

'Michael! Don't you talk about your nanna like that! You wait until you get old and can't control your bodily functions,' she snorted. 'Talk of the Devil – your dad's here with her now, so no more fart or false teeth jokes! I'd better go and see how lunch is doing, and put the kettle on. Can I leave you to finish laying the table?' Irene looked at her watch. 'The others should be here shortly, too.' She gave Mick her sweetest smile – he had been in a strange mood recently, like something was bothering him. It was nice to see him in a better frame of mind today. And he'd even bought his father a card and a pack of After Eights!

Once everyone was seated around the dining table, with Mick and his nanna strategically seated at opposite ends of the big oval, Irene carefully tapped a teaspoon onto her empty wine glass.

'Well, happy Father's Day to you, Dennis, my love, and can I just say how nice it is to have all the family together.'

A murmur of agreement rippled around the table. Kenny and Sally-Ann exchanged furtive smiles, while Baz and Claire surreptitiously bumped thighs together under the table.

'Right then,' continued Irene, 'I guess the men would like a beer with their lunch, if you could sort that out, Kenneth. Would you like a glass of red or white, Sally-Ann?'

'Erm, just a lemonade for me, thanks. I fancy something sharp and refreshing.'

'Same here,' chimed Claire. 'I think I would prefer a fizzy, cold drink, too.'

Irene raised her eyebrows at the two girls.

'Okay… Erm, Barry, could you go and get some lemonade out of the fridge? I think there's a bottle of R-White's. There's also a bottle of Dandelion & Burdock. I can't remember when the pop delivery is due next.'

As had become the standard food joke at family gatherings, Irene went to retrieve two Arctic Rolls out of the freezer for dessert while the rest of the Watkins clan helped to clear away the main-course dishes.

Unseen by the others, Kenny took this as his cue to retrieve a little package from his jacket pocket, then came and sat at the table next to Sally-Ann. Again, furtive glances were exchanged in anticipation of the family sitting back down.

With two slices of Arctic Roll now set in front of everyone, Kenny stood up to hug his dad and give him the little parcel.

'Happy Father's Day, Pops. Hope you like it.'

Dennis shook the package and gave it a little squeeze.

'Well, it doesn't feel like a bottle of Brut 33 or Old Spice,' he laughed, as he began tearing off the paper. He blinked curiously at the little pair of white crocheted bootees in his hand. 'I don't think they'll fit me…' Then he grinned as the realisation hit him. 'Seriously? Am I going to be a grandad?' Dennis's eyes lit up and sparkled at the heartwarming news. He stood up to shake Kenny's hand and give him a manly clap on the back, then went to hug Sally-Ann.

Irene squealed in delight at the news before also going to give the new parents-to-be a loving hug.

'Oh, my word – I'm going to be a granny! I'm so excited!' she gushed.

Claire and Barry exchanged glances with a grin and a nod. Barry took the Father's Day card from his jacket pocket and passed it to Dennis, who tore open the envelope and then read the card. His eyes widened, causing his eyebrows to peer above his reading glasses.

'No way! Seriously!'

'What? What is it?' asked Irene.

Dennis shook his head and laughed in disbelief at the news that was written inside the greeting card.

'Would you believe it – we're going to be double grandparents, Irene!'

Irene's face dropped in one of delighted shock, before clapping her hands and shrieking in excitement.

'Seriously? Oh my goodness, I don't believe it! More additions to the Watkins clan...'

'Mam, can we start on the dessert? The Arctic Roll's beginning to melt,' commented Mick among all the jollity that was taking place. He scowled at the thought of squawking, smelly babies around the house.

'What? Melting. Yes, yes, of course! Tuck into dessert, everyone,' flustered Irene, as she sat down to rejoin the family meal after giving Claire and Barry an excited hug.

'So when are the babies due? I'd better start knitting...'

'Mam, it's still early days,' laughed Kenny. 'You've got until the beginning of February next year. No stress!'

'Same for us,' added Claire. 'Our due date has been given for the beginning of February, too.'

'Well, well, well,' laughed Dennis, his face a picture of happiness. 'So, when did you two ladies find out that you're pregnant?' he asked.

Sally-Ann spoke up first.

'Kenny and I had a suspicion that I was pregnant at the beginning of this month, then had it confirmed at the doctor's on Wednesday. Dr Elliott teased us that some magic must have happened in Monaco, and called it our "honeymoon baby".'

Claire laughed. 'Well, that explains why Dr Elliott gave us a strange look on Friday when we went to have my pregnancy confirmed, and get an approximate date. She calculated back that it must have happened around the time of the wedding. Fancy that, we're having our first babies at the same time!' She went around the table to take her best friend into her arms.

Irene took a long drink of her white wine, then looked around the table at her family. Everyone seemed to be smiling except Michael, who was busy making a mess out of his Arctic Roll. She took the opportunity to make him feel included.

'Isn't it wonderful news, Michael? You're going to be an uncle twice over!'

Mick nodded and gave a fake smile, masking his zero-fucks-given inner thoughts. He glanced over at the wall unit and looked at the box of After Eights – his father's favourite chocolates, and the card – both carefully chosen. They had even been paid for not stolen! Yet in his mind, his Father's Day contribution paled into insignificance – trumped once again by his older brothers.

Satisfied that her youngest offspring seemed happy, Irene topped up her glass, then raised it in a toast.

'Well, here's to the next generation of Watkins. Cheers, everybody.'

The family raised their glasses in unison and clinked them together.

'Oops! Excuse me!' giggled Irene's mother, as a little fart escaped. 'I may have eaten a few too many sprouts...'

19: Catch-up

The heat and cloying smell of greasy bacon and fried onions hung in the air at Naylor's Little Café, causing Sally-Ann to gag as soon as she walked inside. She put her hand over her nose, then scanned around for her best friend.

As was usual at this time of the afternoon, the place was swarming with mothers, buggies, and toddlers stopping off for a cuppa before collecting older siblings from the nearby infants' school.

A hand shot up and waved from the far corner closest to the counter. Claire was here.

Like a competitor in a game of *It's a Knockout,* Sally-Ann weaved her way through the chaotic throng, trying her best to avoid pushchair wheels, shopping bags, and free-range kiddies.

She pulled out a chair and sat down opposite Claire at the little two-person table; a table still littered with crumbs and a smear of HP sauce, presumably from the previous diner. Rolling her eyes, she grabbed a handful of paper napkins from the dispenser and wiped the surface over.

'Couldn't you have chosen a better place for our catch-up?' she chided. 'My sense of smell is off the scale with sensitivity at the moment.'

'Soz, Sal. I have such a craving for sausage sarnies – I can't get enough of 'em.' She patted the tiny swell of her stomach. 'I think this little one will come out looking like a sausage!' she laughed. 'Anyway, I'm going to order a sausage cob and a mug of tea. Would you like anything?'

Sally-Ann shrugged. 'Just a cuppa for me, thanks. And some earplugs. I've been to quieter race meetings!'

Once Claire returned to their table with their order, she tucked into her food with gusto while Sally-Ann looked on in pregnancy-sickness disgust, and gently sipped on her sweetened tea.

After swallowing a satisfying mouthful of her cob, Claire grinned, her eyes twinkling with merriment.

'Well, look at us two, eh! Best mates since infant school, and both expecting our first babies at the same time. Who would have thought it? Were you on your way to the factory office when I saw you this morning? I never got a chance to ask you, it was so busy today.'

'Yep. The office girls thought it was funny that I'm having a honeymoon baby! They've scheduled the start of the Christmas break as the start of my maternity leave.'

'Me too. We'll be going on maternity leave at the same time. Did you know that the office will be taking bets during our last week? The factory lasses can pay 50p to guess our due dates, the baby's sex, and weight. The closest two will each win a box of chocolates, and the rest of the money raised will go towards a baby gift. They also said that we can join in and bet on each other's babies!' She took another mouthful of her sausage cob.

'That sounds like a lot of fun,' laughed Sally-Ann. 'It's nice that the office always does something like this when one of the girls is leaving, or not well. I don't care what anybody says about the factory; it's a great place to work. So, how's the pregnancy going for you? How are you feeling?'

Claire grinned, then wiped her mouth with a napkin.

'I feel absolutely fine. No morning sickness, or not much, at least. And I know this sounds weird, but I feel *really* sexy! If this is being pregnant, then I think we'll be having a football team!'

'Ugh, I wish I could say the same,' sighed Sally-Ann. 'I feel sick all day long, I'm as tired as shit, and already getting puffy ankles. If this is being pregnant, I think we'll stop at this one,' she chuckled. 'God knows how bad the actual birth will be... How did your mum take the news, with you and Barry not being married yet?'

'She's as happy as Larry and looking forward to being a grandmother. She's also offered that we can go and live with her, if we want to.'

'And do you want to?'

'Not a chance! Anyway – top secret news – we went to view a lovely little house last week. It's for sale with Wilton's Estate Agents, and not too far from the factory. It needs a bit of renovating, but Barry's pretty sure that his dad will chip in and help with the work. We put in an offer the same day, and after a bit of to-ing and fro-ing, we finally negotiated a price. It's a deceased estate, so it's the family who's selling it. I think they were happy to let it go to a young couple just starting out rather than a builder who would just rip it to pieces.'

'Whereabouts is the house, exactly?'

'It's that little semi on the corner of Crofters Lane and Quarry Lane. The one that overlooks the allotment gardens. It only came up for sale last week, so we jumped in straight away. You're the only one we've told, though.'

'Ah, I know which one you mean. It's in a lovely spot. Well, good luck, eh. At least you're in a good position, being first-time buyers.'

'That's what the negotiator said at Wilton's. We've got a reasonable deposit and no other debts, so it's not like we're time-wasters. If all goes well, we should complete the purchase by the end of September. Plus, we've got some other news...'

Sally-Ann's eyes widened, expectant.

'Other news? Besides having a baby and buying a house, what other news could there be? Unless... Unless you're getting married?'

'Bingo! Yes! Barry asked me to marry him, and I said yes. Well, of course, why wouldn't I say yes? I'm having his baby and we're buying a house together. My God, we're being so grown up!'

Bitten by the curiosity bug, her friend pressed for more information.

'Do you have a date in mind?'

'Yeah, somewhere around the beginning of November, near Barry's birthday. We've decided to have just a small registry office ceremony, and then go out for a meal. Just our closest family. By the way, we haven't told anybody about that either, so keep it to yourself.'

'Can I at least tell Kenny?'

'Nope! Please try and keep it a secret. We want to make a grand announcement after we've fixed the date with the registry office.'

'So you don't want to have a big wedding like we had, then?' asked Sally-Ann.

Claire looked at her friend like she was from another planet.

'Sal, I'll have a huge baby bump by then! Hardly a cause for wearing a virgin-white dress,' she laughed. 'Nah, just something short and sweet – after all, it's the meaning behind the vows which is important, not how much you spend.'

Sally-Ann groaned in frustration at the prospect of having to keep more secrets, before downing the last of her tea, then looking at her watch.

'Well, I'd better get going. I need to grab a bit of shopping before heading home. I've no idea what we're going to have – everything I cook seems to make me feel sick. It's a good job that Kenny likes salads or sandwiches. That's about all I can stomach at the moment. I don't know how I managed to get through the meal at their house yesterday without puking. Kenny's started having something from the chippie or takeaway at dinner time just so that he can get a hot meal once a day. Talk about compromises!'

20: Card Sharks

From his concealed vantage point in the laurel bushes of Ridge Gardens, Mick crouched low and peered intently towards the black BMW, which had just pulled up in the little car park by the main gates. He could just make out the two burly figures of his suppliers in the front, having some kind of discussion. The driver looked at his watch, prompting Mick to take a look at his. It was almost noon.

It was almost pay-up time.

He felt the pager vibrate in his jacket pocket.

Mick grinned to himself and ignored it, giving him a feeling of empowerment. Like hell he was going to cough up two hundred quid! Yes, he'd played cards with the men, but in his mind, they'd clearly rigged the game so that he would lose. It seemed that for every hand he played, they always had something to top his. So much so that he ran out of goods to put on the table and started playing with IOUs. Well, he wasn't going to be ripped off! He always brought plenty of quality gear to trade – stuff that was worth much more than the allocated gambling value. Some of it was new and unused, and still in the box. They'd even called him their little Artful Dodger, their young protégé. And in return, they were his Fagins; the overseers of a motley den of thieves.

12:05 – The doors of the BMW opened, and the two darkly-suited men got out, causing Mick to shrink further back into the bushes. His pulse began racing with a mixture of nerves and excitement.

The bigger of the two men checked his watch again, then scanned around the car park. The other guy shrugged his shoulders as they exchanged some kind of conversation. They both leaned against the car and began sharing a cigarette between them, killing time.

12:15 – With the cigarette now finished, the big guy crushed the remains into the gravel. He glanced at his watch and scowled before speaking to his colleague, who gave a nod of agreement. After a final cursory look around, the two men got back into the car.

Again, his pager vibrated, and again he ignored it.

The driver gunned the BMW into life, his irritation evident by the spray of gravel which the tyres kicked up as they drove off.

A deep sigh of relief escaped from Mick as he exhaled away his pent-up tension. Though he'd escaped their retribution today, he knew they would still need some kind of payment.

But that was a worry for later.

Right now, it was time for a calming smoke!

Using the same mode of stealth as for his nocturnal activities, Mick quietly made his way through the deep, herbaceous borders of Lodge Gardens towards the rear of the huge, concrete bandstand. With a practised art, he nimbly stepped onto some of the stronger branches so that he could climb onto the concealed concrete plinth at the back.

Once he was comfy and settled, and sure that he wasn't going to be disturbed, he took out his pack of Rizla papers, tobacco, and weed, and began rolling himself a calming joint.

He took a deep inhalation and closed his eyes, setting his mind free along with the smoke...

With her curiosity piqued at the sound of a car pulling up in front of their driveway, Irene moved over to the bay window, mug of coffee in hand, to peer discreetly from behind the curtains. From just beyond the neatly clipped privet hedging, she observed two car doors opening, then two large, smartly dressed men getting out of a black car. They paused and looked towards the front of the house. After some kind of discussion and a nod, the two gentlemen walked up the driveway, their stride purposeful.

'Are we expecting anyone, Dennis?'

Her husband looked up from his Saturday newspaper.

'Not that I know of. Why?'

'Well, there are a couple of blokes just coming up our driveway. They look like insurance men, or double-glazing salesmen, if you know what I mean. Business-looking, in a fancy car.'

She jumped, almost spilling her coffee, as a heavy knock came on the side door to the kitchen, rattling the glass panel.

Seeing that Irene looked a little nervous at receiving unexpected visitors, Dennis did his best to reassure her.

'Stay there, I'll go and get rid of them. Probably just Jehovah's Witnesses, or something.'

'Hmm, they don't have briefcases with them – they don't look like Jehovah's Witnesses.'

The heavy knocking on the glass panel came again. Dennis could see the dark, fuzzy, abstract shapes of the two men beyond. He opened the door sharply and stood up straight as he faced them, as if to say, "Who dares knock at my door without invitation!"

The larger of the two men, clad in a dark suit and long leather overcoat, spoke first, before Dennis had even managed to say a word. The other man, slightly shorter but a little wider, bristled beside him, as though he was spoiling for a fight.

'Is your Michael at home?'

Dennis quickly sensed that this was not a standard, friendly visit.

'Our Michael? No, he's not in. Are you the police? Is he in some kind of trouble?'

At the mention of "police", the two men sneered and snorted. The leather overcoat man spoke again.

'No, we're not the police. But yes, he's in trouble. D'ya know where the little shit is?'

The tone of the man's voice caused a rush of nervous adrenaline to flood through Dennis, spurring him to reply with as much authority as he could muster, given the circumstances.

'I told you, he's not at home, and I've no idea where he is. Can I pass on a message when he gets home?' Dennis sensed Irene come into the kitchen behind him.

She tried to look over his shoulder at the two men standing on their threshold.

'What is it, Dennis? What's going on? What do they want?'

'They're looking for our Michael...'

'But he's not here.'

'I know, I told them that. Just stay back, Irene.'

She moved closer to Dennis, unwilling to do as he had asked. If this matter concerned her little boy, then she needed to know what was going on.

The leather overcoat man seemed to be the spokesman for the pair of visitors.

'Your Michael owes my boss two hundred quid, and noon today was pay-up time. He didn't pay. So now we're here to collect...'

'Two hundred pounds!' exclaimed Irene, her voice a little more high-pitched than she meant it to sound. 'How can Michael owe someone two hundred pounds? Did he borrow it?'

The two men laughed, though it sounded more fiendish than humour.

'No, lady. He didn't borrow it. He gambled, and he lost. And now he owes,' growled the overcoat-man.

Irene stepped forward in defence.

'But he doesn't have that kind of money! How can he pay you back?'

'That's his problem. But we're not leaving here without the two hundred quid...' He moved his overcoat to one side to reveal a baseball bat belted to his waist. A baseball bat that looked well-used. 'That's a nice-looking Rover you've got there, sir. It would be a shame if it got damaged.' He put his hand on the baseball bat as if for emphasis. 'Or maybe we should just take it? Michael often gambles with goods on the table, instead of cash. A nice car like that should be worth at least two hundred quid.'

Dennis understood the meaning of the man's actions. He gently pushed Irene behind him. It was time for her to keep her mouth closed.

'Look, we don't want any trouble. Any gripe that you have is with Mick, not with us. We haven't done anything wrong. You don't touch that car!'

He pointed his index finger at the man, endeavouring to be stern.

The man's eyes narrowed, and he took a step closer towards the doorway.

'I don't give a flying fuck how we get the money. But we're not leaving without it. And if we don't get it, well...' He pointed to the baseball bat and smirked, 'you'll just have to give me the keys to your Rover. Or maybe you have a fancy TV?'

Dennis racked his brains for a solution. He just wanted to be rid of the men from his doorstep without having to give away all his hard-earned worldly possessions.

'Will you take a cheque? I'm good for the money, I promise you.'

Overcoat-man looked at Dennis as if he'd just arrived from another planet. He furrowed his brow and moved his face closer, his scowl menacing.

'Do we look like we take cheques? We deal in cash and goods to the value required... Capice?'

Dennis swallowed hard. He turned to Irene, his eyes pleading with hers to do exactly as he was about to instruct her to do.

'Irene, can you do a sweep of the house to find all the cash that you can – my wallet, your purse, and whatever's in the office safe. And my Pierre Cardin watch – that's worth a few quid.'

'B... But, Dennis...'

'Just do it, woman! GO!'

'And no funny business, missus,' snarled the shorter man. 'Don't think about trying to call the cops or screaming for help. Remember, we've got Billy the Baseball Bat on our team. I'm sure you don't want us to hurt your husband...' He left this last comment hanging in the air for Irene to grasp; an ominous reminder that the hard men were the ones in control, and not vice versa.

Nodding her understanding of the situation, and with her legs feeling like jelly, Irene did as demanded, grateful that she had been sent on this mission and not left alone in the kitchen to guard against the two hard men getting in. There would have been no way she could have held them back.

On returning with all that she could scrape together, she was relieved to see that Dennis had maintained his position by the door and hadn't let the goons over the threshold. She put everything onto the table to be counted out.

'There's £160 in cash, and this Pierre Cardin watch. It's a genuine designer watch, not any old knock-off,' she added, making sure that they understood its value.

Leather-coat man raised his hand and, with a grunt, forcefully pushed his way past Dennis, his patience having worn thin from doing business on the doorstep. Irene stumbled backwards, shocked by this blatant invasion of their home space, and the realisation that the threat had just gone up another level. He headed for the table and re-counted the cash just to prove a point of distrust, while his partner held his position in the doorway, blocking any escape for their victims.

'You want to be careful keeping this much cash in the house. There are a lot of unsavoury people out there who could break in and steal it. It's much safer to keep it in the bank,' he grinned, his tone menacing. He appraised the quality of the watch and nodded. 'This is a very nice timepiece, I'll give you thirty quid for it. So, that means we're still ten quid short.' He eyed Irene's string of pearls. 'Are they genuine?'

Irene's hands shot to her throat defensively. 'These were a present from my husband after the birth of our first child!'

'I don't give a shit about your sentiments – they could have been a gift from the Queen for all I care!' The large frame of the goon started to push his way towards her, ready to grab the necklace.

'Don't you dare lay a finger on my wife!' yelled Dennis, his sense of protective duty overcoming his fear.

'Or what? What are you going to do about it?' The goon's hand shot to the handle of the baseball bat, a stark reminder that they were the ones in control of the situation.

Dennis nodded to Irene.

'Do as he says, my love. Give him the pearls.'

'But... B... They were a gift from you...' murmured Irene, unwilling to let them go.

'And there will be more gifts in the future. Let him have them. *Please.*'

'Do as your husband says.' Leather-coat man held out his large, bear-like hand towards Irene, making her recoil.

She tentatively unclipped the string of pearls and held them out for the goon to grab and inspect.

'Very nice.' He pulled a little cloth bag from his pocket and slipped the necklace and watch inside, then put the cash into his inside breast pocket. 'Well, I think this concludes our business.' He buttoned up his leather coat, covering over the threatening view of the baseball bat. 'Give our regards to Michael, won'tcha? And perhaps you might give him a message from the boss. Don't mess with the big fish. Comprende?'

'Yes, yes, I'll pass on the message. You can be sure of that. Now, would you please get off my property and leave us in peace!'

The two men tipped their foreheads in mock servitude, before turning on their heels and heading away from the house.

Dennis swiftly closed and locked the door, although he knew this would be a useless barrier if these men were determined to get in. A glass panel was no match for a baseball bat.

Irene ran into his arms, and he held her tightly, both caught up in their moment of fear and grateful to have survived a potentially dangerous situation. He kissed the top of her head, then sighed, lost in his thoughts. A feeling of abject disappointment overwhelmed him. How could they not have seen the signs that Michael was mixing with bad company? That he was gambling. But then again, isn't that the whole point of gambling – being able to hold a straight poker face? Give nothing away.

'I'll fuckin' kill that boy when I get mi'hands on him... How could he bring something like this to our door!' he snarled, his pent-up anger now overriding the fear. 'This is not the way we brought him up. Why would he need to do something like this?'

Startled at his sudden outburst, Irene pulled away; her superhero had changed back into her grumpy husband. She chose to channel her nervous energy into putting the kettle on, banging around with mugs and the teapot as she did so.

'Don't start, Dennis. We don't know all the details. We don't know how or why he got mixed up in all this. He's just young and gullible.'

Dennis turned and sat down, then slammed the palm of his hand down hard on the kitchen table, causing the spoon in the sugar bowl to jump out, spilling sugar granules everywhere.

'There you go! Defending him. You're always bloody defending him, no matter what he does. Mick's not gullible – he's a manipulator. Don't you see that! There isn't an honest bone in his body.' He paused to massage his temples, his fingers still tingling from hitting the table. 'I don't know where he gets it from, all this lying and cheating. 'Cos that's what he is – a liar and a cheat. He doesn't get it from my side of the family, that's for sure!'

'Oh, so what're you saying, eh? That my family are liars and cheats? Sod you, Dennis Watkins!'

Irene grabbed the now-boiling kettle and tried to pour water into the teapot, sloshing some over the edge in her shaking anger.

'Argh! Oh, for fuck's sake!'

Ignoring the puddle of water on the worksurface, she came and sat with him at the table, plonking the teapot between them. Tense, quiet moments passed by, each preoccupied with their chaotic thoughts, trying to make sense of having just been violated in their own home. Her throat suddenly felt naked without the string of pearls. How could one ever replace such meaningful memories?

Irene broke the tension first as she poured out two mugs of tea.

'Sorry for being angry at you, my love. I'm just in shock, that's all,' she murmured. 'It's not every day we get debt collectors on our doorstep, eh? And certainly not ones wielding baseball bats...'

Dennis laughed quietly before replying.

'I'll be honest with you – I was shitting myself!'

Irene laid her hand on Dennis's and chuckled with him.

'Well, I never would have guessed. You seemed quite cool-headed to me. But this has certainly got me thinking about all the things that have gone missing from around the house. My Cartier watch and other bits of jewellery. Do you think that could have been our Mick?'

Dennis took a drink of his tea, then sighed.

'I wouldn't be surprised. And all the local break-ins – that's probably our Mick, too. Remember what the bloke said – Mick often puts goods on the table, not cash.'

Irene suddenly gasped and put her hand to her mouth as if in shock, her eyes wide.

'I hope to God it wasn't our Mick that broke into Kenny and Sally-Ann's house while they were away on honeymoon! All those wedding presents that were stolen. All the small stuff. Yet nothing was damaged. Remember?'

'Aye, I remember. No fingerprints, nobody saw anything out of the ordinary. There was nothing that the police could use to trace the culprit. The little git, I'll kill him if I ever find out that it was him! To steal from your own brother. That's low...'

Tears were beginning to well in Irene's eyes.

'What are we going to do, Dennis? How are we going to approach this with our Mick? If he's running up all kinds of gambling debts, then he clearly needs help. God knows what else he's messed up in? Gambling leads to all kinds of crime to feed the addiction. Remember old Roger from just up the road? He lost everything – the house, the lot.'

Dennis nodded.

'Aye, that was quite the scandal,' he concurred. 'And that bloke from your office – your old boss. Oh, what's his name? McCormick? That's it – Miles McCormick. Didn't he end up in prison after being caught embezzling money from the office? And that was because of gambling, wasn't it?'

Irene blushed at the mention of his name and flustered a little before replying.

'Miles. Yes, yes, he lost his job and his freedom. I remember being questioned at work about the missing money. It was just before I went on maternity leave, pregnant with our Michael. It was an awful time...' Her eyes faded and glazed over while she replayed the memory of the office scandal in her mind. They had been torturous, emotional months of uncertainty.

'He lost his membership at our Rotary Club, too. We didn't need that kind of bad egg in our group. Whatever happened to him? He just vanished off the radar. Did you ever hear anything from him after his release from prison?' asked Dennis.

Her voice wobbled, and she shook her head.

'He, er, died a few years ago after falling from a hotel balcony. He was at a poker tournament in Leeds. The police found a half-empty bottle of Glenfiddich in his hotel room, and he had a glass in his hand when he fell. Barbiturates were also found beside the bed and in his bloodstream. Did he fall, or was he pushed? Or was it suicide? No one will ever really know. The police never found any signs of a scuffle or any other fingerprints in his room.'

'You seem to know a lot about it,' Dennis commented.

'Just office gossip. We hear all sorts. He never really managed to get his life back on track after prison, and just went right back to gambling. I, erm, I went to his funeral...'

'You did? You never said anything.' Dennis looked at her quizzically.

'Well, I suppose someone from the office had to go. I'd worked with him for many years, and despite everything, he was a nice guy. Generous.'

'Aye, he was certainly generous with his charity donations for any of our Rotary fundraisers.' Dennis shook his head. 'Then again, I guess you can afford to be generous if you've been stealing the company's money...'

Look, can we just leave talking about Miles? We need to figure out what we're going to do about Michael.'

'You're right. Sorry, yes. What are we going to do about that little shit? I'm tempted to just throw him out. Let him fend for himself. I don't want to live under this kind of shadow, with trouble coming to our doorstep.'

'But he's only eighteen, Den. He's not capable of fending for himself yet. He needs help, not rejection,' defended Irene.

'Only eighteen! Bloody hell, Irene – I was labouring on building sites when I was his age – and bloody 'ard work it was, too. Not fannying around like our Mick. Helping out at the butcher's is hardly back-breaking. Anything to avoid hard work, the lazy sod. It's about time he grew up.' Dennis began squeezing his hands together, his frustration starting to reach boiling point.

'Oh, here we go! "When I was a lad..."'

Dennis glared at his wife, causing her to shrink back a little.

'Don't you dare mock me, Irene. Both Kenny and Barry have worked like navvies since the day they left school. And yes, I realise that Kenny has only just left home at twenty-three, and that Barry still lives here. But they've both saved hard over the years, as well as contributing towards their keep. Kenny even had enough money saved for a good deposit on that little house of theirs. They've never brought this kind of shame home with them.'

Irene sighed heavily, her mind swirling. What was happening to her tidy, organised life? She topped up her tea, her eyes on the verge of tears. A shuffling sound caused her to look up, as she noticed Dennis going to the bar area to grab himself a calming slug of brandy.

'Two hundred fuckin' quid! Two hundred! We can wave bye-bye to getting a new company van this year. Or going on holiday. All our hard work – *PUFF* – gone! You can bet your sweet life we'll never get a penny of that money back. I'll fuckin' kill him when I get my hands on him...'

Hearing the scuffle of footsteps on the doorstep, they both looked up at the dark but recognisable shadow fumbling with his key on the other side of the glazed door.

Growling like a banshee, Dennis launched himself at Mick as he entered the kitchen.

'Come here, you little bastard! I'll fuckin' kill ya...'

21: Liar Liar

Before Mick had even taken two steps over the threshold, Dennis grabbed hold of his son by the lapels of his jacket. He swirled him across the floor in an aggressive waltz, leaving a trail of black scuff marks from Mick's trainers on the cream and beige Cushion Flooring. Dennis slammed him against the tall fridge, causing the jars and bottles within to clatter with the impact.

The two Watkins males faced each other, Mick's eyes wide with surprise, his pupils dilated; Dennis's eyes narrowed in fury, his pupils similarly dilated. Each could smell the breath of the other, one sweet from weed, the other of hot tea and brandy.

Dennis roughly took hold of Mick by the jawline and throat, causing Irene to scream and try to intervene, grabbing her husband by the sleeve of his sweater.

'Dennis! Please! Don't hurt him...'

He shrugged his arm, then glared at his wife. Irene read the unspoken message loud and clear and backed off. Den returned his gaze to his son and gave him another body slam against the fridge.

'Do you know who we've just had a visit from, eh? Two friends of yours...'

'Two friends...?' Mick's eyes suddenly widened with the realisation as to who the visitors were. Having read his pager messages while he was smoking his joint, the second message now made sense –

U R late

You will regret this

He opened his mouth to speak, but words refused to come.

With anger raging in his veins, Dennis roughly shuffled Mick towards the kitchen table and shoved him into a chair, causing it to almost rock backwards. He stood over his son, imposing and hostile, his breathing ragged. Without breaking eye contact with Mick, he sat down opposite, next to Irene.

Now under interrogation, Mick looked at them both, then adjusted his position slightly so that his hands were under the table, unseen. He began to fidget with his fingers; his nervousness, rather than the July heat, making his core temperature rise.

'I'll ask you again – why would we get two hard-hitters, or debt-collectors or whatever the fuck they are, on our doorstep demanding money? Money that *YOU* owe them,' snarled Dennis, as he pointed an accusatory finger at his son.

'I, erm, I don't know. What debt collectors?' Mick could feel his palms damp and sweaty as he rubbed his hands together.

Dennis slammed his fist onto the table, causing both Irene and Mick to recoil in surprise.

'Don't lie to me, you little bastard!' he snarled. 'You know full well who I'm talking about. Two goons came here threatening us with a baseball bat for money – money that you owe them. Gambling debts. Two hundred fuckin' quid...'

Mick swallowed and blinked. His fuzzy mind began easing itself into some semblance of comprehension. He was supposed to have settled up at noon, but didn't have the money, so avoided going to the meeting point at Lodge Gardens car park. Then, after his foolish act of no-show, chose to get stoned behind the bandstand.

Yet in his naiveté, he never expected them to track him down. He never expected this. Damage limitation being his only option, he chose to skirt around the truth and give them a softer version of the reality that he was mixed up in.

He took a deep breath.

'Okay, it all started when I first got the part-time job working on the butcher's stall on the market, and helping with the deliveries. I got chatting with a couple of guys – they sell bent gear out the back of a van; you know, dodgy knock-off stuff. Anyway, they offered me good money if I could help supply them with the odd bit of gear. They made it sound so easy. Exciting. It just kinda snowballed from there...'

'Well, they must have seen you coming, you bloody fool. Didn't you stop to think about what you were getting into?' growled Dennis, shaking his head in disappointment.

Mick shrugged. 'Not really. Once I'd done the first job, I became addicted to the thrill of the chase. The adrenaline rush of getting in and out of somewhere unseen. Poking around in people's houses, and such like. Easy money.'

Irene's face was aghast at what she'd just heard from her son.

'But you started working at the market stall when you were sixteen. Do you mean to tell me that you've been prowling around and stealing all this time? That you get a thrill out of going into someone's house and taking their hard-earned stuff! Leaving them feeling like they've been violated.' She paused for a moment while her mind tried to comprehend the reality of Mick's behaviour. 'Don't you remember how Kenny and Sally-Ann felt when they came home from their honeymoon to find out that they'd been burgled? They were devastated. It took them ages to feel comfortable again in their own home, even with the extra security. Didn't that make you think about changing your ways – your own brother a victim of crime?'

A flush rose to Mick's cheeks as he fidgeted with his hands under the table, balling them into fists of frustration.

Dennis interjected, as he lunged his hand towards Mick, threatening to grab him. 'Unless, of course, it was you! Did you break into their house and steal stuff while they were away?'

Mick shook his head vigorously in denial.

'No! I would never do something like that to my own family! What's the old saying – you don't shit on yer own doorstep? I even helped to clean up afterwards, remember?'

Dennis came around the table and grabbed Mick by the hair. 'I swear... No, I *PROMISE* – if I *EVER* find out that it was you who did over our Kenny's place, I'll break your fuckin' neck!' He pushed Mick's head forward in disgust, almost banging it on the kitchen table.

Mick could feel his heart hammering in his chest. Shit was getting real. Very real. Never in his wildest fantasies could he have imagined things coming to this. He thought about the little boy who had died as a result of drinking some of the stolen booze. And now threats were appearing on his doorstep.

'What about all the other local break-ins? All the stuff that's gone missing from here, from us? Watches and stuff. Was that you?' Irene had tears in her eyes at the thought that one of her children could do such a thing. How had he turned into such a teenage delinquent right under their noses?

'I admit, yeah, I did some of the break-ins. I needed the cash. But I never took anything from home, I swear.' He tapped his fingers on his thighs while remaining poker-faced.

'But what if people recognise their stuff being sold out of the back of this van, as you say?' she asked.

Mick's eyes lit up as though he were now the spokesperson for some grand corporate enterprise, explaining the company's business plan.

'Ah, well, that's the beauty of the scheme, you see. These guys move about the country, going from market to market, so they never sell anything in the area where it was nicked. They have a team of guys who lift stuff for them so that they can circulate around different areas. It's then sold as "reclaimed" or "repossessed" goods.'

As soon as Mick had explained how the scheme worked, he wished that he'd thought before speaking, and could suck the words back in. Realising that he'd naively said too much, he began jiggling his legs under the table, his nervousness increasing.

'Well, you make it all sound so simple!' retorted Dennis, his voice loaded with sarcasm. 'And pray tell, how the fuck did all this turn into gambling? How come you ended up in debt to the tune of two hundred fuckin' quid?'

Mick sighed. 'Sometimes when they come into this area, we'll have a bit of a lad's night, and play a few rounds of cards. Easy at first. But then it started getting a bit heavy. A bit serious, like. When I don't have much stuff to give them, I do IOUs.' He refrained from telling them that he was also caught up in a bit of dealing on behalf of the guys – for a percentage, of course. But he knew to keep his mouth shut about this side of the "work". He'd once borne witness to their use of the baseball bat on one of the dudes who had tried to twist on a deal, and it wasn't a pretty sight. In a way, he was grateful that his parents had opened the door to the goons and not him. At least he'd been spared a beating, and it had only cost him a bit of his parents' money – so far, anyway...

'IOUs to a bunch of crooks? Well, that just confirms what a complete and utter arsehole you are! You are in *way-y-y* over your head with this, my boy. Way over your head. Let me give you a piece of free advice – if the police *EVER* have to pay a visit to this house because of you, I can guarantee that you'll be slung out on your backside. But not until I've knee-capped you first with my sledgehammer...'

Mick blanched. He was being threatened from all sides. It was time for some calming tactics if he was to come out of this unscathed.

'Look, I'm really sorry for all this. I admit that I'm in way over my head with these guys. The least I can do is pay back the money I owe you. And quit with these guys.'

He gazed with pleading eyes at his mother, hoping for some sympathy. Surely she would accept his apology and proposal? But all he got in return was a look of disdain and disappointment. A look that he rarely saw from Irene.

He had lost his only ally.

Equally disgusted, Dennis snorted his contempt at Mick's offer.

'We don't want your dirty money. We don't want the spoils of your ill-gotten gains. And as for quitting with these guys, well...' He shook his head. 'You're just in cloud-cuckoo land, lad. They've got their claws into you. You'll never be free. You've seen their faces, you know their game.'

Mick swallowed hard.

This was one of those rare occasions when he had to concede that his father was right.

22: Home Sweet Home

Before walking up the paved pathway, Barry encircled Claire with his arms as they stood on the pavement looking up at the front of the house, both grinning broadly. The brickwork glowed in the late September sunlight, as if welcoming them home. He gently rubbed her baby bump, then kissed her on the cheek and nuzzled her neck, before speaking.

'Crikey, I can't believe it's really ours!'

Claire snuggled into his arms, feeling all warm and emotional.

'I know – I'm so excited! We'll soon have the whole package when we get married in November,' she gushed.

Like a child with a new toy, Barry held up the bunch of keys and jangled them.

'Right then, Miss Jones – shall we go and take a look at our humble new abode? After you...'

Once inside, one of the first things they noticed was how clean everything had been left; carpets vacuumed, paintwork wiped down, and the citrusy fresh smell of lemon cleaner.

As they went from room to room, they could see that some smaller pieces of furniture had been left behind, as well as the carpets and curtains. There was even an ornately carved, old mirror on the wall in the hallway, in ebony black. Claire traced her fingers over the intricate woodwork of the frame; the mirror reminded her of the one in Snow White. She peered at her reflection, then laughed.

'Mirror, mirror, on the wall. Who's the fairest of them all?'

Knowing that he would be in serious trouble if he didn't give the right answer, Barry ventured some kind of apt reply before continuing his boyish exploration of the house.

'You are, my fair queen. Hey, come and look under here...'

Barry opened the storage cupboard under the stairs, only to find that they had also left the Hoover and an ironing board, prompting him to tease Claire about her domestic responsibilities, for which he received a playful punch.

They headed into the clean but functional little kitchen towards the rear of the house. It had obviously served the previous owner well, but would certainly need to be upgraded as soon as funds allowed. However, it would do for now.

Claire beamed with delight as she noticed that the old lady's family had left a vase of flowers on the little worktop – presumably cut from the pretty, well-maintained garden at the back. Even though the old lady had passed away, the family had still taken care of the grass and garden until the sale had gone through. Just that alone gave Barry and Claire a warm feeling – the house and the old lady had certainly been loved. An envelope was propped up against the vase of flowers, addressed to "*The New Owners!*"

Claire picked it up and carefully opened it, taking out the *Good Luck in Your New Home!* card. She read the little message out loud;

Dear Barry and Claire,

We hope that you will both be very happy in your new home. This was a home full of love and warmth, laughter and joy. We have many happy memories of growing up here, and hope that you will make many more!

We have left a few things for you here and there to help give you a bit of a start.

Wishing you all the best!

Eunice, Joan, and Brian xxx

Claire wiped a tear away from her eye with her index finger.

'Aww, how sweet! We'll have to save this card, it goes with the history of the house.'

She stood the card against the vase of flowers, giving it pride of place.

'Shall we go and take a look at the garden, and in the shed?' she asked. 'Maybe they've left a lawnmower behind for you!'

Barry rolled his eyes and grinned.

'Touché!' he laughed. 'I suppose I deserve that...'

23: Congratulations!

'So, I now pronounce you husband and wife. Congratulations to the new Mr and Mrs Watkins!'

The registrar beamed at the newlyweds. Though he had been conducting ceremonies for years, each one still felt special, as unique as each couple that was taking their wedding vows. He gave Barry a little wink.

'And now you may kiss your bride!' he chuckled.

A blush rose to Barry's cheeks as he took Claire's hands in his, the happy couple sealing their marriage with a tender kiss.

The small congregation of their immediate families gave a gentle round of applause as Barry and Claire turned towards them, grinning. The newlyweds then turned and thanked the registrar, both giving him a hearty handshake.

Not wishing to burden Claire's mum with any wedding expenses, they had opted to keep everything as low-key and low-budget as possible. Rather than book an official photographer, the families all flashed away with their pocket cameras while Barry and Claire signed the register. The registrar then obliged by taking a few group shots for them beside the floral decorations, giving an extra splash of colour to the photos.

In keeping with minimised costs, the Watkins menfolk reused their suits from Kenny and Sally-Ann's wedding, as did Irene, in her flattering two-piece lilac coloured outfit. She also wore her fur jacket to keep out the November chill. With their ever-expanding baby bumps, both Claire and Sally-Ann were left with no choice but to buy new outfits. Claire had opted for a champagne coloured two-piece, comprising a lacy calf-length dress with a matching morning coat, prompting this as the colour theme for the men's buttonhole roses. The biggest clothing surprise had come from Claire's mum; normally well-known for her thriftiness, Mrs Jones had splashed out on a new frock, albeit one that she would be able to reuse for any other occasion, as required. After all, it was her only daughter's wedding!

Acting as "father of the bride" to Claire, Uncle Ted looked polished and resplendent in his doorman's tuxedo, normally worn when he was on the door at the Sports Club and Grill. He beamed with pride at his niece, happy that he'd always been on hand to help whenever she and her mother needed anything. Though he might be known as a tough nut and legend in the world of doormen, he was a gentle giant where his family was concerned. Taking note of the time, he called everyone together, his voice authoritative.

'It's a quarter to twelve, folks. We'd better get going – the table's booked for noon, and it's going to take us at least ten minutes to leg it across town on those bloody cobblestones!'

With one final round of handshakes and thank-yous to the registrar, the wedding party headed out onto the Town Hall steps for a quick photo shoot. The gloomy, indigo skies of November suddenly burst open with a small ray of sunshine, casting a radiant glow over Claire.

As they hurriedly made their way towards Glumangate and The Queen's Head Berni to enjoy a celebratory meal, Mick took up the rear of the group. Once again, he was the odd one out; everyone else was paired up – even Claire's mum had linked arms with her brother, Ted.

He watched Claire from behind as she excitedly made her way towards the Berni. A rush of warmth and adrenaline weaved its way through him as he recalled the memory of being with her at Kenny's wedding back in the spring. Neither of them had spoken about the incident since, and he found it hard to look her directly in the eye. Goodness knows what she must think of him. But how could he speak to her about it? What would he say? After all, they were both drunk. She probably didn't even remember, nor had she shown any further interest in him. He sighed inwardly. And now here she was, married to his brother, and having his baby.

Mick briefly wondered if he would ever experience any of this domestic bliss – the joy of sharing his life with one special person. With his mind distracted, he found himself absently bumping into Friday shoppers and office workers, all hurriedly going about their business. He noticed his mother up ahead, waving to him to get a move on, as the rest of the family disappeared inside The Queen's Head. He waved back to acknowledge that he'd seen her, and increased his pace.

Before entering the pub, Mick took a deep breath to steady himself. He had a long day ahead of him, from which there was no escape.

A day of social torture.

And even worse, a day of emotional longing which would not conclude in the same way as Kenny's wedding.

24: The Stork is Busy! - 1979

With afternoon visiting time in full swing, the maternity ward buzzed with excitement as new parents and grandparents cooed over the new arrivals.

Sally-Ann tried to sit up in bed, feeling very uncomfortable down below, her face a mask of pain and exhaustion. Little Rebecca Jayne had made her way into the world a week ahead of her due date, and being quite a large baby, had made for a long and slow delivery. That said, the pregnancy itself had not been easy for Sally-Ann, having suffered from every conceivable ailment for the duration. An early arrival and painful birth was just the cherry on top. It was certainly something that she was in no hurry to repeat!

She looked down at her newborn daughter, with her chubby, wrinkled face and shock of dark hair, lying content and snuggled in her pink crocheted blanket. How on earth was she sleeping through all this noise! A sudden surge of maternal hormones caused Sally-Ann's boobs to start throbbing. She closed her eyes momentarily to shut off the world around her and took a few deep breaths.

Breathe in...

How am I going to get through this?

Breathe out...

This is only day one...

Breathe in...

Please tell me it gets easier...

Breathe out...

Tears were beginning to wet her lashes. Sally-Ann blinked them away and forced a smile.

The enthusiastic chatter of the new grandparents was only adding to her post-birth trauma, sowing the seeds for a massive headache. But then again, it was Irene and Dennis's first grandchild. And it was a sweet blessing for her own parents after losing a grandchild almost two years ago. She could understand their hyperbolic joy.

Noticing and recognising his wife's discomfort, Kenny gently lifted the little bundle from her arms so that he could move the crowd away from the bed and give Sally-Ann a bit of quiet space. She gave him a weak smile, which he reciprocated with a wink.

Sometimes it didn't need words to communicate.

Seeing the ward nurse come through the door and ring the little bell to signal the end of visiting was like music to Sally-Ann's ears. She had lots of sleep to catch up on and a pile of magazines, which she looked forward to reading.

As if by magic, baby Rebecca took this as her cue to wake up and start grizzling, causing Sally-Ann's boobs to tingle and start leaking. She sighed as this defenceless little one reminded her that *she* was now top of the food chain.

Oh, how she was desperately looking forward to seeing Claire at this evening's visiting time. Her best friend had been her rock during their pregnancies. Although Claire was effortlessly sailing through hers towards the imminent birth, she had always made time to help Sally-Ann get through her worst days. Always found time to help, or to make her laugh. She had certainly been grateful that they had shared the journey of their first pregnancies at the same time, even if their experiences had been polar opposites. If Claire's birthing experience went as easily as the pregnancy, the baby would pop out with ease!

Feeling like she was carrying the weight of five baby elephants, the now-overdue Claire waddled into the kitchen, her gait wide and ungainly. She carefully lowered herself onto a chair, half expecting it to break under her weight, then rubbed her over-extended belly and sighed.

'C'mon, you! Hurry up. I feel like I'm about to split open.'

Still dressed in his PJs and robe, Barry followed her into the kitchen, one hand behind his back, and the other ruffling through his unruly mop of hair. He came and kissed her, then kissed her bloated belly.

'Good morning, you two! And Happy Valentine's Day!' He pulled his hand from behind his back and produced a boxed, padded card and a single red rose.

'Aww, that's so sweet, thank you! I didn't get you anything, sorry... I'm just too nervous to go anywhere now that I'm overdue.' She held her eyes downcast, embarrassed.

'No worries, my sweet. Anyway, I'll put the kettle on while you open your card.'

He yawned again, feeling like a few more hours of sleep wouldn't have gone amiss. After just finishing a week of nights, he was finally getting some much-needed rest days. That said, it was hard to sleep when there was a "baby whale" rolling around at your side, and she had been particularly restless during the night with backache.

Claire took the padded card out of the box, and *awwwed* at the design; two bunnies kissing, holding heart-shaped balloons. She hugged it to her chest and grinned happily.

'You big softie! Thank you. And a red rose...'

'Because you are like a beautiful rose – all red and prickly...' he teased. 'Just kidding! Because you are as beautiful as a rose – that's what I meant to say.'

She playfully slapped him on the backside as he squeezed past her to get the teapot and tea bags. Not wanting the rose to spoil, she grabbed the edge of the kitchen table and used it to support herself as she stood up. Suddenly gripped by an almighty pain around her abdomen, she let out a yelp of surprise.

Shocked into action, Barry quickly put down the kettle, then went to his wife's aid, just as she was gripped by another pain.

'Shit! Are you thinking what I'm thinking?' he asked, half in panic and half in jest. 'Here, sit back down. Maybe I should call the hospital?'

'There's no need to worry,' she laughed. 'Babies take ages, especially the first ones. Look how long Sally-Ann was in labour. Let's just time how far apart they are before we panic.'

She took Barry's arm as he carefully lowered her onto the chair, only to be gripped by yet another contraction. Her waters broke with an unexpected gush, soaking her nightshirt, creating a small, warm puddle around their feet.

They looked at each other, eyes wide.

'Erm... Okay. Maybe we do need to panic...' she panted, rubbing her lower abdomen.

'I'll just get you a dry nightshirt, then I'll give them a call. Wait here...'

Claire looked at Barry with mock disdain and rolled her eyes.

'I'm not going anywhere...'

A deep heaviness settled into her groin and pushed against her pelvic bone, causing her to grimace.

'Ooohhh! Change of plan! Maybe we should go straight to the hospital, eh? My overnight bag's in the hallway, ready to just pick up.'

With his hands now shaking from a mix of nerves and excitement, Barry slowly guided his wife towards the front door, then helped her to step into her boots before slipping on his own.

'Towels! Wait here, I'll just go and get some towels for the car seat,' he shouted, abandoning Claire momentarily while he shot upstairs to the bathroom.

By the time he had come back down the stairs, Claire was being gripped by another contraction. He looked at his watch and realised that they risked being snarled up in the morning rush-hour traffic.

Shit! Shit! Shit!

But what choice did they have? They had to go now! And to hell with any speeding tickets – in fact, a police escort might be just what they needed to make it to the hospital in time, if the contractions were going to continue at this intensity.

Once he had eased Claire onto the towel-covered front seat of the little Renault 5, Barry threw her overnight bag onto the back seat, then set off, both of them still dressed in their nightwear. He chuckled to himself at the irony of the situation.

My first day off in ages, and I haven't even managed to get a cup of tea yet!

After taking a shortcut through the back roads, Barry joined up with the main A632 by the coking plant. Luckily, he hit a moment when the traffic was flowing freely, but they were still at least six miles away from the hospital. Claire moaned as she was gripped by another contraction, her waters still leaking out onto the towels.

The closer they got to Chesterfield, the more congested the roads became. He tapped his hands on the steering wheel, impatient at being stuck at a red light.

Another contraction.

Green light.

He carefully drove the Renault around the Lordsmill roundabout, in the direction of the old hospital, only to become snarled up in a queue of slow-moving cars and buses. Even the Crooked Spire of St

Mary's Parish Church seemed to be twisting its head more than usual, as if curious what all the fuss was about.

Another red traffic light.

Another contraction.

Green light.

As he neared the large roundabout by Holywell Street, Claire let out a guttural moan.

'Barry!' she screamed, panting like a dog with heatstroke.

'Hang on! Hang on! We're nearly there.'

'What am I supposed to do? Push the baby's head back in!' she retorted.

Barry blanched.

'You've got to be kidding – oh, fuck!'

He quickly indicated his exit and shot into the hospital car park, pulling up as close as possible to the front doors, much to the chagrin of the ambulance drivers.

'You can't park here, mate,' one of them shouted, striding towards the car.

Barry opened the driver's window and stuck his head out.

'It's my wife – the baby's coming! The head is out! Quick – she needs help...'

Suddenly geared into action, the ambulance driver rushed to their aid, while the other one ran inside to shout for assistance.

And there, on St Valentine's Day, little Nickolas Aron Watkins made his speedy entrance into the world in the front seat of his mother's car.

The Domino Effect: 1983-1985

25: The First Domino Falls – 1983

With eyes closed and deep into listening to Motörhead's latest album, Baz lay on the sofa, strumming his fingers along with the guitar riffs. As much as he liked Robbo when he was in Thin Lizzy, he still couldn't quite shake the feeling that he was a little too melodic for Motörhead. He missed the rawness of Fast Eddie.

He sensed a draught of air and movement in the sitting room.

Taken aback by the distressed, tearful look on his wife's face, Baz slipped off the headphones, leaving Lemmy & Co playing to themselves – they might be having *Another Perfect Day*, but Claire certainly didn't appear to be.

Like a small child, she stood motionless while Baz helped her out of her coat, before guiding her towards the sofa to sit down. He quickly turned off the hi-fi system, quieting the LP he'd been listening to.

'Claire. Claire, love. What's wrong? What is it?'

She closed her eyes, squeezing them hard. But it still couldn't stop the flood of tears from escaping. A choking sob followed, mixed with a runny nose and garbled words.

'S-S-Sally-Ann. I've just seen Sally-Ann. In the supermarket. And, and…' She wiped under her nose with the back of her hand before continuing. 'Sally-Ann's pregnant again. She and Kenny are having…' Her voice slipped to an almost inaudible level. 'They're having another baby…' she whispered. She looked directly into Baz's eyes. 'They're having another baby. It's so unfair,' she sniffled.

Baz blinked a few times while he absorbed this joyous yet unwelcome news. Kenny and Sally-Ann were now expecting their *third* baby, while he and Claire still hadn't managed to get beyond their first. Not for the want of trying – yet each month offered disappointment on top of disappointment. Maybe that was the problem – too much stress? Trying too hard. Not relaxing and letting Mother Nature take control. It just wasn't fair.

He sighed and pulled his wife close, holding her in his arms until her tears subsided and her breathing settled into an even rhythm. Baz kissed her tenderly on the nose, then looked at her, before using his thumbs to gently wipe away the wetness under her eyes.

Claire took a few deep breaths to compose herself before speaking.

'Sally-Ann wanted me to be the first to know. But I could tell that she seemed embarrassed to tell me. They're going to break the news to the rest of the family next weekend, when we all go out for Father's Day. Then again, it's not like she'll be able to hide it for long, is it?'

'No, not really.' Baz sighed, his ego a little deflated. 'Father's Day! It's becoming a habit…'

He could already picture the look that his mother would give them – she was still eagerly awaiting another grandchild from his household.

'I know – that's what I said to Sally-Ann. She said that this one's their wedding anniversary baby, just as Becca was a honeymoon baby.' She gave Barry a wan smile. 'This one is due sometime in February, next year. Not bad, eh, for someone who hates being pregnant!'

Sensing his wife's hurt and frustration, Barry tried to ease the tension with a light-hearted retort.

'She's like a baby factory. Three little 'uns in six years! Imagine the stretch marks,' he grimaced.

Claire shrugged, nonplussed, her eyes once again welling up with tears. 'Where are we going wrong? I don't want to sound clichéd, but my body clock is ticking. I'm not getting any younger...'

'Claire, you're only twenty-four! You make it sound like you're an old maid.' He took her hands in his. 'Maybe we should get some professional help? I'm up for it, if you are?' His eyes sought hers. 'How about we make an appointment with Dr Elliott, and see what she advises? Maybe it's time to have some tests done?'

For the first time in ages, Claire's eyes sparkled with hope.

'Do you think so? Do you think it's worth a try?' she asked.

'I *know* so. It just seems so strange that we managed it once, but nothing's happened since. Yep, let's do it. Let's see what's going on. Or, what's not going on...' He laughed lightly at his own joke.

Claire soon caught on with his positivity.

'You're right. Maybe it's just a simple fix, like a blocked tube in one of us. A quick poke with a needle to clear the blockage, and voila! Baby No. 2.'

She exhaled deeply, letting all of her frustrations escape. It felt like a ton-weight had just been removed from her shoulders with Barry's logical suggestion. 'Promise me one thing, though – don't tell anyone about this. I don't want our private bits to be the next topic of gossip.'

Baz laughed. 'Not a chance. Our private bits are our business, nobody else's.'

Claire suddenly took note of the quiet room. 'Talking of babies, where's our Nick?'

'He's with mi'mam and dad. They came to get him on their way to pick up Becca. They're taking them to Queen's Park to feed the ducks with the weather being so nice, and maybe go for a row on the boating lake if it's not too busy. Then perhaps go for a Wimpy. My mam even suggested taking them to Clark's to be measured for some summer sandals.'

Claire scowled at the way Baz's parents always managed to go overboard with Saturday treats. Her own mother had often said to her how inadequate she felt in comparison.

'Well, that would explain why Sally-Ann only had Lou-Lou with her, and not both of the girls,' she commented.

Sensing that his wife was about to complain about their lavishness, Baz jumped to their defence with a light laugh. 'Hey, it's a grandparent's prerogative to spoil their grandkids. That means it's just me and you for tea. Fancy ordering a Chinese takeaway?' he suggested.

'Definitely! Give me the menu! I'm in the mood for some sweet and sour prawn balls and egg-fried rice. And pass me the Yellow Pages while you're at it, so I can find the phone number for the doctor's surgery. I'll give them a call first thing Monday morning.'

Baz laughed. 'Yeah, maybe I've got sweet and sour balls, too!'

26: The Journey Begins

Just as Baz had predicted, Sally-Ann and Kenny's third-baby announcement had prompted raised eyebrows and pleading looks from his mother. While their news might have made a great Father's Day "present", Baz and Claire felt like they had given Dennis the gift of disappointment. Even Mick had a smirk on his face, as if to say "failure!". It had been a major challenge to refrain from punching his younger brother's smug face. Mick had never even had a steady girlfriend, so he was even further away from parenthood than they were. Yet as tempting as it was to reveal their desperate quest for fertility, Baz and Claire had managed to remain tight-lipped. The last thing they needed was Irene breathing down their necks for monthly progress updates.

But, at least they were doing something positive about it, and were now sitting in the doctor's surgery, ready to start their journey.

Dr Elliott looked up from her notes and smiled at the young couple, putting them instantly at ease. Her caring bedside manner was well-known and well-respected by all her patients, and her smile and eyes always seemed to sparkle with joie de vivre, which meant that she had a sizable waiting list for people wishing to enrol at Blue Dykes.

'So you've been trying for another baby for over three years, is that right?'

Both Claire and Baz nodded in unison, then looked at each other, each taking a deep breath.

'Well, that is quite a long time without success, so let's see what we can find out, shall we? I want to start by building up an overall picture of your sexual activity and general health. Would you say that you are fairly active, and what contraception are you using?'

Claire took the initiative to speak up and answer for them.

'I would say that we are fairly active – maybe not every day, but yes, we enjoy sex. We haven't used any contraception for years. I went on the Pill after Nick was born, but came off when we decided to try for another baby. We used condoms for a short while, just until the Pill was out of my system.'

Claire shuddered involuntarily at the memory of faffing about with condoms.

Dr Elliott added to her notes, then asked, 'And what about your periods, Claire? Are they regular? Do you have any problems at all, such as endometriosis? Any abdominal discomfort or heavy bleeding?'

A slight blush rose to Claire's cheeks – talking about periods always made her feel uncomfortable.

'They seem to be fairly regular. Yes, I get grumpy beforehand...'

Baz sniggered and mumbled some unheard comment under his breath, but she could guess he was concurring about her mood swings.

Claire dug at him playfully with her elbow before continuing. 'I have the usual mood swings and cramps. Some months are better than others, but generally they're regular and bearable.'

'Hmm, okay.' Dr Elliott scribbled down Claire's answers. 'Let's take a look at your general health. Do either of you drink, smoke, or take any medication?'

Baz took up the reply. 'We like to go out at weekends. I'll have a few pints, and Claire enjoys the odd glass of wine. Same with smoking; these days it's only socially, maybe the odd cig when we go out. And no, we don't take any meds or do drugs.'

'Okay. Have you ever suffered from anorexia, Claire? Or any other eating disorders?' the doctor asked.

Claire shook her head. 'I like to watch my weight, just like any other woman of my age, but nothing that would be considered a disorder. I don't live on lettuce leaves and water, if that's what you mean.'

'Have either of you suffered any STDs? Anything like that?'

Again, head-shaking from both Claire and Baz.

The doctor bridged her hands under her chin while she contemplated the next move.

'First, I'm going to weigh and measure both of you and take your blood pressure. Then I'll send you through to the nurse for a blood test. That way, we can check your general blood health, your hormone levels, and get your blood type. It should take about a week or so to get the results back. Make sure you stop by at reception on your way out and book another appointment with me to go over the findings.'

'And then what?' asked Claire.

'It depends on the results. It might just need a course of hormone treatment to kick-start things. Otherwise, the next step would be to send in a request to the Royal Hospital for further tests for both of you. Just if we need to dig a little deeper.'

'What kind of tests, Doc?' asked Baz.

'Claire would need to go for an ultrasound, and I would also arrange for a laparoscopy.' The doctor turned to face Claire as she spoke. 'That's where the surgeon will make a little keyhole incision just below your belly button so that he can insert a flexible camera. Then your stomach is inflated with gas to expand the area. He'll be able to check your ovaries and fallopian tubes, and see if there's any sign of endometriosis. Look for anything that could present fertility problems.'

Claire winced at the thought of a camera probing around in her belly.

'Don't worry, it's under general anaesthetic. You wouldn't feel a thing. As for you, Barry, I would arrange for a semen analysis and sperm count testing. Again, that would give us any indications of potential fertility problems.'

Barry squirmed uneasily in his seat and blushed as he asked, 'Erm, how do they do that, exactly?'

The doctor smiled at him, her eyes giving their trademark twinkle.

'You have to provide a sperm sample, Barry. And yes, you have to help things along to get the sample out of your body and into a jar...' She raised her eyebrows slightly, then winked at him.

The penny suddenly dropped with Baz as to how he needed to get the sample out, causing him to grin and blush again. He coughed to cover his embarrassment.

'Ahhh, I see...' he grinned then laughed, his cheeks flushed pink.

Claire also grinned at the vision of Barry alone in a cubicle with a copy of *Playboy* or *Men Only* and a specimen jar.

'So, there's no quick fix then, Doc?' Claire sighed at the longer-than-anticipated road ahead.

Doctor Elliott shook her head. 'No, sorry, Claire. There's no "quick-fix". This is a journey of months, not days or weeks. But have faith – you've waited this long, so a few more months won't make any difference. We have to be patient with Mother Nature.'

After making a few more notes, the doctor reached for her stethoscope and blood-pressure cuff.

'Right then, let's get this show on the road, shall we!'

27: Testing Times

Disappointed by the inconclusive results from the preliminary tests carried out by Dr Elliott, a frustrated Barry and Claire were now at the next stage of their infertility investigations.

After checking in at the reception desk, they scanned the waiting room of the hospital's Obstetrics and Gynaecology Department for a place to sit. The seating was arranged around the edges, giving the room a spacious feel, and each bank of seats had a coffee table of well-thumbed magazines within easy reach.

They chose seats close to the oscillating fan, which was blowing a welcome breeze around the room. July and August had not only been unbearable because of the heat, but equally unbearable while they waited for their appointment. Meanwhile, Sally-Ann was starting to bloom with her latest pregnancy as she headed into her second trimester, a painful visual reminder to Claire and Baz that they still had a long way to go.

To pass a little time while they waited, they began whispering their curiosity-guesses to each other as to why others were there. To one side of the room sat a young couple, the girl quietly sobbing and dabbing her eyes with a tissue, while her partner put his arm around her shoulders and held her tightly. It seemed fair to say that they would be facing some challenging times ahead. On the opposite side sat two pairs of what they presumed to be mother-daughter combos. Perhaps they were concerned mothers taking their young daughters for contraceptive advice? Or maybe it had gone further than that, and were seeking a termination.

Radio Hallam played unobtrusively in the background, filling the otherwise hushed void of the waiting room, muffling the private conversations that were taking place within the consulting rooms beyond.

A compassionate-looking nurse came through to talk to the young couple and led them off to one of the rooms.

Claire sighed heavily and took hold of Baz's hand for emotional support. It felt warm and comforting, compared to her cold and clammy hand, indicating her nervousness.

'I've never been under a full anaesthetic before,' she whispered. 'What if I don't wake up?'

Baz squeezed her hand to reassure her. 'You'll be fine, Claire, don't worry. And if you don't wake up, then I'll sue them for compensation and become a rich widower,' he laughed, trying to lighten her mood.

Their attention was diverted by the pre-op nurse coming towards them, her stride purposeful, clipboard in hand. She smiled at Claire as soon as they made eye contact, then gave her a reassuringly strong handshake.

'Good morning, Mrs Watkins. Can I just check your date of birth, and confirm that you haven't eaten anything since midnight?'

'Of course – it's ten-three, fifty-nine, and no, I haven't eaten anything.'

'Great. Okay, if you'd like to follow me, and I'll help you to get settled in.'

Feeling like she was going off to the gallows, Claire hugged Baz before picking up her little hold-all and leaving him behind.

'See you later, my love.' She gave him a little wave as she walked across the waiting area, her legs slowly turning to gloop with nervousness and anticipation.

Baz waved back and waited until she'd turned the corner before heading off for his appointment. He sensed a wave of nervousness tingling in his underpants – if only Claire could be with him to lend a *helping hand*.

He only hoped that he could perform on demand...

28: The Day of Reckoning

'I was called into the office today to take a phone call from the consultant's secretary at the hospital. They've got all the results together now – the ones from our tests.' Claire looked at Baz and gave a wan, nervous smile. 'They want to meet with us to go over everything. Oh, Baz – what if it's all bad news!'

Barry took hold of Claire's hand. 'Mi'gran always says, "don't start worrying about owt, unless you know what it is you're worrying about". I think that's pretty good advice, love. Let's just wait and see what they tell us before we start worrying.' He kissed her on the back of the hand.

She sighed. 'I know... You're right. Anyway, I've made the appointment for next Monday, 19th, at 10:00. So you'll need to put in for a rest day from work.

'Yep, no problem. I'll get that sorted. So, that's the day of reckoning, eh!' He looked at her. 'And whatever the results, there's no judgment on either part. No blame. Okay? We're in this together.'

Claire kissed the back of his hand in response. 'Yep, we're in this together.'

A combination of the mid-September heat, together with the sun streaming through the window of the consultant's office, had turned the room into a sauna. Baz could feel sweat running down his back, a blend of heat and nervousness.

The consultant opened the folder on his desk, ready to be the bearer of news, good or bad. He scan-read the first page, then cleared his throat and took a sip of water as if for dramatic effect.

'So, here we are. I have all the results from the tests that both of you went through, as well as the blood-test results from your GP. As Dr Elliott will have explained, your general blood health seems fine, no anaemia or anything, and Mrs Watkins's hormone levels were fine, so no cause for concern there. Which meant, of course, that we needed to dig a little deeper and look at other areas or possible causes for infertility.'

He then looked at Claire, ready to address her with the gynaecological findings.

'From the blood tests that were carried out here, your hormone levels appear to be normal. The scan and X-ray results are all clear – no visible anomalies. Similarly, with the laparoscopy results – no blockages or visible anomalies. A little endometriosis, but nothing that should affect your fertility in any way, Mrs Watkins.'

Claire exhaled loudly, and her shoulders visibly relaxed with the news she had just been given. However, this meant that the problem possibly lay with Baz. She sensed that he had tensed up in preparation for receiving his results.

'Right then, Mr Watkins – let's have a look, shall we?' The consultant paused for a moment while his eyes scanned over the paperwork. 'I'm afraid the test results are not so favourable for you. As you know, your testosterone levels are very low. Similarly, the results show that your sperm count is also very low, and what few sperm you do have are of inferior quality.' He looked up at Baz, his eyes conveying compassion. This was always a tricky moment for patients, and one that he never enjoyed sharing. 'Have you had any recent or serious illnesses which could account for this?'

Baz looked puzzled. 'Such as? I mean, I've had the flu a couple of times. And I had chickenpox when I was a kid.' He trawled his mind before being hit by a light-bulb moment. 'Then, when I was about seventeen or eighteen, I had the mumps. I got them after a trip to Ibiza with the lads.'

The consultant snapped his fingers together. 'Ah-ha! Strange that nothing was in your medical records about this.'

'I never went to the doctors about it. One of the other lads got it too, and was diagnosed, so I just went along with what he had. We both had exactly the same symptoms.'

'Ttch! You should always go and see a doctor if you fall ill after being abroad. Mumps is extremely contagious and can contribute to male infertility, especially if severe. Particularly if both the testes were badly affected – if they became very swollen. It's called orchitis. It's rare, but it can happen.'

'Oh, they were very swollen!' concurred Baz. 'Like tennis balls.'

The atmosphere in the room suddenly chilled, and the air stilled while Baz digested the news. He let his hand slip out of Claire's, and his mind went into overdrive.

'So, if I had a bad dose of this when I was seventeen, could it have affected my fertility?' he asked.

'Yes, that's highly likely. Your body was at a crucial point in its development,' came the explanatory yet unwelcome reply from the consultant.

Claire's eyes suddenly widened, while Baz's eyes did the opposite. They narrowed, as he directed his gaze towards Claire. He took a deep breath before asking his next question.

'Does this mean I'm unlikely to have fathered any children since that time? Because the mumps affected my fertility?'

Claire swallowed hard. Her mind swirled and buzzed with panic as she tried to calculate the events of the past. Baz looked directly at her, while she avoided his gaze and looked down at her lap.

'But we have a son,' he continued. 'How can that be?' Barry's voice began to wobble and crack. 'Claire – tell me... How can we have a son if I've been infertile all this time?'

Hot tears began to fill Claire's eyes and spill over. Her body began to shake as she began to sob.

'I don't know, Baz. I just don't know! I've *always* been faithful to you.' She graciously accepted some tissues from the consultant. 'Oh, no! Oh, no! It can't be... It can't be...'

'It can't be what, Claire?' Baz stood up out of his chair to face his wife and grab her by the shoulders. 'What are you not telling me?'

Claire's tear-laden, guilt-ridden gaze met Baz's.

'It was at Kenny and Sally-Ann's wedding reception…' She paused for a minute while she gathered her thoughts. 'I'd had too much to drink, and it was hot in the room. I felt a bit queasy, so I went outside to get some fresh air. You offered me your jacket – don't you remember? Your Mick must've followed me outside. Anyway, we got chatting, innocent at first, but then he tried to kiss me, and stuff.'

'And "stuff"? Are you saying that he raped you? That he forced you to do something against your will?'

Claire shook her head. 'I just did it to stop him from pestering me.' She looked intently at her husband. And he, in turn, was looking at her in complete shock and disbelief.

'I pushed him away. Honestly!' she continued. 'But you know what a charmer he is…' Claire blushed as she dragged up the memory. 'He told me that "his balls were aching for me", and that he "just needed to empty them". Sorry to sound so crude. But that's what he said.'

'Well, that's some chat-up line!' sneered Baz, his voice full of contempt.

'He said that he just wanted to feel what you feel. He promised to pull out at, you know, at the right moment. And I thought he had. I felt, you know, his stuff on my thigh. It was over so quickly. I think it was his first time. I didn't think any more of it.'

'Ugh! And then what?'

'I just went inside to the bathroom to get cleaned up.'

Barry's stomach began to roll over and tie itself in knots at the images floating around in his mind.

'And what did he do?'

'He just thanked me and staggered off. Said he was bored. That's when he left – straight after, you-know-what. Don't you remember – he left the reception early? We've never mentioned anything to each other since that night. Like it was a dream, or something.'

'A dream!' he snarled. 'This is a fuckin' nightmare! I'll kill the bastard! I swear I'll fuckin' kill him! And you! How could you, Claire!'

The consultant coughed lightly to remind them he was still in the room, a witness to this sudden revelation.

'Could you sit down, please, Mr Watkins. Let's not do anything rash. Let's just take a moment to take stock of the situation. Judging by the results of your test and the confession from Mrs Watkins, there is a distinct possibility that the child was fathered by your brother. The withdrawal method is extremely unreliable, particularly when people have been drinking.' He wrote a few notes into their case file before looking directly at them. 'As painful as this revelation is – for both of you – I think the next step would be to take blood samples from your brother and your son to help determine paternity. We already have samples of your blood, Mr Watkins.'

'How does it work?' Barry asked, his voice small.

'In simple terms, all humans carry a unique gene code, and children inherit half from their father and half from their mother. By doing an HLA test on the white blood cells, we can, with reasonable accuracy, determine paternity to within ninety-five per cent. If that's what you both want, of course?'

Baz closed his eyes in disbelief and sighed before opening them. He blinked back tears and tried to speak. 'We came here looking for answers... Well, we certainly got some unexpected answers, eh, Claire?'

In his mind's eye, he pictured Nick – the little boy that was, in all probability, no longer his biological son. The little boy whom he had loved and nurtured for the past four and a half years. A child who should be his own.

Claire tried to reach out to him. 'Nick could still be yours, Baz. I know the possibility is remote, but it only takes one healthy sperm. Maybe we were lucky. Please, let's do the blood tests to be sure.'

'And what if Nick isn't mine?' he hissed. 'What if he's Mick's kid? Then what? Nor does it change what you both did!'

'Let's hope for the best, eh? I don't want to lose either of you,' she whispered. 'Please, Baz. Let's try and work this out, for Nick's sake. He's the innocent one in all this. Let's do whatever is best for him.'

Baz stared hard at his wife.

'If there's one thing I'm proud of, it's that I've never hit a woman. But right now, Claire Watkins, I could slap you for what you've done to this family. To *our* family. This should have been a day for planning our next baby. I... I... I have never felt so cheated in all my life.'

Claire burst into tears. It was the loneliest, lowest moment that she had ever experienced.

29: Blood Brothers

The journey home from the hospital was eerily silent, save for the tyre hum of their car and that of other traffic. A contradictory feeling of volatile mourning permeated the air, for the loss of all that they had, and all that was about to change.

Claire noticed that Baz's knuckles were white as he gripped the steering wheel. Nervousness writhed around her stomach, fearful that Baz might drive the car off the road in anger. And an even bigger sense of fear for what was to come was making her feel nauseous. Her mind raced.

What would happen once they got home?

How would Baz react behind closed doors?

She looked at her watch – it would still be a while before they needed to pick up Nick from the Infants' School. Plenty of time to discuss, and hopefully persuade Baz that it was an insane mistake on her part. One that she'd even forgotten about. She never even imagined that Nick was not Baz's son; they had so many of the same traits.

As if on autopilot, Baz navigated the car home, clipping the kerb with the passenger-side wheel as he parked the car, making Claire jump. She said nothing.

They walked up the front path in silence, Baz ahead of Claire. His fingers fumbled as he tried to direct the key towards the lock, causing him to swear under his breath. Once inside, he almost closed the door in his wife's face before running up the stairs and slamming the bedroom door, rattling the jamb.

Claire stood motionless at the foot of the stairs, her stomach flooding with adrenaline. With an overwhelming sense of defeat, she burst into tears, sobbing like she'd never sobbed before. She sat on the bottom step, taking a moment to steady herself.

Breathe.

Breathe.

She began retching and heaving as she choked on her breath and the hot, salty liquid from her tears and mucus. If this was how she was feeling, she couldn't even begin to imagine how Baz was feeling right now. This was a million-dollar kick in the balls for him. In the blink of an eye, he'd gone from being a father into a long, dark tunnel of uncertainty. Of having it all snatched away from him. It was sick. It felt like some cruel joke had just been played on them both.

One stupid, stupid moment.

One that meant nothing...

But that one stupid moment would now change everything.

Once inside the sanctuary of their bedroom, Baz leaned against the door while he tried to compose himself, taking steady, even breaths. His heart banged in his chest, and his legs shook, not only from the exertion of running up the stairs, but from the personal blow that had just been delivered by the consultant and his wife.

It's unlikely that he could father children.

It's unlikely that Nick is his son.

In the heat of the moment, he wanted to smash the bedroom to pieces; he wanted to smash his brother to pieces. He even felt like smashing Claire to pieces.

Yet he wouldn't.

He couldn't.

Confused and dejected, he walked over to the dressing table and picked up their wedding photo. Even though they'd only had a simple Registry Office ceremony, Claire still looked radiant, her champagne coloured outfit glowing in the weak November sunshine. It was just possible to see the swelling curve of her baby bump, pregnant with Nick. Although they knew that they would marry, they had decided to bring the wedding forward because of the pregnancy.

Funny how Sally-Ann had also fallen pregnant at the same time as Claire – Kenny and Sally-Ann's honeymoon baby, as they called it. As best friends, Claire and Sally-Ann had done everything together, even having their first babies at the same time, and with brothers, no less.

Except one of them wasn't the brother it was meant to be.

A rush of adrenaline surged through his veins and tingled along the length of his arms to his fingertips, making it tempting to destroy the photo, but instead, he placed it back on the dresser.

With the weight of a thousand men on his shoulders, Baz went and sat on the end of the bed and just stared blankly at the wall.

He pondered the situation.

Would Mick agree to a blood test? Would he even acknowledge that he'd fucked Claire? That he'd possibly impregnated her. And if he did agree to the test and was proven to be Nick's father, what then? Would he have to pay something towards Nick's upkeep?

What would become of his marriage to Claire? Of his relationship with Nick?

Would Mick want to take the child from him? Highly unlikely, given Mick's self-centred character.

So many questions...

He sighed. His head began pounding with the onset of a headache.

A gentle knock at the bedroom door brought him back to the moment.

'Baz, it's me... I'm really sorry. Can we talk?'

Tears began welling in his eyes at the sound of Claire's voice.

'I need more time. I've got nowt to say to you.'

He could hear scuffling sounds on the other side of the bedroom door.

'Please, Barry...'

Now it was Claire's turn to choke back tears. She leaned her forehead against the door. 'Yes, I made a mistake. A big mistake. I admit that. But please don't let it tear our family apart. Please, Barry...'

He looked across at the wedding photo.

He pictured his wife at the other side of the door, equally distraught at the news they'd just received. But she'd still done wrong, hadn't she?

His vision of Claire darkened and changed to one of her in her bridesmaid's dress, hitched up so Mick could gain access. Even though she wasn't married to Baz at the time, she'd still gone behind his back. And with his brother!

But Mick was a smarmy, arrogant bastard who could charm his way into or out of anything. As he'd done with Claire – he'd charmed his way into her knickers. Baz ran a quick mathematical calculation through his mind – Mick would have just turned eighteen a few weeks before Kenny and Sally-Ann's wedding. Mick, the April Fool!

Fire began to rise in his belly, and he clenched his fists. The heat burned his chest as bile and acid rose, exiting from his mouth and nose. He retched again, puke splattering across the carpet.

From the other side of the door, Claire could hear his muffled retches. Taking a brave step, she eased the door open to peep in. Geared into action by the sight of Baz throwing up, she ran to the bathroom to get a glass of water and a cold, wet face cloth. Now was not the time for disagreements.

'Here, take this...' She proffered the glass of water, doing her best not to spill any on him.

As tempting as it was to knock her hand away, he graciously took the drink, eager to swill the sour taste of puke from his mouth. After a few refreshing mouthfuls, he gave the glass back to her, swapping it for the cold face cloth. He closed his eyes and held it over his face, relishing the coolness against his skin.

Claire's voice broke through his moment of self-care.

'It's almost time to pick up Nicky from school. Do you want me to go?'

Baz shook his head. 'I'll go. I need some fresh air to clear my head.' He gave his face and hands one more wipe over before tossing the cloth back to Claire. 'We both need some space to think.'

Claire nodded meekly. She kept her head down, unable to meet Barry's gaze.

'I... I'll get the carpet cleaned up while you go. Please don't say anything to Nick yet. We need to talk this through first.'

'Too fuckin' right we need to talk this through. But no, I won't say anything.' He sighed heavily as he headed out of the bedroom. 'What a mess. What an absolute fuckin' mess...'

30: Bowled Over by Emotion

Their little boy chatted away in the back seat, innocently unaware of the drama now unfolding around his paternity. He'd had a good day at school – storytime had been his favourite. And playtime. That had also been a favourite. And during Play-Doh time, he'd made a purple dinosaur. *Rarrgh!* Nicky mimicked the roar of his plasticine dinosaur. And he got to play with the Fuzzy Felt today because he'd been good at saying the alphabet. It had been a busy day! Though he'd only started school two weeks prior alongside his cousin Rebecca, he was already sounding like an old pro.

Baz looked in the rearview mirror to check the traffic behind him before indicating. His eyes caught sight of Nicky smiling at him. He forced a smile back.

'And what did you have for lunch?' asked Barry.

'Fish fingers and mashed spuds. I asked the dinner lady for an extra one 'cos I was still hungry, so Becca gave me hers. I like fish fingers.'

'That was kind of Becca. I hope you remembered to say thank you.'

'Of course I did. Can I go to school again tomorrow? I really like school. Becca doesn't like school, though. She cried today when Aunty

Sally dropped her off. Did you like school, Dad?' With his curious little mind in overdrive, Nick yawned.

'Aye, it was okay, I guess...' Scuffling sounds from the back seat of the Renault caused him to glance around, only to see Nick settling down for a snooze without really hearing his father's reply.

The adorable sight of the little boy now peacefully sleeping jagged at his heart. White hot anger began simmering inside. A feeling he knew well and tried to keep in check. He'd been in a few situations at work that had caused him to lash out in anger. Dickheads who had made his blood boil. And yes, he'd received a reprimand for his behaviour. But this was a whole new level of anger building within – like a seething volcano, the pressure building ready to erupt.

Rather than go straight home, he decided to drive around for a while, taking the opportunity to have some quiet time to think while Nick was having forty winks. Different scenarios began playing out in his mind. Different ways that he could hurt his brother. This was a matter of revenge. Of personal pride and honour. This was a matter of making his brother pay for what he'd done to the family. Red mist fogged up his rationale. He could feel his temples pounding. A car beeped behind him and brought him back to the present moment. How long had he been driving around, distracted? The sound of the beeping car woke Nicky.

'Are we home yet, Dad?'

'Almost, Nick. We'll be home in just a jiffy.'

'Good, 'cos I really need to pee...'

Baz changed gear and manoeuvred the car in the direction of home. His head buzzed, and his heart began thumping hard with pent-up aggression.

Time to put plans into action.

Arriving back at the house, Baz left the engine running, then helped Nick inside so that he could run upstairs to the bathroom without wetting himself.

Alerted by the sound of them coming in, Claire came through from the kitchen. She spotted Nick disappearing into the bathroom at lightning speed. Guessing that he needed assistance, she headed towards the stairs, only to be distracted by a rummaging noise coming from the storage cupboard beneath.

Baz emerged from the cupboard with his leather sports holdall. He unzipped the bag to retrieve his cricket bat.

'I didn't think there was any cricket practice tonight.' Then the penny suddenly dropped. 'What're you up to?'

Baz just glared at her, his eyes burning with fury.

'It's best you don't ask...' he hissed, keeping his voice low. Yet the malicious intent came across loud and clear.

She tried to grab his arm to hold him back, but he just shrugged her away with force, the cricket bat inadvertently banging into the ornate mirror, cracking the glass.

'Baz, no! Please! I'm begging you...'

But her plea fell on deaf ears. Claire looked at the broken mirror, and her heart sank. As much as she tried not to feel superstitious, it seemed like an appropriate metaphor, making her anxiety even worse.

Suddenly aware that Nick had come out of the bathroom, Claire's maternal instincts kicked in to shield him from Barry's anger. Rather than risk any kind of physical confrontation with her husband in front of Nick, she instead gave him one last pleading look and silently mouthed *'Please don't'*, only to be roughly shoved to one side as he exited, slamming the front door behind him.

The next sound she heard was Baz revving the engine of their car as he shot off. She had a good idea where he was heading.

Different scenarios began playing out in her mind, and none of them were good.

'Where's Daddy going? Is he angry with me? I peed my pants a little bit.' Nick held his damp underpants aloft for his mother to see.

'No, he's not angry with you, my love.'

Claire decided to deflect any more of Nick's questions with an invitation to go and get some clean, dry underwear, then a glass of milk and some biscuits. But the sick, uneasy feeling in the pit of her stomach told her that this was not going to end well.

With tears blurring his vision, Baz navigated his way through the afternoon traffic on the short drive across Castle Ridge towards his parents' house. His stomach still felt light and sensitive from his earlier bout of nausea, and his head pounded and spun with a million questions. He glanced across at the cricket bat lying on the front passenger seat, causing him to tighten his grip on the steering wheel.

Although Baz had a reputation for having a quick, fiery temper, he had managed to keep it suppressed over recent years, particularly with having a small child at home. But today – right now – he knew that the flame had been lit on his fuse, and he was ready to blow up. And that shit-head younger brother of his was about to take the full force of the blast.

As he eased the car onto the driveway, he noticed that Mick's Capri was parked just in front of the garage door. Good – that meant the lazy bastard was at home.

The red paintwork shone in the afternoon sun, and the chrome sparkled, glinting into his eyes. The Mk1 Capri was Mick's pride and joy – the only decent thing that he owned, and the only possession that he hadn't sold, or used to wheel-and-deal with. To do such a thing would be akin to selling his own mother, seeing as how it had been an 18th birthday present from her.

Like a knight about to slay the colossal dragon, he took a deep breath and grabbed hold of his trusty cricket bat, wielding it like a mighty sword. He strode towards the car, his vision focused purely on its destruction. Oh, what a way to hurt his brother!

He swung the bat, smashing each of the back lights in turn. He swung again, bringing it crashing down onto the sloping back window.

And again.

And again.

Baz screamed in fury, unleashing his anger.

He cleaved into the boot lid, then began systematically working his way along the passenger side of the car, creasing the back wing and door.

SMASH! Onto the front wing.

SMASH! Onto the headlights.

Then the driving lights. *SMASH! SMASH!*

Broken glass began littering the driveway.

WHACK! Onto each of the wing mirrors.

WHACK! Onto the bonnet.

And again.

And again.

Next came the turn of the chromed front bumper, until it resembled nothing more than crumpled tin foil.

The mighty dragon began to buckle and bend from blow after blow, no longer able to breathe fire and burn through the streets of Castle Ridge.

With his breath now coming in heaving gasps, Barry paused for a moment to get a better grip on the cricket bat, the palms of his hands hot and sweaty. Using the cuff of his rugby shirt sleeve, he wiped the sweat from his brow and hands. It felt satisfying to look at the car, something so beautiful, but now destroyed.

Just like his marriage.

He looked up at the sound of the front door opening to see a wide-eyed, younger brother looking at him, his face agog. Unaware of the destruction taking place outside until he'd taken off his headphones to go for a pee, Mick had been alerted by the unusual cacophony coming from the driveway. A curious peek out of his bedroom window ignited an Olympian sprint down the stairs, his need to pee forgotten.

Baz grinned in malicious victory, then started striding towards Mick, pointing the cricket bat at the accused.

'What the fuck have you done to my Capri!' screamed Mick. 'Are you fuckin' insane!'

'I've done to your car exactly what I'm going to do to you, you little bastard!' Baz took a swing towards his brother, connecting with Mick's forearm as he held it up in defence. He swung again and again, each blow connecting with some part of his brother's body.

Whack! Mick's shoulder.

Whack! Mick's forearm again.

Whack! His left kneecap.

Mick went down, writhing in agony on the front path.

'Stop, for fuck's sake! Stop!' Tears began streaming from Mick.

Another blow hit his hand as he held it aloft for mercy, smashing into his knuckles and fingers.

Baz stood over him, breathing heavily from the exertion, his face red and his eyes manic. He slipped the cricket bat under Mick's chin – the knight pointing the sword at the dragon's throat.

'Get in the house – *NOW!*' he ordered. Baz was suddenly aware of twitching curtains, as the neighbours began tuning in to the fracas. This would certainly give them something to talk about!

'What's going on? Please, Baz, tell me!' simpered Mick, trying to push the cricket bat away from his throat.

Baz stepped to one side to allow his brother to get up and limp his way into the house. He followed behind and slammed the door behind them.

Mick tried to slither upstairs to escape out of the way, but Baz grabbed him by the ankles and pulled him back down, before grabbing hold of his long hair. With the prisoner in his grasp, Baz pushed Mick towards the lounge area, then threw him forcefully into one of the armchairs.

'I want some answers from you, you little shit...' he snarled. 'Have you ever had sex with my wife? Have you ever had sex with Claire?'

Stunned by the accusation, Mick's mind went into overdrive as he sought for answers.

'Wha... What do you mean?'

'It's a simple question, Mick. It has one of two answers. Either yes or no. He lunged towards his brother and grabbed him by the hair, his face now centimetres from Mick's. 'Have you ever had sex with Claire?'

Mick's eyes widened as a deeply buried memory suddenly ignited a blurred flashback.

'Once. Yes, just once. But it meant nowt, honestly. It was a long time ago, at our Kenny's wedding reception. You weren't even married back then. It was only a quickie.'

'You bastard! Do you know what you've gone and done! You've broken my family, that's what you've done!' he screamed, covering Mick's face in spittle. He let go of his brother's hair, pushing his head back as he did so.

Tears of anger were beginning to well in Barry's eyes, but now was not the time to let them spill over. Mick would only construe it as weakness. Barry straightened up, then pushed the cricket bat hard into his brother's crotch. Mick winced.

'Well, it turns out that Nicky is probably your kid, not mine. Your quick shag with my wife got her pregnant...'

Mick struggled to comprehend the accusation that had just been laid at his door. 'Bbb... But... I don't get it. What do you mean, "Nicky's mine"?'

Barry took a deep breath. 'Because Claire and I have been trying for another baby for years. A little brother or sister for Nicky. But nothing. So we've been to the clinic for some fertility tests. And do you know what those tests have just revealed?'

Mick shook his head.

'Those tests have just revealed that I'm infertile. I fire blanks. So that can only mean one thing – that Claire has been with someone else. And that someone else was *YOU*, you bastard!' He let the words sink in.

'But how do you know it was me, and not some other bloke?'

'Because I believe Claire's answer. Besides, you've only got to look at our Nick to see that the apple didn't fall far from the family tree. He's got the same colour eyes as you and Mum.'

A rush of bravado coursed through Mick's veins – the same type of adrenaline rush he got when cruising the Mk1 through the winding lanes of the Peak District, or when setting up a deal.

Time to retaliate.

'You can't prove it! You can't prove that Nick is mine!' he squawked.

'Oh, yes, we can! And we're going to. You're gonna go for some blood tests, matey! You're not worming your way out of this one, you little shit. We're going to prove that you're the father.'

'And then what? What if I am?' Mick's eyes narrowed. 'What do you expect me to do about it, eh! Do we swap? Are we going to swap places?'

The sound of the front door clattering open and then closed brought them back to a different kind of reality. Alerted by the neighbouring jungle drums, Irene had received a call at work to let her know that two of her lads were fighting in the front garden and one of them was running rampage with a cricket bat.

Both Barry and Mick looked up as their mother walked into the lounge, their eyes transfixed on her, like wild animals caught in headlights. Equally transfixed, Irene began to scream at the bloodied sight before her.

Instinct told her that this was a situation that would have far-reaching consequences.

And her instincts were never wrong.

31: The Domino Effect

'S*TOP! PLEASE STOP!*' screamed Irene, as she strode towards her sons, much like she would have done when they were arguing and fighting as little boys. Except this situation looked far more serious than squabbling over toys or childish teasing. With Herculean strength, she tried to pull Baz away from Mick, while doing her best to avoid the cricket bat.

'*STOP!* Will someone please tell me what's going on!' she demanded, sandwiching herself between the two brothers.

Baz roughly shrugged his mother's hands away from his shirt, breaking one of her fingernails close to the tip. Irene winced at the sharp, stabbing pain, while automatically sticking the now bleeding index finger into her mouth. She glared at Barry, her face red.

After taking a few moments to regulate his breathing, Barry spoke up, his words hissed and venomous.

'Your golden boy has *REALLY* gone and done it this time! Ask him. Ask him what he's done...'

Irene locked eyes with Mick. The situation itself told her that it was serious – so serious that his brother would come around and smash up Mick's beloved Capri, and then start on him. A knot formed in her stomach. She had become accustomed to bailing Mick out of minor scrapes or deals that had gone wrong. But she sensed that this must involve Barry, or the family, in some major way.

'Well? What is it? What have you done this time?'

'Nowt! Nowt that he can prove!'

'Bollocks! That's bollocks, Mick. And we will prove it, even if I have to drag you for the paternity test myself. I'll slit your throat to get a blood sample, if I have to!' Baz began lifting the cricket bat towards his brother.

'Put that down!' screamed Irene. 'What paternity tests? What's going on? Will somebody please tell me!'

Baz took a deep breath, knowing that the forthcoming words would tear his heart out. 'It turns out that Michael might be the father of our Nick.' He surprised himself by how quietly he spoke. His shoulders suddenly sagged, the burden of sadness weighing him down.

Irene's mouth dropped open, lost for words. A heavy silence permeated the moment.

'Wha... What do you mean, "Mick might be Nick's father"? I don't understand...'

An icy cold chill ran through her veins, and she felt the sudden urge to sit down before her knees gave way. She headed for the sofa, and Barry followed suit. He placed the cricket bat across his knees before taking up the threads of the explanation.

'Claire and I have been trying for another baby for years, without success.' He looked directly at his mother. 'And then when Sally-Ann announced this third pregnancy, well, it just tipped Claire over the edge. So we decided to go for some fertility testing.' He could see that he now had his mother's full attention. 'Anyway, cutting a long story short, it appears that I've probably been infertile all along, which raised the question as to who fathered our Nicky.' Baz glared at his younger brother while drumming his fingers on the cricket bat, agitated. 'Claire confessed that our Mick had pressured her into a quickie at Kenny and Sally-Ann's wedding reception...'

Mick began grinding his jaw, ready to speak out in his defence, but Barry cut him off.

'Not a word, Mick. Not a fuckin' word.' He continued the story for his mother. 'She swears she's not been with anyone else. That it was just a drunken one-off. But... Well, you can see what a shit-storm it's created. The question is, where do we go from here? I want... Nay, I *INSIST* that our Mick takes a paternity test. We'll have to get Nick blood-tested, too.'

Irene blanched. The realisation of her own past deeds rushed to mind, bringing forth a heated blush to her cheeks. Her perfect world could start crumbling around her if she wasn't careful. And all the gossip that would follow... Damage limitation was essential if they were all to come out of this unscathed. She pondered for a moment before replying.

'But is it *really* necessary to put such a young child through all this? To suddenly find out that you might not be his father? And then what? Have you honestly thought this through? What about all the knock-on effects, Barry? Can't you just let sleeping dogs lie?'

'Let sleeping dogs lie! Are you joking? Yet one more time that the golden brat gets away with something! No! This is a huge fuckin' deal,

Mother, and not one that I'm letting him get away with. Not this time! You might think the sun shines out of his arse, but I certainly don't...'

Irene cringed at the stinging accusation, then exhaled loudly, wishing she could just wave a magic wand and make all this go away.

'I'm not meaning that Mick should be absolved of any responsibilities. I just think that it's unfair to Nick. Does he really need to know? Does he need to go through all this when we could keep it a secret among ourselves?' A little light-bulb moment came to mind. 'Maybe you and Claire could adopt a little brother or sister for him? It would be an easy-enough explanation – that you wanted to help some other little boy or girl find a new mummy and daddy. Forget all this fertility hassle.'

'Yes, Mum, adoption could be a solution. It's a nice sentiment. But I still want Mick to accept *this* responsibility. This is a big fuckin' deal for me. Don't you get that? And if it is proven that Nick is *his* son, then I would be more than happy to legally adopt him as my own and explain everything to him when he's old enough to understand. Let some semblance of family life resume in the meantime.'

That final comment seemed to lessen the sting for Irene. Yet some nagging doubt about the blood-testing and paternity-testing still plagued her.

She looked at Mick, her hands flexing with an underlying nervousness. With the situation between the boys now a little calmer, she eased herself away and headed towards the kitchen.

'Right then, I think we'd better take a look at those injuries, Mick. I'll see if there's a bag of frozen peas in the freezer to help cool the swelling. And your hands look like they need some ice, too, Barry.' She sighed.

Just like the old days...well, almost.

Once she had changed Nick into some clean underpants and trousers, Claire kept her promise of sitting down with him and sharing a post-school snack of some biscuits and a glass of milk. This was their undivided time together while Nick told her all about his day. And what a busy day he'd had!

Knowing how perceptive he could be, despite his young age, Claire put on her most attentive face, masking her inner turmoil. It gave her the mental respite she needed from the day's unfolding reality. Letting her motherly focus slip was not an option if she was to make it through to his bedtime without collapsing into a heap of tears.

With snack time completed, Nick chose to play with his train set as his next task from the list of entertainment options provided by his mother. He would save colouring for later, and storytime for after his bath, while they had a bedtime snuggle. He had it all planned out...

As he fell into his imaginary world of being a train driver, Claire looked at the innocent child crawling around on the floor with his train set, a child blissfully unaware of the mayhem about to be unleashed within the family. She shuddered, knowing that the little boy she gazed upon – her son – had, in all likelihood, not been fathered by the man she loved. The man who was now shunning her for her five-minute misdemeanour.

How were they going to explain this to everyone? And especially to Nick himself? How would she be judged? As some kind of trollop? Or the victim of drunken pressure? Would anyone feel any sympathy for her situation? Her stomach felt nauseous at the mere thought of losing all that she had.

'What time will Daddy be home from cricket practice?' came the voice of the steam-train driver, interrupting her thoughts. 'He forgot to take his bag, didn't he. Silly Daddy!'

Brought back to the moment, Claire mentally chastised herself for having lost focus. But how could she not? There were a million-and-one questions to be asked. None of which she had the answers for.

Realising that Nick must have seen Baz leave with his cricket bat, she stumbled for a reply.

'Erm, I'm not sure, my love. I think it's just you and me for tea. Are you getting hungry?'

The sound of his tummy rumbling made him giggle as he nodded his affirmation.

'Yep. And it's rumbling for dippy eggs and soldiers.' He suddenly remembered his manners. 'Please and thank you, Mummy. Two eggs, please.'

'Okie dokie, Casey Jones. Two dippy eggs coming right up. You carry on playing and I'll let you know when they're ready.' She smiled down at him, holding back the tears. They would have to wait until she got into the kitchen, out of sight.

'My name's Nick, silly! Who's Casey Jones?'

'Ah, he was a train driver on a kids' programme I used to watch when I was a little girl. I used to love following all his adventures. His train was called the *Cannonball Express*.'

'Wow! What a cool name for a train! I think I'll call my train that...'

And with this newfound knowledge, Nick went back to playing with his train set while his mother forced herself to hum the theme tune to *Casey Jones* in a bid to quash her melancholy mood.

Apart from her son, fear and uncertainty were her only other companions right now.

32: Coming Apart at the Seams

Guessing that Nick was already in bed, Baz crept into the house as quietly as he could. Every fibre of his body felt shredded – it had been a very testing day, and it wasn't over yet. Now he had to face Claire. He kicked off his trainers and put them up onto the shoe rack before going into the metaphorical lion's den, cricket bat still in hand.

Claire glanced up at her husband as he entered the sitting room. She met his gaze with a meek look before casting her eyes over the damaged cricket bat. Deep gouges and dents were testimony to some kind of destruction having taken place, as were the streaks of red paint – or was it blood? She swallowed and fiddled with her wedding ring, hoping that it was the former.

'I'm guessing that you went to see your brother?'

'No shit, Sherlock! Yes, I went to see the bastard...' he snarled, still feeling pent-up.

'There's no need for that kind of talk, Baz. And keep your voice down...' Claire went to the television and turned off the nine o'clock news, transforming the room into a void of tense silence.

Barry came and sat in the armchair opposite his wife. The moment he sat down, the mental and physical exertions of the day suddenly overwhelmed him. His shoulders sagged, his muscles ached, and the focus seemed to leave his eyes.

'Sorry... Yes, I went over there.' He looked at her. 'Don't worry, he's still alive, and not in hospital. He's admitted what you two did at Ken's wedding reception. But in typical Mick-style, he doesn't want to accept any responsibility for Nick.'

Hearing the words of her infidelity spoken out loud pained her as much as it did Barry. Yet, it was the truth; there was no escaping it. She nodded towards the cricket bat.

'What happened to your bat? It looks a bit bashed up,' she asked.

'Let's just say that he won't be driving the Capri for a while...'

Claire's mouth fell open. Barry had certainly taken his revenge to the max if he'd damaged Mick's beloved car.

'Barry! You didn't! Won't you have to pay for the damage to be repaired, or pay some kind of compensation?'

'Pay for damages? Fuck that! He owes *ME* for damages – damages to my life! To *our* life.' He looked at Claire. 'Anyway, he's going to take the paternity test. And if he is the father, then I'll just adopt Nicky as my own. I'm the only father the kid's ever known, so I don't see why that should change. We can explain things to him when he's old enough to understand. We'll also need to take him for a blood test. Poor sod...'

'Aye, that's not going to be easy,' she concurred. 'He hates needles. I erm, I presume your parents know what's going on?'

Barry nodded sagely before replying. 'Let's just say, you and Mick are not the flavour of the month. Mam had a meltdown because one of the neighbours called her at work about me and Mick fighting outside. Then she started worrying about all the gossip that's bound to follow, and all the trauma for our Nick. Dad had all on holding himself back from punching us. It was a right old shouting-match and fiasco. In the end, he just pissed off to the Sports Bar to drown his sorrows, which set Mother off again. By the way, have you phoned your mum to let her know anything about this?'

Claire shook her head. 'No, I never got the chance with Nick being around. You know how much he listens in, even when he's just quietly playing. I'll pop round and see her tomorrow morning after I've taken Nick to school.'

'What time did he go to bed this evening?'

'The usual – around eightish.'

'So, you could have called her this evening,' he countered, his tone sarcastic.

'Don't start, Barry. You know my mum has to look in on Nanna in the evenings since she had that fall, and make sure she's okay. Like I said, I'll go and see her after I've taken Nick to school. This is something that needs a face-to-face conversation. I'm going to call work first thing tomorrow morning and put in a sick day.'

'I've no doubt that Dad will tell Kenny all about it tomorrow, at work. You'd better get in touch with Sally-Ann, so that she doesn't get second-hand information. I can't imagine they'll be very happy with you and Mick, seeing as how it happened at their wedding reception. Jeez, Claire!'

Tears began filling her eyes as she took a moment before asking the million-dollar question.

'And what about us?'

Barry hung his head for a moment, then shook it.

'I dunno, Claire. I just don't know.' He looked up and met her tear-laden gaze. 'On one hand, I don't want to rock the boat because of Nick. Yet on the other hand, I feel cheated. So cheated. Like you're soiled goods. I can't believe that you took your wedding vows knowing what you'd done... That hurts, Claire. That *really* fuckin' hurts.'

Empty moments passed as each became self-absorbed with their jumbled thoughts. There was no straightforward path out of this situation. Barry broke the silence first.

'It'll probably be months before we get all the answers. You've broken my heart, Claire. Smashed it to pieces.' He sighed before continuing. 'I really want to tell you to piss off, to leave us. That's just how angry I feel. But for Nick's sake, I'll let you stay, and we'll try to pretend that everything's normal when he's around. I'm going to sleep in the spare room for the time being. Maybe once everything's sorted and we know for sure, I'll feel different. I don't know. My head is exploding with all this.' He began drumming his fingers on the damaged face of the cricket bat, agitated.

'My head is exploding, too, Barry. You're not the only victim in all this. I feel sick to my stomach for my stupid five-minute mistake. I was drunk, and yes, I should've known better. And now I'm paying the price – a damned heavy price. But please don't let it break us up – don't let Mick win...'

That final comment got Baz's attention.

33: Don't Let Mick Win

Barry listened intently to the sound of Claire's snuffles and quiet sobbing permeating through the dividing wall between their bedroom and the spare room in which he lay, and it touched him somewhere deep inside. He'd known her for long enough to realise that it was as she'd said – a stupid, drunken teen mistake, a five-minute one-off. It wasn't as though she'd had a torrid long-standing affair with his brother. She just wasn't that kind of girl. She was downright straight and honest, and he could well imagine that it had been a moment of weakness, put under pressure by Mick.

But what will happen if Mick is proven to be Nick's father? Just the knowledge of it being a *possibility* had created enough of a shit-storm. The muscles in his hands and arms still ached from the exertion of smashing the Capri to smithereens. Oh, but the satisfaction it had given! It had been worth it just to see the look on Mick's face. Smug bastard. Not so fuckin' smug now, eh! But at least he had agreed to take a blood test to see if they could determine paternity. That was a start. Plus, of course, they still had to arrange for Nick to take a blood test, as well as inform the rest of the family what was happening.

He adjusted his position and folded his hands behind his head on the pillow. And he had to admit, he still loved Claire. Very much. It wasn't something that he was just going to be able to switch off. Maybe he could forgive and forget? Move on. Just get the paternity stuff sorted out, then try to get back to some kind of normal life?

What did Claire say before they went their separate ways up to bed? "Don't let Mick win".

Tears filled the corners of his eyes, and he sighed in the darkness. Judging by the sounds of Claire's continued sobbing, sleep was unlikely to happen for either of them tonight. He felt sorely tempted to go to her.

But she was certainly right about one thing. They couldn't let Mick win. They couldn't let him break up the family. This would need a united front if he and Claire were going to get through this and protect Nick.

As his mind slowly returned to the present moment, he was aware of only silence, save for muted external night noises. A silence that indicated Claire had now fallen to sleep.

He listened to the soft calling of an owl and the gentle rustling of the leaves. The owl received a counter-reply. For a brief moment, he wondered what their conversation was about. His thoughts then drifted towards a conversation which he and Claire had had, before making the appointment with the specialist to go over their results – a conversation in which he'd said there would be no judgment and no blame, whatever the outcome. True, it wasn't the outcome that either of them had expected.

Far from it.

But they were in this *together*.

They had to present a united front if their marriage was to survive the fallout from this revelation, as well as for Nick's sake. Having already witnessed first-hand his parents' reaction to the news, he knew their strength would be in their unity. If Claire was going to take a sick day from work tomorrow, then so would he.

Now in a calmer place, Baz turned onto his side and wriggled around under the covers until he found a comfier position, before closing his eyes and letting sleep claim him.

34: Another Domino Topples Over

No longer able to focus on his sporting newspaper, Dennis tossed it to one side on the sofa and swapped from his reading glasses into his everyday pair.

'What's wrong wi'ya, woman? You've been pacing around like a cat on hot bricks all evening.'

Irene took a slow, deep breath, in through the nose and out through the mouth, before turning around to face her husband.

With her mind having been in turmoil for days, she knew the time had come...

'It's just all this business with the blood testing and stuff. Seeing if Nick really is Mick's kid.'

'But I thought that the boys had already agreed that if Mick's proven to be the father, then Barry will legally adopt him. End of story. Isn't that what the family meeting's about tomorrow night? To open the envelopes and go over the HLA results together. As a family.' Dennis looked across at the envelope addressed to *Mr M Watkins*, perched on the mantelpiece, waiting to be opened. Barry had similarly received theirs today for Nick.

'Yes, I know. But... It's... Well, the results could likely reveal more about Mick than we really want to know.'

'You're not making any sense, Irene. What about the results?'

Feeling apprehensive and with her hands shaking, she sat down in the armchair nearest to Dennis. Close enough for honesty, yet far enough away to create a safe, confessional distance from the reality she was about to disclose.

'If the paternity tests are based on a 50/50 from the mother and father, there's a possibility that...' She took a breath. 'There's a possibility that the tests could show that Mick isn't your son...'

Irene's words hung in the air. After all these years, they were finally out. Heat began rising through her core, causing her face to flush, while her hands fidgeted with a confessor's agitation.

Silence, like a broad icy chasm, formed between them.

'What do you mean?' Dennis's eyes bore into hers as he shook his head with incomprehension. 'You'd better start talking, woman!'

Irene took a deep breath through her nose, then exhaled, ready to offload all that had been burdening her conscience for well over two decades.

'It was after I'd returned to work at the Regional Offices – once Kenny had started at infants' school, and Barry was old enough to go into the creche. It was nice to feel important again – as myself – as Irene. And not just as Mum, or a housewife. Anyway, I'd only been back a short while when I got that big promotion, remember? The one to become Miles's PA.'

'Miles McCormick? The bloke who was sent to prison?'

Irene nodded before carrying on.

'We worked well together, but then he began showing me a lot of attention. I felt flattered, I suppose. Little things at first, like finding a surprise bunch of flowers on my desk as a thank-you if a meeting had gone well; that kind of thing. It made me feel special. Then, somehow, an affair just developed...'

Dennis flinched inwardly at the word "affair", as though an icy hand had just squeezed his heart.

'You had an affair with that sleazeball?'

'He wasn't a sleazeball, Dennis. Okay, maybe he was overly charming and a bit flash. But he showed me *attention*. Attention that wasn't connected to homelife. Like I said, I just got sucked in by the thrill of new affection.' Seeing the hurt in her husband's eyes, her voice began to crack and waver as she continued. 'Anyway, he began to enjoy the high-life a little too much, and started going to the casino in Sheffield, or the local dog-tracks. It was a habit that needed funding when the wins didn't happen. The more he lost, the more he started cooking the books, so to speak. And drinking – he began drinking heavily, too. I suppose he knew that the walls were about to come tumbling down.'

'The big embezzlement scandal?'

Irene nodded.

'But this came at a time when I'd just found out I was pregnant with our Michael. I crossed my fingers and hoped that he was yours. They were difficult days, with the court case and everything. I was just grateful to know that I would be leaving to have a baby. To get away from it all.'

'And did he never question the pregnancy? Did he ever ask whether the baby was his, or not?'

'Yes. Yes, of course he did. But we knew that our affair had remained a secret – I never caught wind of any office rumours or snide comments when I announced the pregnancy to my colleagues. Everyone was genuinely thrilled for you and me, and our surprise late addition to the family.'

She paused while she gathered her thoughts and memories from those frantic months. 'Miles was already in prison by the time Michael was born, so I put everything behind me and just got on with our lives. There was never any contact after that.'

'And was he married when you had your dirty fling? Did he *cheat* on his wife?'

The way Dennis emphasised the word *cheat* came like a slap to Irene.

'No, Miles was already divorced.'

'Yet he knew that you were married with kids. You two make me feel sick! Well, karma got hold of him, didn't it!' Dennis glared at his wife, causing Irene to shrink back a little.

'When the embezzlement came to light, Miles at least had the decency to clear my name with the police,' she defended. 'They were satisfied that I wasn't involved in any way. And that's when we stopped our affair. Or rather, I stopped our affair. I knew what we'd been doing was wrong, and I now had the baby to consider. It's a mistake that has burned me up ever since.'

Dennis sneered his contempt at her confession. 'So you had enough of a conscience not to cheat people out of money, but not enough to care about cheating on your husband. Was I so invaluable to you? Was Miles worth more?'

He sat quietly for a few moments while he gathered his thoughts, before continuing. His stomach floated with the hurt and adrenaline associated with receiving bad news, while his bottom lip quivered with the next question – a question which he could only whisper. Yet he made sure that his wording bit deep into her guilty conscience.

'And how long did the affair last? How long were you two *shagging* each other behind my back?'

Irene blushed as she answered. 'Probably around six months, something like that... I can't remember exactly. Maybe eight months?'

Her words stung him hard. All those months equated to a full-blown affair, not just a quick office fling and a grope in the copier room.

'So, every morning when you kissed me goodbye before we went to work – that kiss – *OUR* kiss – meant nothing. All those times we made love... I bet you were thinking of him. Or probably just closing your eyes out of duty...'

'It wasn't like that, Dennis! Of course I loved you!'

'Loved me? Ha! Not enough to keep your knickers on!' His voice began rising in intensity, releasing his pent-up fury. 'I've worked my fuckin' fingers to the bone for this family. And all this time you've been harbouring this secret. This dirty fuckin' secret! You disgust me...'

'Dennis! I've said I'm sorry...'

'Oh, and that makes everything alright, does it?' he snarled. 'Do you know how hurt I feel? That my wife doesn't know who fathered one of our children?'

Irene cast her eyes downwards, unable to face her husband, lost for words. Now in full flow of raging anger, Dennis continued his tirade.

'Right under my own fuckin' nose, we've probably got a cuckoo in the nest! Honestly, this is like something from an episode of fuckin' Dallas. It wouldn't surprise me if JR walked into the room next!' he screamed.

Irene flinched as he ranted, trying to hold her emotions together.

'I suppose we need to tell Michael? Or should we wait until you've taken a blood test – until we know for sure?' she asked.

'What, and feed more lies to the family? Things like this are a festering wound, Irene. The longer you leave it, the worse it becomes. Until it bursts open, like it's doing now. Of course we tell Michael – he has a right to know. And we'll tell the rest of the family at tomorrow's meeting. It involves them, too. I'll be absolutely honest, Irene – this has knocked me for six...'

'Oh, for God's sake, Dennis – don't you think you're being a bit overdramatic! This happened over twenty years ago. Can't you forgive and forget, like Baz did with Claire?' she defended. 'And let's be honest, you would never have known about any of this if Claire's thing hadn't happened.'

'Don't blame Claire for all this! You were the one who had a seedy love affair while married with a family. A five-minute drunken shag hardly compares with what you did!'

'Do you know what – I wish I'd kept my mouth shut!'

'And I wish you'd kept your legs shut, then maybe none of this would have happened. I think you should pack a bag and move out. Go to your mother's. Go anywhere you fuckin' like. I need some time to think this through...'

'Are you serious? You want us to separate?' Irene looked at her husband, crestfallen at such a suggestion.

'I'm deadly fuckin' serious.' He shook his head.

'B... But what if the paternity tests show that Mick *is* your son? Then what? You're the only father he's known.'

'I didn't say that I was going to stop being Mick's dad. I said that I was going to stop being your husband. You've lied. You've cheated. And you've kept a dirty secret all these years.' He glared at her and shook his head. 'I'm sorry, Irene, but the trust has gone.'

Tears began to well in Irene's eyes before spilling over into choking sobs. She gasped for breath as she tried to speak.

'And–then–what?'

'I don't know, Irene. I just don't know. But if there's one thing that I do know – this is going to kill Mick. This is going to kill the boys...'

35: How the Mighty Fall

Claire stirred Baz's coffee, then tapped the teaspoon on the side of the mug before passing it to him, and picking up her own. She took him gently by the arm so that she could whisper into his ear before they went into the dining area.

'What's wrong wi'yer mam and dad? They've hardly said a word to each other since we got here. And your Mick looks like he's in shock, too. Like summat big's happened. Do you think they've already opened the letter?'

Barry shook his head.

'Nah, I saw it on the mantelpiece when we first got here. But whatever it is, it's bad. They didn't want any of us to bring the little 'uns. Like this is for grown-up ears only. Beats me...'

As they entered the dining area, they took note that Dennis and Irene were sitting apart, at opposite ends of the large dining table, with Mick sitting closest to Dennis, and Kenny and Sally-Ann seated opposite. Barry took the seat next to Mick, and Claire sat by her husband, putting her closest to Irene.

Claire looked across at her best friend and smiled wanly, receiving a similar smile from Sally-Ann in return. From the corner of her eye, she could see that Irene's hands were shaking, and she looked visibly ashen and drawn.

Clearing his throat before speaking, as if officiating at some kind of board meeting, Dennis looked around at his family.

'Thanks for coming over. We've got quite a bit to deal with tonight, none of it easy. But whatever the news, let's deal with it like mature adults, eh?'

As he stood up to go over to the mantelpiece, Dennis put his hand on Mick's shoulder and gave it a reassuring squeeze. He passed Mick's letter to him, while Barry pulled his envelope from his inside pocket.

They opened their letters simultaneously, each scanning across the words. The family waited in tense silence.

Mick and Barry looked at each other, then gently nodded their acknowledgement of the contents. Barry spoke up first.

'The results confirm, to within a ninety-five per cent plausibility of paternity, that Mick is the father.'

A ripple of murmurs went around the table while the family absorbed the information. Mick held his eyes downcast before speaking.

'I'm really sorry for all of this, Baz. And to you, Claire. It was stupid of me, and it was wrong.' He looked from under his eyelashes at Claire and blushed. 'I admit that I had a crush on you, Claire – I just wanted what Barry had. A nice girl. Something I don't think I'll ever have.'

Barry put his hand over his brother's and gave it a gentle pat, which caused tears to spill over in Mick's eyes. He wiped them away with his sleeve, then continued.

'Anyway, in light of this,' Mick held up the letter, 'Barry's going to formally adopt Nicky as his own. After all, Barry's the only dad he's ever known...'

The two brothers gave each other an awkward hug as their unspoken way of saying sorry for the pain that they'd caused each other.

Dennis nodded and shook each of them by the hand, then went and hugged Claire. While standing, he yet again cleared his throat, then took a breath. His bottom lip wobbled slightly as he spoke.

'Your mother and I also have something to share with you. Sadly, not good news.'

Mick closed his eyes. Having already been given the devastating news about his own paternal quandary the night before, he knew what was coming. He braced himself.

Sensing that this was something major, the room fell quiet, all eyes on Dennis. All, that is, except for Irene, who held her eyes downcast.

'Your mother and I are separating, I'm sorry to say.'

A noisy hullabaloo babbled around the family as they absorbed the news.

Dennis sighed, then continued.

'Unfortunately, something has come between us, which, at the moment, we can't resolve. So, we've decided to separate for the time being.'

'No! *You* decided that we should separate!' yelled Irene.

'What's going on, Mum? Dad? Will someone tell us, please!' Kenny spluttered, barely able to get his words out from shock.

'With all this paternity testing going on between Mick and Barry, your mother had a bout of guilty conscience, and confessed to having had a *love affair* many years ago. About twenty-three or four years ago, to be exact. An affair which possibly resulted in a pregnancy.'

The family looked around at each other, wide-eyed and speechless, before looking at their mother. Then the penny dropped with Kenny.

'What – you mean our Michael? Our Michael's not your son?' He looked at his father in disbelief.

Dennis shook his head in sadness.

'We're not sure, Ken. So our next step is for me to take the same HLA test and see what it shows.'

'And what about the other guy? The one with whom Mum had the affair? Won't he have to take a test?' asked Barry.

'In normal circumstances, yes. But he died many years ago. The scumbag fell from a hotel balcony at a poker tournament. But at least Mick and I will be able to see whether there's a paternal connection, or not.'

'Fuck! This is big news!' exclaimed Barry. This time, he put his hand over Mick's in a show of solidarity. 'Well, no matter what the outcome, you'll always be our shithead little bruv, won't he, Ken?' He gave Mick a brotherly push before turning his attention to his mother.

'Well, I'm shocked, Mam, I have to say. Who was it? Do we know the bloke?'

Irene tried her best to hold her head up with a modicum of dignity, while her eyes teared up, ready to spill over. Her voice cracked as she spoke.

'It was someone I used to work with at the Regional Offices. A chap called Miles.'

'What? The crook?' spluttered Kenny. 'I might have only been little, but I can remember you and Dad talking about something bad that had happened at your office, and some bloke had gone to prison because of it. Was it him?'

Irene nodded meekly.

'Yes, it was him.'

The family rippled with murmurs of "Wow..." while they digested the information that they'd just been given.

Dennis tried his best to soften the blow with a little humour as he ruffled Michael's hair.

'Aye, so not only have we got one cuckoo in the nest, there might also be a cuckoo's cuckoo. But, if we all rally round and stick together, we can get through this.'

Realising what he'd just said, his eyes clouded over as he looked across at Irene. 'Although this doesn't change our situation. I still need the separation while we work this out. The affair might have happened years ago, but it's all too painful for me.'

Feeling like a stranger among her own family, and with everyone looking in her direction, Irene nodded; her very soul feeling shredded and defeated.

'Well, keep me updated, won't you? I have a right to know the outcome...' She stood up and smoothed the creases from her skirt before making her way out of the dining area, ready to leave.

'Aye, we'll do that. Goodnight, Irene.'

'Night, Den. Night, everyone.' She nodded towards her family, unable to meet their gazes.

A muffled chorus of shocked goodbyes accompanied her out of the door and into the night.

36: Contemplating the Future

A heavy, shocked silence fell over the family as they heard Irene's car drive away. As the sound of the engine faded into the distance, the sniffles from a now sobbing Dennis cut through, bringing them back to the present moment.

Kenny went over to his father and put his arms around his shoulders, to be joined by his other two brothers. Claire and Sally-Ann looked at each other, their eyes and minds tuned in as if to say this was turning out to be way more complicated than anyone could have ever expected. Sally-Ann gestured to her friend for them to head into the kitchen. This was going to need a large pot of strong tea.

By the time they came back into the room, the Watkins males had moved through to the lounge area and were chatting quietly. Sally-Ann poured tea for everyone, then left them to put in their milk and sugar. She sat beside Kenny, waiting for an update.

'Thanks, love. You're a good lass,' acknowledged Dennis. 'Anyway, I called the surgery today, and I've booked an appointment so that Mick and I can get the HLA blood tests done. And even if the results show that I'm not Mick's biological dad, I'm the one who raised him, and to me, we've always been father and son. Nothing will change in that respect.'

'So why bother with the tests, then?' asked Kenny.

'Because now that we know about your mother's affair, we'll never stop wondering. At least this way, we'll know for sure, and move on with our lives, one way or another.'

Barry was equally curious to know more. 'And if Mick is your son, what about you and Mum? Will you get back together?'

Dennis sighed heavily and shrugged his shoulders. 'I dunno. This has knocked me for six, I can tell you. Yes, I know it happened years ago, but it has left us with far-reaching consequences.'

He took a sip of his tea, his mind racing with thoughts, yet empty of answers. 'I just need some time to process all of this. You of all people should understand that.' He noticed that Claire was blushing.

'I didn't mean that with any malice, Claire.' He gave her a weak smile. 'Anyway, let's just try and keep the lid on this for now. As far as people need to know, your mam and I are just having a bit of a bumpy moment and separated for a while.'

The family murmured their agreement. Although in Dennis's mind, this wasn't just a bumpy moment; it was like a typical Derbyshire road – full of potholes, and with shoddy repairs that didn't last. He was not even sure if the potholes in his marriage could be repaired...

As Barry and Claire drove through the bottom end of Castle Ridge to pick up Nicky from her mother's, a heavy silence descended over them, each deep in their own thoughts after the latest revelation within the Watkins household.

Barry sighed, then broke the verbal void.

'You're quiet, lass. What's on your mind?'

'Oh, just all this business with Mick, and now your mum. It's such a lot to take in.' She sighed, then began rummaging in her handbag for her lip gloss.

'I know,' concurred Barry. 'Who'd have thought it? I would never have expected this in a million years. Not mi'mam. It just doesn't seem like something she would do. I guess you never really know someone.'

Claire rolled on a slick of gloss, while her mind absently recalled something her mother had once said about Irene – that she was "all fur coat and no knickers". Although in that instance, she'd meant that Irene was a superficial snob, yet under the surface, she was no better than anyone else. Somehow, the "no knickers" part seemed appropriate, given the shocking news of her affair. Claire looked at Barry and gave him a wan smile before speaking.

'D'ya know, I never thought I would hear myself saying this, but I feel sorry for your Mick. Christ, it's no wonder he's so messed up in the head.'

'What, having an ex-con for a father, you mean?'

'Possibly – although we don't know for sure. I wouldn't be surprised, though. We know that dodgy dealing is in Mick's genes.'

'Aye, he's no angel, that's for sure,' he concurred. 'Let's hope that our Nicky takes more after your side of the family, eh!' Barry looked across at his wife, his smile optimistic. 'Big kick in the balls for Dad, though. I wonder if Mum would have ever confessed to the affair if all this paternity stuff hadn't come to light with Nick?'

Claire felt the colour rise to her cheeks, knowing that she was, in part, a catalyst in this whole toxic mess. She shrugged and exhaled a little louder than she meant to, feeling the weight of the past months on her shoulders.

'I guess we'll never know. Do you think there's anything we can do for Mick to try and make up for all the shit he's going through? I feel so responsible.'

'Well, it's funny you should say that, 'cos I feel a bit the same way – especially after smashing up his car. Although I must admit, it felt good at the time...'

'Barry!' she chided. 'Anyway, what's your idea?'

'I've seen a car for sale that I can just about afford – I've got enough in my Halifax account, if I can barter the guy down a bit. It's an Escort Mk1 Mexico. Looks pretty smart in the sales ad. I was thinking of buying it for our Mick.' He looked at Claire, hoping for her approval of the idea.

'Is the Mexico the one that looks a bit like a rally car?' she asked, her knowledge of cars vague at best.

'That's the one. They have strengthened body panels, and this particular one has fancy driving lights as well. It's Maize Yellow, with a black stripe.'

She ventured a small joke. 'I think it sounds like Mick's kind of car – especially if it's got strengthened body panels,' she chuckled.

Barry gave her a wry grin and furrowed his eyebrows. 'Ha! Ha! Very funny,' he chortled. 'So, you're okay with the idea, then?'

'Yeah, absolutely. And I'm more than happy to chip in with the cost – I've got a bit in my savings account, too,' she offered.

'Brill. I'll give the guy a call when we get home. That should at least make our Mick easier to spot when he's out driving. There's no hiding from the world in a yellow car!'

37: Honey

Hearing the sound of an engine stop and the slam of a car door, Nick jumped up from his game of *Operation* to look out of the front window.

'Dad's here with the car!' he screamed, his voice full of excitement. He ran into the kitchen to find his mother just as Barry came into the house, his smile broad.

'Wow – that is some motor! I wouldn't mind keeping it for myself,' he exclaimed, throwing the keys into the air and catching them with all the flourish of a kid with a new toy.

Nick eagerly led his mother out of the kitchen, almost crashing into Barry's legs.

'Slow down, cowboy! Where's the fire?' laughed Barry, taking Nick by the shoulders.

'I want to see it! I want to see it!'

Barry took his son by the hand to slow him down a little.

'Well, how about you two get your coats on, then we can take a look at the car we've got for Uncle Mick. And, if you're really good, you can ride with me while we take it to him. How does that sound? Mum can follow behind in our boring car…' He winked at Claire, who rolled her eyes, but with a grin.

The family piled outside onto the pavement to take a look at the Mexico, the paintwork and chrome glowing in the late October evening sun.

'Ta-da! So, whaddya think, then?'

'Wow, it looks fantastic! Better than in the pictures,' gasped Claire.

'Aye, I took it to Auto-Shine on the way home to have it waxed and valeted.' He stroked the paintwork, careful not to smear fingerprints on it. 'They've done a bloody good job,' he concurred. 'Look, it's even got fluffy dice!' he laughed, pointing to the pair of dice hanging from the rear-view mirror.

'It looks like a big, shiny, honey bee! The big lights look like eyes. Can we keep it, and call it Honey?' Nick pulled on his dad's hand.

'I agree with Nick – can we keep it, and give Mick our old Renault?'

Barry raised his eyebrows in mock consideration before shaking his head.

'Sorry, babe – it's already in Mick's name, and I've paid half a year's insurance for him…'

'Damn!' she laughed.

'So, shall we go and deliver *Honey* to Uncle Mick?'

Barry opened the passenger door so that his beaming son could climb into the back for a ride, then fastened his seat belt. He winked at Claire before jumping into the driver's side.

'We're going to take the long way,' he grinned. 'Race you there!'

Barry eased the Mexico onto the driveway as quietly as possible, so as not to raise any awareness of his little ruse.

Sat quietly at the table with a cuppa and the crossword, Dennis got the fright of his life when Baz and Nick burst into the kitchen. Claire followed in behind them, having just arrived in the little Renault.

Too excited to contain himself, and without even stopping to greet his grandfather, Nick ran upstairs, shouting,

'Uncle Mick! Uncle Mick, come and see! Quick! C'mon.' He banged impatiently on his uncle's bedroom door, waiting to lead him downstairs.

'But you have to cover your eyes when we get to the bottom,' he instructed, 'and I'll guide you to Dad.'

Puzzled but amused, Mick played along with Nick's request, only to be met with a set of dangling keys at eye level when he took his hands away.

'They're for Honey!' squawked Nick, with hyper-enthusiasm.

Mick looked from the keys to his brother, then down at his little nephew, his face puzzled and crumpled with questions.

'Who's Honey?' he asked.

Barry took hold of his younger brother's hand and dropped the set of keys into his open palm.

'These belong to Honey... And Honey belongs to you.'

'C'mon, c'mon. Put your coat on, Uncle Mick. I'll take you and show you.'

Mick did as instructed and allowed himself to be led outside, followed by the rest of the family.

His face was agog when he saw the gleaming Mexico on the driveway. He looked from the car, then to Barry.

'This is Honey!' explained Nick. 'Cause it looks like a yellow bumblebee.'

'But... But I don't understand...'

Barry came and hugged his younger brother.

'Look, I felt really shitty after smashing up the Capri. That car was your pride and joy, and it was a present from Mum. Yes, I was pissed off at the time, but I shouldn't have taken it out on your car. I hope this makes up for it, and you'll accept the Mexico as an apology? I've put half a year's insurance on it, too.'

Mick had tears in his eyes and was lost for words. He reciprocated his brother's hug, then went to hug Claire.

'Wow! Fu... I mean, this is amazing. Thanks!' With boyish enthusiasm, he grinned at Barry. 'Can I take it for a spin?'

'Only if I can come with you?' laughed Baz.

'C'mon – let's all go,' suggested Dennis, feeling a dose of youthful vigour returning. 'Gimme a minute to lock up the house!'

38: Smoke Without Fire

As Mick sauntered up the driveway towards the side of the house, he took note of grey smoke seeping out from the open kitchen door, followed by the launch of an oven tray, a black smoking mass, and a few choice words.

Changing his pace to a sprint, he almost collided with his father in the doorway. Coughing and spluttering, and gasping for air, Dennis took a moment to steady himself before bursting out laughing.

He sat down on the doorstep and took a few deep breaths.

'How hard can it be to cook a ready-made meal?' Dennis looked up at Mick and shook his head in defeat. 'I thought I'd cook summat nice for us, so I got one of those family-sized frozen lasagne things from Farmfoods when I did a bit o'shopping today.'

'So what went wrong?' laughed Mick.

'A combination of not reading the instructions and forgetting that I'd put it in the oven. I got distracted in the garage. You know how it is once I get in my man-cave...'

'So, I guess we need a Plan B for dinner, then?'

'Aye, I guess so. Shall we just go up to the Sports Bar and have scampi and chips?' Dennis gave Mick a hopeful smile as a way of avoiding any more attempts at cooking.

'That sounds like a very good Plan B, Dad. Just let me go and get washed and changed out of these smelly butcher's clothes.'

As they entered the kitchen, Dennis nodded towards some post for them propped up by the sugar bowl on the table. Mick followed his gaze, then looked at Dennis.

'So, this is the day of reckoning, eh?' He gave his father a weak smile, nervous as to what the contents were about to reveal.

'Aye, the HLA test results have arrived. That's why I was going to cook summat nice, whatever the outcome.'

The two men looked at each other and nodded sagely.

It was time to find out their truth.

Such a life-changing moment meant that the envelopes were opened carefully along the gummed edge rather than just torn open. They each read their results, eyes scanning across the contents, while they absorbed the words.

Dennis closed his eyes and took a deep breath before speaking.

'I'm sorry, lad. I was hoping for better results than this.' He laid the letter on the table in front of him. 'The tests show that we're not a match, to within a 95% certainty.'

Mick looked across at Dennis, his eyes filled with tears. His voice cracked as he spoke.

'You'll always be mi'dad, no matter what it says on paper. I'll always be a Watkins.'

'Aye, you'll always be a Watkins. C'mere...' Dennis stood up to give Mick a reassuring hug, both men lost in this shocking but quiet moment of revelation.

'So what happens now?' asked Mick. 'Am I supposed to change my surname to McCormick? How does this affect things with the family?'

'I'll tell you what happens now, mi'lad – let's both get washed and changed and get some food inside us. We can't think on an empty stomach.'

'Plan B?' laughed Mick.

'Aye, Plan B...'

Mick wiped his mouth on the napkin and burped courteously, replete from a plateful of scampi and thick-cut chips, followed by a bowl of ice cream. The Sports Bar and Grill never failed to live up to its reputation for quality dining at a reasonable price.

Much had been discussed over their evening meal, with both having agreed on two things. One: It would be wise to take legal advice concerning any name-change, if needed, and his "new" family, should he wish to approach them. Dennis knew of a reputable Solicitor and fellow Rotarian, Frank Bryant, from Bryant & Harding. He dealt in legal matters, including family law. And, two: They also needed to update the Watkins clan with the results, starting with Irene.

While Dennis went to settle the bill for their meal, Mick went to use the payphone to call his mother and arrange an urgent meeting to give her the paternity news. But not only that, he was already burning to know more about his blood-father, Miles McCormick.

39: The Good, the Bad, and the Intriguing

Mick plumped the pillow vertically behind his back as he relaxed on his bed, his hands clasped behind his head and legs crossed at the ankles. His mind was conversely exhausted from all the information his mother had given him about his biological father, yet was exploding and excited as to what to do with it.

She had begun by telling him how the affair with Miles McCormick had started, which, although it was something his father had already told him, he wanted to hear his mother's version – the real version – not the one that Dennis may have twisted to suit his cheated heart.

Strangely enough, Dennis didn't want to know more than he already knew when Mick offered to fill in the blanks after he met with Irene. As he said, what he didn't know couldn't hurt him.

It transpired that Miles had always been a bit of a ladies' man. His then-wife, Sadie, had finally had enough and divorced him a year or so before his affair with Irene. The divorce was anything but amicable, with McCormick having to provide an alternative home, as well as stump up a sizable settlement to keep Sadie in the lifestyle to which she had become accustomed. She had a very wealthy social circle, to say the least.

Not only that, but their teenage son, Alistair, had just started at the prestigious, private secondary school, Repton, as a boarder – all of which needed paying for. Local schools in Castle Ridge had never been good enough for Alistair.

Luckily, Miles was able to retain his NCB Manager's villa. It was his one saving grace, and one that would act as a nearby love nest for him and Irene.

With Alistair now safely ensconced in boarding school, Sadie was free to come and go as she pleased, eventually starting a relationship with a property manager who sold villas to Brits out in Marbella. Always the one to enjoy a bit of glamorous sunshine, Sadie spent more time abroad than at home, flying Alistair out during the school holidays. By the time Alistair had left school then graduated from university with a business degree, he was already well-versed with the wheelings and dealings of the Marbella money-men.

It was during this time that his father was imprisoned for embezzlement, so in a way, it was a blessing to be abroad and away from people making any connections – after all, McCormick is not quite the same as Smith or Brown as a name to hide behind. Yet despite the flashy lifestyle, Alistair was a solid Derbyshire lad at heart, and soon became bored with the flaky falseness of those around him. He longed for something more stable and a business of his own.

It was after his father died in the hotel accident, and he inherited what small amount remained of Miles's estate, that Alistair decided to permanently return to the family home and set up his business, leaving his mother behind in Marbella.

One of the things that Alistair learned during his upbringing and the accompanying lifestyle, was that people often bit off more than they could chew to keep up with the circles in which they mixed. This often led to cars and boats being repossessed, and he knew that this was a job that he could do. He had no qualms about knocking on someone's door and taking what was owed. If you can't pay for it, you can't own it. Simple.

However, there are not many people with such expensive tastes in Derbyshire, when compared to the Marbella set, so his door-knocking was to retrieve smaller items, such as TVs and other household goods, as well as the odd car or caravan. This led to him becoming a legitimate agent for selling off these repossessed items, and apparently now had a flourishing business trading in cheap, second-hand stuff.

This was as much as Irene had learned from local sources while trying to keep tabs on anything connected to Miles. Their affair might have been long since over, and Miles might be long since dead in the ground, but there was always something that had a hold over her. And perhaps it was connected to Michael? Deep in her heart of hearts, she had always suspected that he was Miles's son, but tried to bury the thought.

Now it all made sense.

After his mother had confessed her paternity suspicions to Michael, he could understand why he had always felt slightly different or unconnected to his brothers. Not just because he was younger, but because of the *biological* differences. He wasn't one of them.

Reflecting on all that he had learned this evening, Mick was intrigued by his older half-brother – for that's what Alistair was. Strange how they had both ended up in a similar kind of wheeling and dealing market, though Alistair's business sounded way more successful and legit than his own dodgy dealings.

He sighed and started formulating plans to try and track him down. Maybe he could join Alistair in business? After all, he did have a wealth of "experience", albeit shady, in this kind of thing. It could be a good way of going straight and blowing out the illegal parasites with whom he'd become ensnared.

Perhaps he was a McCormick, after all.

40: Reality Check

With the paternity news now having been relayed to the rest of the family over Sunday lunch, the results had not been taken particularly well by Barry and Claire. Any sympathy that they'd had for Mick in recent weeks had evaporated the moment the results were announced. The reality of the domino effect was kicking in, a reality which meant that little Nicky didn't carry any Watkins blood whatsoever.

He really was the cuckoo's cuckoo.

Even harder for them to bear was the knowledge that they would one day have to break this news to Nick. It had been hard enough facing the fact that Mick was Nicky's biological father – but now this! Irene had a lot to answer for, messing up everyone's lives! Could they really still look at Mick as a Watkins?

The biological enormity of the situation was having such a profound effect on Claire that she began verbally resenting Sally-Ann and Kenny for having such a perfect little family, causing Sally-Ann to storm out, and Kenny with divided loyalties.

Mick's face was ashen as he listened to them arguing about him, like he was invisible. Did they not realise he could hear what they were saying about him and his mother? He felt sorely tempted to just drive away and never come back.

He hung his head, dejected, and put his hands over his ears.

Dennis could only look on in abject despair at the high drama and accusations being flung back and forth over the dining table, grateful that his grandchildren were spending the day with their other grandparents and not witnessing the animosity of their parents. The once tight-knit Watkins unit was crumbling around him. Although his own wedding vows had stated "For better, or for worse" all those years ago, he could never have envisaged that this is what the "worse" case scenario would play out like.

He silently cursed Irene for what she had done to the family. If only people realised what they were getting into when they embarked on the covert thrill of an affair, and the repercussions of their actions – the enormity of the devastation it causes once everything comes to light.

His chest tightened, as if his heart would break.

Although Dennis had done his best to calm the situation around the table, he conceded that the family would need a few days to digest the information and for the dust to settle. He knew it was just a knee-jerk reaction from the boys and their wives, and did his best to reassure Mick that he would always be a part of the Watkins family.

But for Mick, his new reality was one of being in a familial no-man's-land and an outcast. He no longer felt like a Watkins, but nor did he feel like a McCormick. An overwhelming need to track down his half-brother, Alistair, enveloped him.

But where to begin?

The local telephone directory seemed like a good place to start.

Mick looked at himself in the hallway mirror and tried to envisage what Alistair might look like. Would they share any of the same features and mannerisms? He would hopefully soon find out.

He settled himself at the little telephone table and opened the directory at M. Sadly, the search drew a blank – there were no listings under the name of McCormick in either the Castle Ridge or Chesterfield areas. He had already hit his first stumbling block.

Then he remembered that his mother had said something about Alistair having returned to his family home instead of staying in Marbella. Maybe she knew where it was located? He picked up the phone and dialled her number.

After chatting with Irene, all that she could remember was that Miles had bought a little detached cottage in Baslow for his ex-wife and son as part of the divorce settlement. This was enough of a clue for Mick to start his detective work on tracking down his half-brother and making contact.

His mother had been reluctant at first, trying to encourage Mick to "let sleeping dogs lie" and be happy with the life that he'd got. But Mick now had the additional leverage of using guilt as a part of his manipulation arsenal to get the information he needed.

Rather than call Alistair out of the blue and risk the phone being slammed down on him, he thought it wiser to try a friendly, face-to-face doorstep approach.

The little village of Baslow in the Peak District was not only quaint and pretty, but also had ideal road links to get to Chesterfield, Sheffield, Buxton, and Manchester. It ideally offered the best of both worlds: remote enough to escape while being convenient enough not to feel cut off.

Mick perceptively noticed, after cruising through the village a few times, that the Mexico was a head-turner, so he opted to leave it in one of the pub car parks. As much as he loved the car, the Maize Yellow colour didn't allow for being incognito.

Struck by an unusual dose of nervousness, Mick chose to explore the village first in a bid to walk off some of his tension. Although not a large village, Baslow seemed to have enough facilities, while retaining the charm of an idyllic Peak location.

The picturesque scenery and fresh air soon worked its calming magic, giving Mick a renewed dose of courage.

It was time.

He headed for the address scrawled on the piece of notepaper.

The cottage itself was located just down a little lane on the far side of the village. It wasn't as large as Mick expected it to be, but then again, there had only been Sadie and Alistair, and he was about to go to boarding school at the time, so it wasn't as though Sadie needed something as large as Chatsworth House, even if she was trying to impress her social circle. The cottage was solidly built of honeyed Derbyshire sandstone and looked as though it had been well maintained over the years.

To the side of the cottage was an open barn area housing a reasonably new, sign-written Transit van; *McCormick's Merchandise.* He was definitely at the right place, and guessed that Alistair must be at home.

A sudden wave of jealousy coursed through him, coveting all that Alistair had. Why couldn't he have been a full brother, and not some half-arsed kid who was brought up in a mining town and had to beg, steal, or borrow for everything that he wanted? But maybe now the tides were turning?

With a surge of bravado, he took a deep breath and slowly walked up the driveway to the cottage.

It was now or never...

With a slight feeling of trepidation, Mick took a breath, then rapped with the brass knocker, and waited. He stuffed his hands into his pockets to try and quell the shaking. A few moments later, the glossy, black door was opened by a fairly tall, tanned, and athletic-looking young man, somewhere in his mid-thirties, with hair and eye colouring similar to his own. His clothing was smart countrystyle, and his watch looked heavy and expensive.

This had to be Alistair.

'Didn't you see the sign on the gatepost?' he sneered, looking down his nose at Mick. 'It says, *"No Hawkers or Sellers"*.'

Mick suddenly felt very small and insignificant.

'I'm... I'm not here to sell anything. I'm here to introduce myself.'

He politely held out his hand towards Alistair. 'My name is Michael Watkins from Castle Ridge, and I'm your half-brother. I'm sorry if this is a bit of a shock or surprise to you.'

Alistair didn't reciprocate by taking Mick's hand but rather narrowed his eyes at him with suspicion. He did a double-take and shook his head, unsure as to what he'd just heard.

'Could you repeat that, please...'

'I said that my name is Michael Watkins, and I'm your half-brother. Your late father, Miles, is also my father.' He waited for his words to hit their target and for Alistair to say something.

Alistair rolled his eyes in disdain. 'So your mother was just another one of his floozies, then!'

This was not going the way that Mick had imagined. Although he was not expecting an "open-arms, welcome home" kind of hug, he was at least hoping for some civility. Hadn't Alistair's mother brought him up with any manners or courtesy!

'Look, I know this must be a bit of a shock to you, but I can prove it. We had a bit of a family issue recently, some paternity thing. After all the testing was done, it seems that the bloke who I thought was my dad, isn't. My mother then confessed that she had an affair with your father, and I'm the result. I just wanted to meet you, that's all. We can forget this meeting ever happened, and I'll just walk away.' Mick cast his eyes down, getting the feeling that he wasn't really welcome.

'Yes, you're absolutely right – this is a shock. And yes, I do want to see some proof...'

Their doorstep conversation was interrupted by the sound of two vehicles approaching from behind. Mick turned his head to take a look, then blanched. He recognised the white Transit van and black BMW 3 Series. They belonged to the two goons with whom he traded his cash and goods for gear and a small percentage.

Seeing that their boss had a visitor, they pulled up in front of the door rather than in the open garage, blocking Mick's escape.

'Well, if it isn't the little shit from Castle Ridge! What the fuck are you doin' 'ere?' snarled the big guy in the long leather coat.

Mick looked at the hard men and then at Alistair, and back again.

Then the penny dropped.

Hard.

Alistair's legit business of the repossession and sales of domestic items was just a front for his backhand stuff and dope dealing. The "good seed gone bad" once the money-greed demon had taken hold. He was the one at the top of the food chain, in which Mick was just a subservient minion.

Alistair looked at his two middlemen and then at Mick. He cocked his head, puzzled.

'Erm, it seems like you three know each other already. So, what's really going on here?' He glared at his two underlings. 'You know the rules! You know your trail shouldn't lead back to me,' he barked.

Mick could sense the tension between the men, causing his own anxiety to rise. How could he bolt out of this situation if the need arose? His mind even envisaged a scenario of being dumped in a bath of acid!

'We didn't know he was here, boss. Honest! It's as much a surprise to us as it is to you to see young Michael on your doorstep.'

Alistair considered what they had just said – they at least confirmed the name that the lad had used when he'd introduced himself. That part of the story at least matched. He looked at Mick and raised an eyebrow.

'Do you have any proof for what you've just told me?'

Mick nodded, then pulled out the letters with the HLA paternity information confirming that Dennis wasn't his father. He gave them to Alistair to look over.

After scanning the documents, his half-brother took a deep breath, then issued orders.

'You two – fuck off, and get some work done. And you,' he indicated to Mick. 'You come with me.'

Alistair stepped to one side to allow Mick into the cottage, whereupon two large Irish Wolfhounds bounded towards him, happy to see a new friend. Mick jerked backwards, almost falling down the steps.

'Don't worry, they're just big daft loonies,' Alistair reassured his nervous guest. 'In here to the left, into my office. Murphy, Fergus, go to your beds.'

The two tousle-haired, grey dogs lolloped towards the kitchen with a reluctant groan.

Alistair indicated for Mick to sit in one of the comfy-looking wing-back chairs before settling down in his own, grand-looking, leather Chesterfield.

'Sorry, the lads can come on a bit strong at times. That's what I pay them for – to deal with my day-to-day business, and to keep any unwanted people from my door. So, what's this about you being my half-brother? Tell me again...'

Once Mick had finished recounting the story just as his mother had explained it to him, Alistair eyed him with a little less suspicion, then nodded.

'Isn't it funny – what goes around, comes around, as they say. Your mother worked for my, sorry, *our* father, and now you "work" for me.' He air-quoted "work". 'What a small world it is.'

Michael tried to assess the situation as fast as he could. Was Alistair being sarcastic, or was he being genuine? He tried to keep the conversation on the lighter side.

'Exactly! Strange that we've both ended up in a similar business, and brought together by a quirk of fate.'

An uncomfortable pause ensued while each man became absorbed in their thoughts. Mick looked around the office and noticed a large, framed photograph hanging on the wall of Sadie and Alistair in sunnier climes – presumably Marbella. He also noticed a silver-framed photograph of a smartly attired businessman on the desk with features and colouring similar to theirs.

Mick broke the silence.

'Is that Miles? I've never seen any pictures of him. Mum doesn't have any, as far as I know.'

Alistair picked up the photo frame and looked at his father before setting the picture face down on the desk.

'Yes, that's Miles, Dad. The family embarrassment. I keep that picture of him on my desk to remind myself how *not* to do business. And yet here I am, lying and cheating my way through life to make money, just like he did. I guess the trick is not getting caught. That's where he failed.'

Mick took a moment to comprehend Alistair's twisted vision of what a fatherly role model should be like. It was certainly not the way he looked at Dennis as a role model. And yet, who seemed to be making the most money? After all, isn't the idea of being in business to make money? That's what had lured Mick into dealing in the first place – extra cash.

'I know it's a bit of a bold suggestion, but seeing as how we're both in this together, what about some kind of partnership? Or, at the very least, maybe a better percentage? I do bring a reasonable amount of business your way, after all. Why can't we both benefit?'

He swallowed hard, his palms sweating. Maybe he'd crossed a line here; when all was said and done, it was the first time that he'd met Alistair.

His half-brother's face suddenly became very serious, his tone sharp.

'You're right – it *is* a bold suggestion. You've got balls, I'll give you that.' Alistair's mind began whirring. One of his "supplier and dealer" guys had now seen his face and knew where he lived. Not only that, he claimed to be related and wanted a share of the profits. The story that he gave about his mother's affair with his – *their* – father, sounded credible. And without a doubt, there seemed to be a clear genetic resemblance between the two of them.

Bored with having been sent to their beds, Fergus and Murphy came back from the kitchen into the office, wagging their tails and happy to see their master. This was the cue that Alistair needed to break the conversation and play for time. He stood up and offered his hand towards Michael.

'Well, thank you for your visit today. It must have taken a lot of courage to make contact. It's come as quite a shock to me to suddenly discover that I have a sibling, as you can appreciate.'

Mick stood and took Alistair's hand to reciprocate the handshake.

'So, do we have a deal?' he asked tentatively.

Alistair snorted slightly.

'No, we don't have a deal. I have to give this a little more than five minutes of thought. I'm not just some wealthy relation that you can free-load off, you know. I need to dot the i's and cross the t's before I enter into any kind of deal, family or not. I'll send word to you when I've made my decision.' And with that, Alistair moved towards the office door to show Mick out, his trusty Wolfhounds at his heel. 'Oh, and one more thing – don't *ever* come here again without my permission or invitation. Is that clear?'

Realising that he was way out of his depth in big business, Mick nodded his servitude.

He didn't feel like a McCormick. Yet.

But perhaps he now had a little more leverage in the game.

Didn't he?

41: Putting Life on Hold - 1984

The tightly fixed jawline and heavy-set body language told Claire all she needed to know without Barry uttering a single word when he came into the sitting room. He plonked himself down in the armchair, throwing one leg over the armrest, and let out a sigh of defeat.

'I take it the news isn't good?' asked Claire.

He looked at her from under his mop of wavy hair, dampened by the March drizzle, sagely shaking his head.

'We officially down tools and go on strike at midnight. The local vote was to show solidarity with the lads who'll lose their jobs in the threatened pit closures. Bastard Maggie and her cronies! Doesn't she realise how many lives are going to be affected by this? How many communities? You can't just close a bunch of pits and throw men on the scrap heap.'

Claire came and sat on the floor by the armchair and put her head against Barry's leg.

'Shit. So what happens next, you know, for the men, and for the country?' she asked, looking up at him, her eyes full of concern.

'There'll most likely be a knock-on effect with other pits going on strike in support. That said, we've heard that the Nottinghamshire miners have voted to continue to work, so there'll probably be a bit of tension with some of the neighbouring pits.'

'Thank goodness I'm still working at the factory, eh. Don't worry, we'll get through it. The strike won't need to go on for that long, will it?'

'Well, that's where Maggie and MacGregor have got us by the balls. The crafty bastards have been stockpiling coal for the power stations, so that'll lessen the initial impact of the strike. But believe me, if you'd have heard the blokes at the meeting – blokes who are normally peaceful buggers – they're going to do their best to bring the government to its knees. If the Tories want a fight, we'll fuckin' give 'em one.' Barry ruffled her hair unconsciously, needing to feel something soft to ease his pent-up anger.

Claire nuzzled closer to his leg, relishing the tenderness in such a fraught moment. They were going to have to tighten their belts, that was for sure. There would be no holiday to the Miners' Camp in Skegness this year, or anywhere, for that matter.

She was suddenly grateful that they lived on the outskirts of Castle Ridge. With a view over allotments to the front, a huge recreational area over the back, and woods, farmland, and countryside within a reasonable walking distance, they had certainly picked the ideal spot to live when they bought the house. At least they wouldn't be facing row upon row of grey estate houses like many of the other mining families.

'Damn! If only I hadn't used most of my savings to buy our Mick that car. Just when the money would come in really useful!'

'Hey, you didn't know there would be a strike. Better that it was invested in the car, and not just used up on bills and baked beans. At least you've got something to show for the money, even if it was a gift for your brother. It was used for something solid, something good. You'll only resent the strike if all your savings just evaporate on bills.'

'Aye, you're right. You always seem to find sense in madness. At least one of us can stay level-headed. But on the plus side, there's some money in the strike fund, so we'll get a few quid if we go on picket duty. It's better than nowt, I suppose.'

'Tell you what – I'll go and make us a cuppa, and then we can make a list of what our average expenses are, compared to what I earn. That should at least give us an overview of how much money we'll need each week,' she suggested, trying to remain positive, even though her insides were feeling chewed up with anxiety.

He kissed Claire on the back of the hand as he helped her to stand up.

'My cool, calm, and collected Claire. What would I do wi'out ya?'

'Well, for a start, you'd have to make your own cups of tea,' she teased, hiding her true fear for the upcoming challenges.

42: Miners United Will Never Be Defeated

Before the sun had even begun to rise, hordes of police transit vans were snaking their way across the country in an organised bid to stop the convoys of flying pickets from reaching their appointed destinations. In a dangerous game of cat-and-mouse, motorway exits and side roads were blocked, and all "suspect" vehicles were stopped, denying the men freedom of movement to help their comrades.

A swarm of police units from the Cheshire area made their way from both sides of the A632 to form a pincer movement at Castle Ridge Colliery in preparation for the 5:30 am day shift starting. At least 30% of the men were still working, and tensions were running high, meaning that this was a target colliery for the flying pickets. Police units from different counties were also converging at other local collieries today in readiness for the planned invasion.

As more and more pickets managed to get through the police blockades or sneak in through back roads, the numbers swelled to over two hundred and fifty, and were still rising, thronging the gates of Castle Ridge.

Frustratingly, the NUM had made very little impact or headway in the early months of the strike due to the government's canny stock-piling of coal in order to fuel the power stations. And as it was now May, the summer months were looming, further lessening the need for coal. Nor did it help the local cause with the majority of neighbouring Nottinghamshire collieries still operating, and a breakaway union, the UDM, springing up against the NUM.

As Barry linked arms with his comrades in order to build a human blockade, a memory flashed across his mind; he remembered Claire once asking him why he'd wanted to go down t'pit instead of learning the building trade like Kenny, or some other trade. His answer was simple – national pride. He saw mining as one of the British heritage jobs, alongside farming and fishing. Without these trades, there would be no food or warmth. These men had a solid camaraderie and passion for the job – and that's why he was standing here now, battling for the very thing he believed in. The fight wasn't just about getting a fair wage – it was a fight to keep men in work and the country running.

The tension swelled as the numbers grew. The men sensed that the scab-buses were approaching, chaperoned by armoured police vans, front and rear. A shielded wall of police moved into position, essentially blocking the men from reaching the buses containing the workers as they crossed the picket lines.

A loud chorus of foot stomping began to ripple through the crowd, bringing forth their voices. Unified chanting began, the gathered throng of voices louder than any choir.

Miners united will never be defeated!

Miners united will never be defeated!

Their pride was as strong as their voices, as they repeated the chant over and over again. Barry chanted along, loud and proud.

Miners united will never be defeated!

Miners united will never be defeated!

As the men pushed slowly forward, they met with resistance from the wall of police shields, each pushing against the other for supremacy.

Who would win the day? The law or the mob?

What do we want?

Work!

When do we want it?

Now!

Maggie out!

Maggie out!

Maggie! Maggie! Maggie!

Out! Out! Out!

Miners united will never be defeated!

Once the buses came into view and began easing their way through the supposed safe passage created by the police vans, the men surged forward, breaking the lines. The vehicles came under attack from clods of earth, half-bricks, glass bottles – anything that could be used as a missile was hurled into the air, only to shatter on impact, causing shrapnel and shards to be scattered across the men.

As the injured fell, scuffles broke out between the police and the pickets; chaos became the order of the day, with both sides losing control. Tempers and emotions were running at maximum, fuelled by their basic instinct of fight or flight. Some of the older pickets within the crowd sensibly began to move backwards out of the fray, while the younger ones stood their ground.

After the vehicles had slowly eased their way through to take the workers in for the day shift, the police tried their best to restore order and get the crowd to back off and disperse. Some of the men, Barry included, took this as an affront; it was like the police were declaring that they had won the battle. The workers had successfully gotten through, aided and abetted by the police – they were nothing more than puppets of Maggie and MacGregor!

The frontline of police changed their formation tactics and created a V-shape to spearhead their way through the crowd and break them up, causing some of the men at the side of Barry to lose their balance and fall to the ground. Angry and hurt from having been knocked over, the men lashed out, kicking at the legs of the officers. In retaliation, the police turned on the men and started using their truncheons.

Seeing the blood, and hearing his comrades shouting for the beating to stop, Barry jumped in and took a swing at the officers, punching one in the face and knocking the helmet from another. He, in turn, took a heavy hit across the arm and elbow from one of the truncheons, causing him to buckle. The next thing he knew, his other arm was being roughly shoved up behind his back, and he was being pushed to the ground, under arrest for assaulting a police officer and for affray. With handcuffs now encircling his wrists, he was lifted up and unceremoniously frogmarched towards one of the waiting Black Mariahs, before being loaded into the back along with other "rioting pickets".

After being taken to Beetwell Street Police Station in nearby Chesterfield, the men were photographed, fingerprinted, and charged for their picket-line misdemeanours. Despite the charges brought against him, Barry still felt a sense of pride for having done his duty in supporting his fellow men in their fight for their right to keep the collieries open and the industry alive.

He might now have a criminal record, but at least he wasn't a scab.

As to how Claire would react to the news?

Well...

He would just have to deal with that battle once he got home.

43: Broken Hearted

The gnawing and growling in Kenny's empty stomach triggered an automatic response to take a look at his watch.

'Bloody 'ell, Dad – it's almost twelve. Time to down tools and head up t'chippie. What say you? Do you fancy some chips and a slab of cod?'

Dennis finished smoothing the patch of plaster at the bottom of the wall before dropping his float into the bucket of water by his side. He wobbled as he stood, feeling a little light-headed and dizzy.

'Are you okay?'

Kenny went to his father's aid and grabbed his arm.

'Aye, I'm fine. I just got up a bit too quickly, that's all. Got a rush of blood to the head. Nowt to worry about.' He gently shrugged Kenny away, then picked up his little hand-brush to wash off his plastering float in the bucket. 'Just let me clean this, then we can go and get summat to eat.'

'It's my guess that you're not looking after yerself properly. Not since Mam left. Why don't you come and have more meals wi'me and Sally-Ann? The kids would love to see more of their grandad.'

Dennis grinned sheepishly, knowing that his son was right. Since Irene had moved out, his evening meals had consisted of ready-made concoctions and stuff out of tins. Plus, Mick had brought a steady supply of bacon, sausages, and steak from the butcher's. He couldn't remember the last time he'd eaten any fresh fruit or veg if he was honest with himself. Many months of too much beer, fatty foods, and rubbish – all compounding to give him indigestion and acid reflux. Rennies and Polo Mints had become his go-to relief aid.

'How about I come over for Sunday lunch, then?' He fumbled in his pockets looking for the keys to the van. 'Here, you drive...'

'Are you sure you're okay? You look like shit, to be honest.' Kenny gladly accepted the keys from his father.

Dark circles under his eyes were another indicator that Dennis was not really handling the bachelor lifestyle. He looked palid and grey. No matter what they thought about their mother's morals, she had, without question, been an excellent home-maker and caregiver to the family.

The main car park in the centre of Castle Ridge was already quite full when they arrived, necessitating a drive-around until Kenny could find a space big enough for the Transit. Typically, this was on the farthest side, as all the other lunchtime visitors had parked as close as they could to the local amenities.

Kenny rolled his eyes when he saw the length of the Friday queue at Naylor's chippie – already out of the door and curving towards the butcher's shop in the next building.

Despite the early autumn chill in the air and a moderate breeze, Dennis mopped his brow and face with his handkerchief, then loosened his collar a little.

'Looks like half of Castle Ridge fancy having chips for lunch today, eh?' he said, as they tagged onto the back of the queue. He noticed Mick in the butcher's shop window and gave him a wave. His youngest son grinned and gave him a thumbs-up in return, before going back to serving his customer.

As the queue inched slowly forward, Dennis found it necessary to lean against the wall for support. Something didn't feel right... A wave of nausea and pain constricted through his stomach and exploded into his chest. His knees began to buckle as though the weight of an elephant had descended on his rib cage, pushing him down to the ground. He tried to grab hold of Kenny, but his hand wouldn't work. Pain and tingling shot up and down his arm and across his jaw.

'K... Kenny...'

As Dennis crumpled to the floor, he bumped into the lady behind, causing her to scream out, alerting Kenny to his father's distress. Realising that Dennis was probably having a heart attack, he shouted for assistance to the others in the queue, while he made his dad comfortable. The lady to the side of them immediately took off her coat and made a cushion behind Dennis's head, while someone further ahead in the queue ran inside the chippie and asked for them to call 999 for an ambulance – *there was an old guy out on the pavement, most likely having a heart attack!* Another person realised who the victim was and ran next door to get Mick from the butcher's shop.

Once Kenny and Mick had made sure their father was safely in the ambulance and on the way to the hospital, they popped inside the chippie to thank them for their assistance. Kenny asked to borrow the telephone so that he could call his mother – even though she and Dennis were separated, it was only fair to let her know the situation.

Just as the call from Kenny was being connected to Irene's desk from the switchboard, she heard the wail of sirens screaming down Colliery Hill and past the NCB offices. Goose-bumps caused the hairs on her forearms to rise, and her scalp prickled; some inner sixth sense told her that it wasn't the police dealing with a picket line fracas. She took a deep breath before taking Kenny's call.

'Tell me that there hasn't been an accident. Is that why you're calling? I've just heard the emergency services go flying past...' Her voice sounded small and shaky as she asked for information.

Kenny sighed. 'Well, not an accident as such, but Dad's just been rushed to the hospital with a suspected heart attack. We were in the queue at the chippie when it happened.'

'Oh, good God! Is he okay? I mean, I know he's not okay, but like... Is he dying? Was it a big one? Sorry, I'm not making much sense...'

'They made him stable enough to transport him, and they're taking him to the Royal. I've got our Mick with me, and we've got the Transit, so we're going to follow on. Do you know whether Baz is on picket duty or not? Can you contact him, and then meet us at the hospital?'

She nodded her answer to Kenny, then disconnected the call.

Irene's temples began pounding as the blood rushed to her head. This couldn't be happening! This was all her fault for what she'd done to the family. For what she'd done to Dennis. It was karma!

The sudden reality of possibly losing someone close hit Irene like a thunderclap. Tears filled her eyes, and she screamed out, alerting her co-workers to her distress.

'Please don't let Dennis die...

Please don't...'

44: Facing the Unknown

The quiet yet purposeful hum of activity was the first thing that struck Irene when she entered the Cardiac Care Unit – like ants in an ant colony, staff scurried to and fro, all with an efficient purpose.

After speaking to one of the reception staff, she and Barry were directed to the family room to join Kenny and Mick, while they waited for news of Dennis's condition. Both Kenny and Mick jumped up to hug their mother and brother in solidarity when they came into the room.

'Is there any news or update? Do we know what's happening? How is he?' blustered Irene, desperate for information.

'Come and sit down,' directed Kenny, leading her to a seat. 'He's stable as far as we know, but they've taken him to run an ECG, and to do some blood tests. This should help the doctors determine how serious the heart attack was, and what the next steps will be.' He gave her an encouraging smile. 'He's in the best hands, Mam. They'll take good care of him, and let us know what's happening as soon as they can.'

Feeling the onset of another bout of tears, Irene rummaged around inside her handbag for a pack of tissues.

'This is all my fault,' she snuffled. 'If I hadn't been so stupid...' She exhaled loudly, expelling her frustration, sadness, and guilt. 'I really can't take much more of this...' she sobbed.

Mick was just about to speak when the cardiologist came into the family room with an update for them. His soothing voice and gentle bedside manner calmly reassured them that, although Dennis had indeed suffered a heart attack, the ECG didn't show any extensive coronary muscular damage.

'That's good, though, isn't it, Doctor?' Irene asked.

'Yes, and no. We still need to determine the cause. We're preparing him for an angiography, which means that a catheter will be inserted into an artery up to the heart, then a special fluid will be pumped into the catheter. The fluid shows up on X-rays, thereby identifying the exact location of any narrowing or blockage. From there, I can decide on the best course of treatment.'

'So, he's not out of the woods, yet, then?'

The cardiologist put a reassuring hand on Irene's shoulder.

'No, he's not out of the woods yet, but at least we'll soon be able to see the wood for the trees, so to speak. We'll have a clearer overview of the next steps to take. Why don't you all go to the cafeteria and get something to eat and drink, and I'll come and talk to you again after the surgery.' He gave them a nod and a small smile, which left them feeling a little more hopeful.

Kenny stood up, then gave Barry a tug on the sleeve.

'C'mon. Let's go and find a phone so that we can call Sally-Ann and Claire and give 'em an update. They must be worried sick. And I don't know about anybody else, but I'm desperate for summat to eat. Mam, could you and Mick find the cafeteria and grab us a table?'

Irene nodded, grateful to have something else to occupy her mind and calm her frayed nerves. Her stomach rumbled, reminding her that she hadn't eaten anything since morning coffee either, having been called away just as her lunch break was about to begin.

Though the uncertainty and waiting were not over yet, they all needed some food for the soul in the meantime.

'Well, look at this lazy bugger languishing in bed!' teased Kenny. 'He'll do owt to get out o'work...'

Dennis adjusted himself on the pile of pillows and pushed the bedside tray table to one side, happy to see his family of evening visitors.

'Aye, that was a bit of a scare!' he chuckled. 'And not one I'm in a hurry to repeat...'

'A "bit of a scare" is an understatement, Dennis Watkins! You frightened the bloody life out of us...' sniffled Irene, about to burst into tears for the umpteenth time that day.

'Ah, you don't get your hands on my insurance money that easily,' he quipped. 'I'm not ready to pop off just yet – I'm made of tougher stuff than that.' He pretended to flex his biceps like some kind of He-Man.

Kenny rolled his eyes and grinned.

'Damn! I'd better cancel that holiday to Barbados then...'

'Ouch, stop making me laugh, I don't want to burst mi'stitches.' Without warning, a cloud of melancholy enveloped him. 'But joking aside, it's been a bit of a wake-up call. One minute you're feeling young and invincible, and the next, you're feeling old and mortal. It's scary.'

'Ufff! You're only fifty-one, not seventy-one, for goodness' sake,' chided Irene. 'You might be mortal, but you're certainly not old!'

She sat on the edge of the bed and took Dennis's hand in hers, giving it a gentle squeeze. A look passed between them both, an unconscious moment of each reading the other's mind.

'I certainly hope so. This little episode has made me realise just how much I love you and miss you.' He gave her hand a gentle squeeze in return. 'Life just isn't the same without you. I think it's about time I did some forgiving and forgetting.' His bottom lip began to quiver, and his eyes welled with tears. 'Will you come home, Irene?'

Irene closed her eyes and took a deep breath, then nodded her acceptance.

'There's nothing that would make me happier, Den.' She took his hand up to her lips and kissed it tenderly before giving him the gentlest of hugs.

A chorus of relieved, happy sighs rippled around the room as the family acknowledged their parents' reconciliation.

'Sounds like you really were "brokenhearted", Den,' laughed Claire.

'Aye, quite literally!' he agreed, with a chuckle. 'Anyway, has the cardiologist given you an update? Do you know the extent of everything connected to the heart attack?'

'Yes, he came and spoke to us while you were in post-op recovery. The angiogram revealed a blockage, so they had to proceed with a coronary angioplasty to help keep the artery open. You'll have to take blood-thinning meds for a while, too,' Irene explained.

'And,' chipped in Kenny, 'you will also need to take some time off work to rest and rehabilitate. I can keep the business running, but just take on smaller jobs that I can do alone. It's not like we're that busy, anyway, with the strike being on.'

'You're a good lad, Ken. Thanks for that,' acknowledged Dennis.

'It also means a change of diet and lifestyle. Less fat and more gentle exercise,' chided Irene. 'Less of my meat and potato pie, and more fish and salads. No more wild living!' she teased. 'Anyway, the cardiologist said that he'll have a full meeting with both of us before you're discharged, and give us all the information about your rehabilitation.'

'Will I still be able to go for a pint?' he asked, his tone hopeful.

Irene shook her head. 'Probably not. You're going to have to live like a monk from now on if you don't want another heart attack.'

'Live like a monk? So does that mean no, erm, you know, hanky panky then?' He winked and nudged a now blushing Irene.

'Eeewww! Dad!' groaned Barry, at the thought of his parents still having an active bedroom life.

'Take it easy, tiger! The kids are listening... Let's just get you nursed back to health before you start raising your blood pressure. Talking of which, here's the nurse to take yours. We'll leave her to do her checks, and see you tomorrow.'

Irene gave Dennis a kiss on the forehead, not only relieved that he was alive, but relieved to be back in his life.

45: Too Close to Home

Mick's heart rate increased on hearing the local gossip just supplied by his mother. According to a news article on Radio Hallam this morning, there had been a suspicious death in Castle Ridge the previous night. Although the name of the deceased hadn't been released, it was reported as the "possible drug related death of a young male individual".

Surely that could only be one of his customers?

But how? And which one?

He never supplied any of the hard stuff. He needed more information if he was going to avoid the police making any connection back to him.

'A drug death? What, here in Castle Ridge? I didn't know there were any junkies in Castle Ridge,' he lied.

'I know! What's the world coming to when this kind of thing reaches our local doorstep? Claire called me earlier, and according to her mum, there was a lot of police and ambulance activity on the estate last night. At first, she thought it might have been kids messing around with fireworks and someone had gotten injured – there were loads of 'em wandering about doing Penny for the Guy. Anyway, turns out it was at one of the houses near the Miners' Welfare. A young lad was found by his mother in the garden shed with dope paraphernalia, whatever that is, and a bag of glue. Her screams alerted the neighbours, of course. One of them ran to the phone box to call for an ambulance. It was too late, though. The lad was already gone by the time help arrived. Cardiac arrest.'

'That's awful. I've been hearing a lot of stories recently about young 'uns turning to glue for kicks. That, and lighter fluid. It's a cheap way of getting high, especially when you haven't got any money coming in,' interjected Dennis. 'And this bloody miners' strike isn't helping. Morale's at an all-time low in the area.'

'Aye, that's true. Sad, but true.' Irene shook her head. 'Mind you, wasn't there something on the news back in September about the strike having been declared illegal? Because there was no national ballot before it began. They're gunning for Scargill more than ever. It's sometimes terrifying watching the picket line at the colliery from the office window. I remember back in May when all those flying pickets came. I've never seen so many police down there. It was absolute pandemonium.'

Realising that the morning coffee discussion was descending into the politics of the miners' strike, Mick surreptitiously fingered the pager in his trouser pocket. He had more urgent, personal matters to attend to. Based on his mother's description of the location, he figured out exactly which house and who the careless young lad was. It was one of his customers, and there were others further up the chain who needed to know.

'Take a seat, Michael. So, there's been a death on your patch? So fuckin' what. That's their risk, not yours, my boy. You supply. End of. What they do, and how they do it ain't your problem. Besides, it was the glue, not the gear, which killed him.'

'I know, I know. But he was only a young lad...' Michael looked up at the two menacing shadows standing over him. He would have preferred talking directly to Alistair, but he had given some bullshit excuse that he was too busy organising a fireworks party with some of the other local businesses.

'Anyway, since when did you develop a conscience?' sneered the smaller of the two men, laughing.

'But what if it leads back to me? To us? What if his mates give up names, and the cops come sniffing around?' Panic was beginning to rise in Mick's voice.

The larger of the two men answered.

'Providing you've got no gear at home – assuming they raid your parents' house, that is – there's nothing they can prove. And *NOTHING* will lead them to us, will it, Micky? Cause you'll keep your big mouth shut. Capice?'

Mick recalled something that his father had once said – that he was never going to be free from these guys. He knew too much about their operation. And not only that, Alistair was at the top of the chain. His half-brother would drop him like a hot stone rather than have his name tagged into it. Or worse... In the short time that Mick had gotten to know him, he realised that Alistair had a narcissistic self-preservation streak.

Adrenaline pumped through him, giving him a sickly feeling in the pit of his stomach.

'I want out of the drug sales. I'll increase my goods and cash to you instead – make up for it that way... I'm more than happy to do the nightwork, if you get my drift.'

The larger man tousled the top of Mick's head in a fatherly way before forcefully grabbing him by the back of the head and hair, his face inches away from Mick's. He laughed maliciously, choking Mick with his rancid cigarette breath.

'You want out of the drug sales! What fuckin' planet are you on, Michael? You're one of our best salesmen. Everybody wants a bit of blow to forget their troubles. No one is buying fancy electrical gear at the moment, even if it is knock-off. Or have you forgotten that there's a miners' strike on?'

'Of course I haven't forgotten! But I just can't do this anymore. I... I...' Mick paused, trying to hold back his tears. 'I want out. If I can't just do the burglaries, then I want out altogether...' He proffered the pager back to the large man, too nervous to throw it across the room. 'Here, take it back. And I won't say a word to anyone. I... I promise.'

A heavy silence hung in the darkened room while the two goons considered Michael's words. A heavy silence, which was then followed by raucous laughter.

'He wants out, and promises not to say a word! Aww, the poor boy's got another death on his hands. Well, boo-fuckin' hoo.' The big goon changed his sarcastic tone into one of control as he began poking Mick hard on the chest with his index finger as he spoke. 'Big money comes with big risks, Michael. Get used to it.' He then gently curled his hand over Mick's, enclosing the pager, before grabbing him by the hair again, ready to emphasise his next comment. 'There *is* no way out, Michael.'

Unable to focus on his driving, Mick pulled up in the nearby pub car park to settle his nerves and his breathing. Tears filled his eyes, and he felt sick to the stomach. He turned off the engine and headlights and let the darkness envelope him, wishing he could just float off into the cosmos.

Yet the more he tried to figure a way out of all this, the more he knew that the goons and his father were right.

There was no way out.

Perhaps if he visited Alistair directly and tried to reason with him face-to-face? He pounded his fists on the steering wheel in frustration as he recalled Alistair's last words to him on the day they first met –

"Don't ever come here again."

46: Community Spirit

The rich, spicy smell of freshly baked mince pies filled the air, enveloping Dennis in a homely embrace as he entered the kitchen. Glad to be out of the early December damp and drizzle, he shook off his coat on the doorstep, mindful not to allow too many drips to pool onto the floor.

'You're looking pleased with yourself – I take it you had a good Rotary meeting?' asked Irene, just as the timer pinged on the oven. She grabbed her oven gloves, ready to take out the next batch of mince pies, before setting in the next.

Dennis took note that she'd been a busy little bee with her usual array of Christmas preparations; a stack of cards was piled up ready to be taken to the Post Office, and a half-empty bottle of brandy stood next to the dark and fruity Christmas cake, obviously having been given another good soaking. And guessing by her merry mood, she'd probably given herself a little soaking with brandy, too. He poured himself a small glass as a winter-warmer.

'Aye, we did. The strike was the main topic of the meeting, as you can imagine. It's creating a very hard winter for everyone – not only the miners, bless 'em, but a lot of the local businesses are suffering as well. Tensions are running high, and everyone's feeling the strain.'

He poured another little glass of brandy for Irene, who joined him at the table once she'd emptied the tray of hot mince pies onto the cooling wire. She brought a couple of cooler ones with her for them to sample.

Dennis took a bite, savouring the rich flavours.

'Bloody 'ell, lass – you make a mean mince pie! Anyway, one of the members, Frank Bryant – the solicitor who helped us with our Mick's stuff – had this idea of organising a Christmas party for all the miners' kids. His son-in-law and family are on strike, so I think that's what gave him the idea. Try to do summat nice for all of 'em. Anyway, he's asking for contributions and help from the local shops, farms, and businesses. Then we can put together some little food hampers for the families, and perhaps a few toys for the kids.'

Feeling the effects of the brandy and the heartwarming nature of the suggestion, Irene could feel tears welling in her eyes.

'Oh, what a lovely idea! I'd be happy to do some baking and chip in with some mince pies, or something like that,' she added.

'I think Frank's wife is going to get the Shirecliffe WI to help with the baking, but I'm quite sure we can find some other way to help out with the party. Maybe we can organise a collection centre where people can bring toys and clothes to donate? Even if it's only some socks and a toy car, every little bit helps.'

'What a great idea!' Irene suddenly had an epiphany as to how she could help. 'I could make some posters at the office, and photocopy them to put up in the local shops and the library, asking for donations.

I'll give this Frank chap a call tomorrow and see what he says. When is the party, anyway?'

'Frank's going to try and book the Welfare on the estate for Saturday 22nd, so that the food will be as fresh as possible for the families over Christmas. He's also drawn the short straw to wear the Santa outfit,' laughed Dennis. 'I managed to escape that job on account of no longer having a beer belly!' He patted his slender stomach, much reduced in size since his heart attack and change of diet.

With the last batch of mince pies now out of the oven, Irene flopped back in her chair, exhausted, causing a puff of icing sugar to fall out of her hair and onto her nose.

Dennis laughed, then dusted the icing sugar away with his handkerchief.

'Which reminds me,' he said. 'Frank's daughter runs the hair salon up in Castle Ridge with another lass. They're offering to do a free shampoo and set for the miners' wives. Give 'em a bit of pampering before Christmas. I think one of the other salons is also going to chip in and help.'

'How wonderful! I think she has Silver Scissors up on the High Street. It used to be her aunty's place before she retired. Well, that's a lovely idea. What a great community spirit – everyone pulling together to help. I must remember to tell our Barry and Claire so that they can sign up Nicky for the party.'

'Aye, they could do with a bit o'cheering up,' concurred Dennis. 'I think this strike is really getting to Barry, and I know Claire's feeling the strain, especially with Christmas coming up. I reckon we should invite 'em here for Christmas Day. Claire's mum, too – then at least Mrs Jones won't be home alone for Christmas.'

'I was just thinking exactly the same,' agreed Irene. 'We always buy too much, anyway. Then we can invite Kenny, Sally, and the girls for New Year's Eve, especially with it being his big birthday the day after. That'll take a lot of pressure off Sally, with her having three little ones to deal with.'

Irene suddenly felt a great sense of maternal warmth; it would be so nice to have the family together this Christmas after last year's disastrous separation of her and Dennis. Maybe his heart attack had been a much-needed blessing in disguise to make them all realise just how delicately the scales of life are balanced, and just how much they all need each other.

'I saw that our Mick's car was in the driveway when I came back. Didn't he go out tonight?' asked Dennis.

Irene shook her head, her brow furrowed as she replied.

'No, he's been in all night. In fact, he fell asleep on the sofa watching that nerdy science programme – what's it called? Tomorrow's World, that's it. He hasn't moved since.'

'Aye, he seems to be staying in a lot more these days. I think that glue-death really rattled him. I'm a bit worried about him, I have to say.' Dennis reached over to steal another mince pie, only to have his hand playfully slapped by Irene.

'Oy, watch your cholesterol, mister!'

Dennis looked at her, puzzled. 'So why do all this baking then?' he teased.

Irene rolled her eyes and smirked. 'Old habits die hard, I suppose... Besides, it's good to have plenty of baking at this time of year. There's always someone dropping in for a visit.'

They both turned around to see a bleary-eyed Mick come into the kitchen, yawning and rubbing his fingers through his tangled mop of earthy, chestnut coloured hair.

'Ooh, mince pies. Thanks, Mam!'

'Hmmm. See what I mean!' she laughed.

47: A Sinister Warning - 1985

Two sinister shadows watched the immediate area surrounding the Watkins' household, and waited. From what they could make out, the neighbours on either side were still busy saying goodbye to 1984; their New Year's Eve parties in full swing, whereas the Watkins' property was already in darkness.

Perfect...

Moving with expert silence, they made their way towards the front door, their senses keened for any unexpected interruptions. They held their crouched positions for a brief second while they prepared themselves for the task ahead.

With a nod from the larger of the two, the other one steadied himself on one knee before setting the spout of the battered green Jerry can into the now open letterbox. He tilted it slightly, liberally pouring the highly flammable liquid through the narrow slit. As the fluid soaked into the autumn-leaf patterned Axminster below, it spread out towards the large newel post at the foot of the stairs.

Next, they doused a long piece of rag with the accelerant, then stuffed it into the letterbox so that it hung inside, before placing the empty canister well away from the danger zone. Primed and ready for a fast exit, the larger of the two shadows flicked open his Zippo lighter.

'With compliments from the boss,' he sneered, then nodded and grinned towards his accomplice as he put the flame near the petrol-soaked cloth.

'Happy New fuckin' Year, Michael...'

By the time the cloth had fallen to the ground inside and ignited the fluid with a ferocious *WHOOMPH*, the two figures had already vanished into the nearby shadows to watch, leaving three generations of the unsuspecting Watkins family to their fire-trapped fate.

As the dense, acrid smoke filled the hallway and puthered upstairs, the licking and leaping flames began to take hold of the wooden newel post and bannister, heading in an upward direction. In their quest for more fuel, the flames bit into the pram near the telephone table, causing the synthetic bodywork to melt and bubble. As the heat and flames grew in intensity, the wax on Dennis's Barbour coat ignited, passing the torch onto the next, and the next, until the wall of coats became a searing mass of flaming orange.

Roused by the screams of his granddaughter on her way to the bathroom, Dennis bolted wide-awake and shot out of bed to see what the commotion was about.

Kenny similarly heard Rebecca's howling screams out on the landing, just as the acrid smell of smoke crept around the slightly open door to the guest bedroom. Realising that he was only clad in his underpants, he wrestled with his sweater and jeans before running out onto the landing, almost crashing into Dennis.

'Becca! Becca! Stay there, don't move! Daddy's coming for you...'

After sweeping his terrified daughter up into his arms, he banged with incessant urgency on Mick's bedroom door with the flat of his hand.

'FIRE! FIRE! Mick, get out of there!'

The heat from the flames began to tingle the skin on his face. Aware that there was no escape down the stairs, he banged again on his brother's door.

Mick's eyes widened with terror when he came out and saw the dancing flames, grotesque shadows dancing with them, creating a monstrous pattern on the walls.

Kenny retraced his footsteps back towards the guest room to help Sally-Ann with Lou-Lou and baby Josephine, while Dennis went to assist Irene, who was by now hysterical, choking on the smoke.

'Quick! Quick!' bellowed Mick, trying to make himself heard over the roaring noise of the fire raging in the stairwell. He gestured for everyone to make their way towards his bedroom, ushering his parents, Kenny, Sally-Ann, and the little girls into his room before slamming the door closed. Having used his bedroom window on many occasions for his covert nocturnal activities, he knew it was the best and safest exit point.

Coughing from smoke inhalation, Mick put a blanket at the bottom of the door to buy them some clean-air time. He flicked the light switch, but nothing happened.

'The fire must've taken the power out,' shouted Dennis, trying to make himself heard over the noise of his frightened family.

'We'll have to climb out of my bedroom window and onto the garage roof. It's the only way out!' Mick yelled. 'This way, follow my voice...'

'I've got a tiny babe-in-arms, in case you hadn't noticed,' screamed Sally-Ann, in her blind panic. The wails of little Louise grew in intensity as she clung to her mother, much like a koala clinging to a tree.

'Don't worry, we won't let anything happen to you or your girls! Now hurry...' urged Mick, as he pushed his bedroom window open to the widest setting. He hopped out first onto the flat roof of the garage and took each of the older girls out one by one, before helping his mother. Dennis came out next, ready to receive the baby and Sally-Ann, while Kenny gently helped them from the inside, before clambering out.

Having executed their urgent escape, clad only in their nightwear, the icy night wind whipped around them, the cold becoming their next challenge.

Mick hopped back in through the window to grab the rest of his bedding, plus any clothing he could find in the dark, then began distributing it to his family.

'Here, take these and put them on. I'm going to jump down and get the ladder from the side of the garage. Kenny, can you guide them down the ladder to me, then go and get help? Shout and scream, and rouse the neighbours! Get them to call the fire brigade.'

After his most recent dialogue with the chain of command above him, he instinctively knew that this fire was no accident. It was a warning. They were guaranteed to be in touch, even if it was only to gloat.

He quickly checked his jeans pocket to feel for the outline of the pager, and waited for them to make contact.

Within minutes, their next-door neighbours, Eddie and Pat, had called for the emergency services and were on the scene to assist. While Pat ushered Irene, Sally-Ann, and the now hysterical girls into the warmth of their house, Eddie stayed with the men while they waited for help to arrive.

As a retired first-aider, Eddie found it impossible to just stand idle when faced with a crisis and calmly took charge.

'Do you have any fire extinguishers in the garage or your work van, Den?'

Dennis shook his head in defeat.

'Aye, in both. But both sets of keys are in the house. They're hung up in the kitchen. Fuck!'

'Maybe I can get into the kitchen, Dad,' shouted Mick, trying to make his voice heard over the noise of splintering wood, while he sprinted towards the kitchen door.

'Mick! No! Don't go back into the house. It's not safe!'

But it was too late; Mick had already put a brick through the glass in the kitchen door, and was trying to get his arm through to undo the Yale latch. Unfortunately, in his haste to help, he only served to make the situation worse by creating a through-draught of air. Hearing the sudden howl of wind and flames from behind the door to the hallway, Mick realised what he'd innocently done. Tears of frustration filled his eyes.

Similarly aware of a sudden rise in the fire's intensity, Dennis kicked the dustbin in frustration. Then it dawned on him – the garden hose reel was located behind the dustbin, and permanently attached to an outside tap.

'Here, take this!'

He handed the end of the hose to his neighbour, who ran towards the front door, dragging out the length of pipe as he did so. Kenny ran to help, feeding more hose off the reel, as his father turned on the water. After tense, sweaty moments of saturating the front door with water, Eddie opened the flap of the letterbox to insert the hosepipe, in the vain hope of dousing some of the flames before the fire brigade arrived.

With the water now flowing freely onto the hallway carpet, Dennis knelt down to peer through the letterbox. The wall of heat from the stairwell stung his eyes, causing him to reel back momentarily, as the hungry flames engulfed the bannister and stair treads, rapidly taking the fire upstairs.

He wrinkled his nose; woven into the acrid smell of burning wood and plastic, another familiar odour pervaded the air, arousing his suspicions.

'Can anyone else smell petrol on the doorstep, or is it just me?'

Kenny murmured his agreement.

'I was just thinking exactly the same thing, Dad. But wouldn't that mean that the fire was started deliberately? That you've been firebombed?'

'And why would anyone want to firebomb me? Unless...'

Dennis spun around on his heels, ready to lunge for Mick. However, the deafening, blue-light arrival of two fire tenders and an ambulance meant that he had to set his anger to one side for the time being.

But the rage in his father's eyes and the pointed finger of accusation didn't go unnoticed by Mick. He closed his eyes, close to tears. This was not meant to happen. He had wanted out of the dealing to *protect* his family. To go straight. Not to drag them down with him.

The pager in his pocket suddenly vibrated.

While the rest of the men were now distracted by the arrival of the emergency services, Mick vanished into the shadows around the side of the garage to read the message.

Consider this a warning. Happy New Year, Michael.

He stared at the words. Panic swirled through every fibre of his body. Although it was tempting to throw the pager as far away as possible, he knew that he was in too deep.

Not only was he being threatened, but also his family.

Mick sighed heavily as he endeavoured to stem the rise of his evening meal, gasping for air as he did so. He leaned his back against the garage wall for support.

Neither his father nor his brother would let the matter rest, of that he was sure. He swallowed hard when he heard more sirens.

The police had undoubtedly been notified that the fire had, in all likelihood, been started under suspicious circumstances. The smell of some kind of accelerant around the doorstep was a good indicator of that.

This was not the start to 1985 that Mick or any of the family had envisaged. They had planned to start the new year with a party for Kenny's 30th. The old year had been hard enough for everyone, what with the miners' strike and Dennis's heart attack, without this!

Mick knew it was time to face the music.

He took one final deep breath before walking out of the shadows towards the police car.

All hell was about to break loose!

From a safe distance, two figures observed the fiery mayhem unfolding at the Watkins' house; rather like a pyromaniac would enjoy being a spectator at the chaos he had created.

The two figures also observed Michael appear from behind the garage just moments after he would have received their warning message; his head and shoulders hung low as he walked towards the police car.

What the fuck was he doing!

They would need to inform Alistair.

48: Turning the Tables

Noticing movement out of the corner of his eye, Dennis turned to see Michael walking towards the police car. Puzzled, he pulled gently on Kenny's sleeve and nodded in the direction of his youngest son. After a brief exchange with one of the officers, Mick was offered a seat in the back of the police car. Dennis closed his eyes and looked heavenwards.

'Oh, God. This cannot be happening. Please tell me that our Mick isn't the cause of all this.'

He looked towards his ruined house, which, mercifully, the fire brigade now had under control. They were just dousing the last of the flames before damping down. With everyone's swift reactions, it looked as though the fire had been contained to the hallway and stairwell, and the rest of the house was just affected by smoke damage. They had had a very lucky escape.

'Let them take the little bastard,' snarled Kenny. 'And if he is involved, I hope they throw away the key! How could he bring this on his family?' Kenny glared across at the police car, hoping that Mick would sense his fury.

And they were not the only ones glaring at Mick.

As the police car drove off towards Chesterfield Police Station, Mick felt strangely calm in the back seat. He had no idea how this would unfold or how it would end, but he knew that he'd reached his limit. Alistair might be his half-brother, but this was not the way to treat family – his real family. After all, being a Watkins was all he'd ever known. And even though Dennis wasn't his biological father, he still had a genetic link to the rest of them. He knew where his loyalties lay. Mick settled his head onto the side window and absently watched the street lights flash by.

Nature or nurture?

That was a question often asked. Although he hadn't been raised within the McCormick household, the nature of the beast – the genes – were still having an underlying sway on his actions. A surge of resentment pushed a flood of adrenaline into his stomach as he inwardly cursed his mother for her love affair. It seems that on this occasion, nature had superseded nurture.

The pager vibrated in his pocket, causing him to shudder, more in disgust than fear.

Although he was going in for voluntary questioning, he suspected that he wouldn't come out of this without some kind of charges being pressed against him. But this meant that he had the power to take others down with him, depending on how much he revealed. He was the one holding all the aces. Just this alone gave him strength.

He was doing the right thing – this had to stop!

Mick glanced down at the pager.

Wrong move. Keep schtum.

Fuck! The sneaky bastards had been watching him all along! His mind raced for a suitable reply – he couldn't risk any more attacks on his family. He surreptitiously keyed in a message.

Damage control. Trust me.

Moments passed by without a reply. Would they trust him?

The police car approached the main Lordsmill Roundabout, ready to turn off towards the police station on Beetwell Street. In a few short moments, he would have to empty out his pockets before being questioned. That would mean giving up the pager.

He could feel his heart rate increase, the pulse in his wrists and temples strong. Mick closed his eyes and took a few calming deep breaths.

Vibration. He took one last look at the pager.

Damage control. Or big trouble.

The police car turned towards the ramp, which led to the underground car park.

He smirked – yes, there would be damage control.

But it would be to save his skin, not theirs.

49: Dampened Spirits

With the weight of the world dragging his soul down, Dennis turned and put his head on Kenny's shoulders, his tears flowing without any embarrassment. At this moment in time, he didn't give a shit who saw him cry.

Having finished damping the embers, the fire crews were now packing away their hose reels and equipment. The misty winter air was laden with smoke and soot residue, adding to the grey mood of all those involved.

Feeling a gentle squeeze on his arm, Dennis looked up to see the sympathetic eyes of Mr Fisher, the senior officer. Although Mr Fisher had served in the Fire Brigade for most of his life, it was clear to see that it still pained him to see a member of the local community in distress.

'We've done all we can here, Mr Watkins, and made the place secure. Someone will be back here in daylight to do a final assessment, but it does appear to be a deliberate act of arson. The police will also need to interview you, to see if you can shed any light on the situation.'

Dennis nodded sagely.

'Aye, we'll help all we can. Mind you, I saw our Mick drive off with the police earlier on, so it's my guess that he knows summat.' He held out his hand to shake that of Mr Fisher's, and gave him a grateful nod. 'Thanks for saving the house.' And then with a wry smile, he added, 'Happy New Year...'

Kenny also shook Mr Fisher's hand.

'You take good care of your dad, d'ya hear. All the best to you.'

'Thanks. I will,' acknowledged Kenny, as they waved off the senior officer.

Kenny put his arm around his father to lead him next door to where the rest of the family were sheltering.

'Right, you heard what the man said. Let's get you inside where it's warm, and get you a cup o'tea.'

'A cup o'tea? Fuck that, I need a double brandy!'

Upon completion of giving their statements to the police, Dennis and Kenny were allowed into the house via the kitchen to retrieve their car keys. With a heavy heart, Dennis peered around the scorched door that led from the kitchen into the hallway to assess the extent of the damage.

A black, gaping mess greeted him, revealing the charred remains of the baby's pram and telephone table. The staircase, though intact, was unsafe to use, and the handrail looked like blackened stumps of teeth, jagged and rotten. There was no way of retrieving anything from upstairs, and the doorways into the Lounge and Dining areas had been secured with wood to stop anyone from entering.

Dennis did his best to hold back the tears as he spoke, exhaling loudly in his anguish.

'Why, eh? Why would anyone do this?'

Kenny came and put his arm around his father's shoulders.

'Well, until our Mick puts in an appearance, I guess we'll never know. You can bet your life that he's involved, the sneaky little bastard. C'mon, let's go and get the girls and head down to our place. We'd better give our Barry a call and let him know what's happened. Some fuckin' thirtieth birthday this is turning out to be!'

Feeling haggard and forlorn, Dennis turned and looked at Kenny, his face one of sincere apology.

'Eh, I'm sorry, lad. I'd forgotten that it was your big birthday today! Look, I know we probably don't feel much like celebrating, but let's try and put on a brave face for the sake of the kids. Let's still have a little party – try and salvage something of the new year. Agreed?'

Kenny nodded. 'Aye, agreed.'

Barry came into the kitchen, his face pale and drawn, his eyes wide with disbelief.

'That was mi'dad on the phone. Kenny's birthday party will be down at their house instead. Apparently, mi'mam and dad's house was torched last night – some bastard set fire to it!'

Claire almost choked on her mug of tea at the news. She could barely speak while her mind computed what Barry was trying to explain.

'Fire? Their house was set on fire? Is everyone okay? I mean, weren't they having a little family party there last night?'

'Aye, everyone's fine, thank goodness. They were all asleep when it happened, but one of the girls noticed the fire when she went to the bathroom. Her screams woke everyone up, thank goodness.' Barry poured himself a mug of tea and sat down with his wife at the kitchen table. 'Eddie and Pat from next door came to their aid, so they stayed at their place overnight. The front hallway and stairs took the brunt of the fire. The rest of the house just suffered smoke damage.'

'My God, what a terrible way to start the new year!'

'I know! But that's not the worst of it – they reckon our Mick might know who did it; that it's somehow connected to his dodgy dealings. He went with the police voluntarily. They haven't seen him since.'

'Humph... Well, that's the McCormick blood running through his veins!' Realising what she'd just said, Claire closed her eyes, wishing she could suck the words back in. She looked at Barry apologetically. 'Sorry, that's not how it was meant to come out.'

He shook his head and endeavoured to salvage her embarrassment.

'No worries. I get what you mean. At least we can see that our Nick isn't following in the McCormick traits. Anyway, Dad said that they're still going to have a thirtieth birthday party for our Kenny, just that it'll be at Kenny's place. They asked if we could chip in with some food and stuff, and to be there for around three.'

'Of course! We'll help in whatever way we can. I'll put the oven on to get hot and bake some sausage rolls. We can take all the leftovers from last night's party, too.'

'Sounds good. Meanwhile, I'll go and have a chat with Nicky and put him in the picture about his grandma and grandad's house. Then at least he won't be too scared if he overhears any grown-up conversations about it. You know what he's like for listening in.'

As difficult as the situation was, the family did their best to put on a brave face for the sake of the kids and Kenny. Once the food started to be devoured, and with some Bruce Springsteen playing in the background, the mood began to lighten, and shoulders began to relax a little. If it wasn't for the fact that Dennis and Irene were dressed in clothes borrowed from Sally-Ann's parents, the day could have almost passed off as a normal New Year's Day and birthday gathering.

They knew plans would have to be made for accommodation, and that wheels would have to be put in motion with the insurance company and repair works to the house, but for today, Dennis and Irene endeavoured to put that to the back of their mind.

On hearing the doorbell ring, Becca, Lou-Lou, and Nick ran to the front door to see who it was.

'Yay, Uncle Mick's here to join the party, Daddy!' shrieked Becca, leading Mick by the hand into the dining room.

The room fell uncomfortably silent as Mick entered, and the tension rose tenfold. Kenny, with fists clenched, could barely restrain himself from lunging at his youngest brother.

Sensing that some very private adult time was needed, Sally-Ann encouraged the kids to choose some snacks from the table, then go with her into the front sitting room so that she could put Becca's new *Thomas the Tank Engine* video on for them to watch.

Mick pulled out a chair and sat down, then took a deep breath. His voice sounded hoarse and cracked as he spoke. He looked directly at his parents, his eyes puffy and filled with sadness.

'I'm really sorry for what just happened, with the fire and everything. I never meant for you guys to be dragged into all this...'

He held his head low, while all around him the family flared up with their anger, voices and tempers raised, as they all flung questions and accusations at him. Mick gave them a moment to simmer down before carrying on with his explanation.

'Yes, there's no hiding the fact that I've been messed up in some serious shit. I've been involved in burglaries, and I've been involved in some dope dealing. I fell in with the wrong crowd, and these are the consequences. I don't feel good about it. That's why I went to the police last night. I want to go straight, so I had to come clean about everything. This has just gone too far.'

'Too fuckin' right it's gone too far!' yelled Kenny. 'My family could have been killed last night!'

Dennis cracked open a can of beer for himself and then one for Mick, pushing it towards him.

'Give the boy a chance, Ken. Let him speak.'

Mick nodded his thanks, then carried on.

'One thing I didn't realise at the time when I started all this was just who else was involved. The guy at the top of the chain pulling all the strings...'

'Well, I certainly remember those two guys who came to the house a few years ago demanding money. Don't tell me there's some kind of Castle Ridge Mafia behind all this!' said Dennis.

Mick shook his head.

'No, not the Mafia. Alistair. Alistair McCormick.

Irene's face blanched at the mention of the McCormick name, while everyone else seemed to hold their breath, mouths open in shock.

'Your other half-brother?' questioned Barry. 'But I thought you two got along just fine? Or, at least, that's the impression you gave.'

'Aye, well. You know me, I can keep a poker face.' Mick looked at Baz and gave him a weak smile. 'He might have a nice cottage in the Peak, and yes, he has an electrical shop over in Bakewell. But it's all just a legit cover for his dodgy dealings. That's why he has the two henchmen – they do all his dirty work.'

Dennis put his hand over Irene's as the memory of their visit still cut a raw nerve.

'So when did you realise that it was Alistair pulling all the strings?' asked Sally-Ann.

'Not until all this paternity stuff came to light. I plucked up the courage to visit him, rather than phoning him out of the blue. Anyway, those two goons turned up while I was there, and that's when we all made the connection. I hoped that Alistair might have cut me a bit of brotherly slack, or given me a better deal. But no. He's just a selfish, narcissistic bastard.'

'So why the fire at Mum and Dad's? Why involve our family like that? Was he jealous, or something?' Kenny snorted his disdain towards his brother, still feeling the shock and strain from the previous night.

Mick shook his head and lowered his eyes, barely able to look at everyone. This was the moment when he would have to take ownership for many of his actions, particularly those in which others had been hurt.

'No, it was because I wanted out. The fire was a warning shot. A reminder that I'm just one of his possessions.' He looked up, his eyes full of remorse. 'Remember the glue-related death on the estate a couple of months ago? Well, that young lad sometimes bought a bit of blow from me. His death was the wake-up call that I needed. I realised that there are real people behind all the money that we take. I don't want to be a part of it anymore.'

Mick noticed that Sally-Ann was looking at him, and could clearly see by the look on her face that she was calculating something in her mind. He realised that he needed to be careful how he worded things, and keep the conversation steered towards the drugs.

In order to buy himself a few extra seconds of thinking time, he took a long, slow drink from his can and allowed them to see that his hands were shaking slightly; a way to show them that he was fearful of what he'd gotten himself into. He continued his explanation.

'Anyway, I called a meeting with his henchmen – Alistair would never do any face-to-face meetings. I told them that I wanted to quit and promised to keep my mouth shut. Just walk away. But, as Dad once rightly told me, I will never be free of them. They just laughed in my face.'

Dennis did his best to refrain from saying "I told you so", but his raised eyebrows said it all. Mick flushed, then nodded towards his father with solemn acknowledgement.

'But how do these guys keep tabs on you? You can't always be near a phone box.'

Mick pulled the pager out of his pocket and held it up for them to see.

'It's called a pager. We can send short messages with it. And this is how I know they were responsible for the fire last night. They sent me a message. The fire was a warning shot. But like I said, they've crossed a line. I might be a piece o'shit in your eyes, but no one messes with my family. My *real* family. That's why I decided to go to the police.'

'Well, good for you,' chipped in Irene. 'It's a relief that you want to turn your life around and get out of all this. What did the police say?'

'There was plenty to talk about. And just to warn you, I am being charged with possession and dealing of cannabis; I had a bit of blow in my jacket pocket. But, that's a small price to pay for what's about to go down.'

Mick gave a smile of relief that he was about to unburden himself from Alistair and the goons. 'It turns out that Alistair's men were watching the fire so that they could report back to him – which also meant that they saw me go off with the police. They sent me a warning message to keep my mouth shut, or else. Anyway, I saw an opportunity to play them at their own game. I sent messages back saying that it was "damage control" and to "trust me". That I would be the fall guy to keep them in the clear. I've already sent them a message to let them know that I've been busted, and the police are satisfied that the fire was nothing more than a turf war with other dealers.'

'So they think they're in the clear?' asked Claire.

'Exactly. But in reality, I've given the police enough info to set up a sting operation so that they can swoop in on Alistair and his men. It's a fair trade-off for the possession charges.' He exhaled loudly. 'I'll finally be free of 'em. I can't tell you how grateful I am to have remained a Watkins and not changed over to my blood name.'

Stunned by Mick's revelations, the room fell silent while everyone absorbed what he'd just explained to them.

'Fuck, that's some serious shit, Mick,' huffed Kenny, impressed by his brother's ingenuity. 'It's like summat out of *Miami Vice*!'

It was the lighter comment that was needed to ease the tension, causing a few sniggers from everyone.

Quick to follow with a tag-on, Barry laughed, 'Yeah, but Don Johnson's much better looking and way cooler than our Mick!'

'What are you all laughing at?' asked Nicky as he came into the dining room searching for more snacks. '*Thomas the Tank Engine* has finished, can we watch something else now?'

Sally-Ann jumped up and took Nick's hand, welcoming the opportunity to bring the discussion to a close.

'Well, I think baby Josephine is awake now, I can hear her crying. Why don't you kids come upstairs and help me, and then we can all have some birthday cake and put some more music on. Deal?'

She scowled towards the adults to signal that the heavy part of the day was over, and it was time to relax back into the party.

With enough intuition to understand what Sally-Ann was implying, the family made the break to stand up and replenish their drinks and swiftly change the topic of conversation; the room once again buzzing with light banter.

But Sally-Ann was having some intuition of her own.

As everyone stood up, her eyes momentarily locked with Mick's, before each glanced away, unsure of what had just crossed between them.

From all that Mick had confessed today, she had some kind of inner feeling that he'd been involved in a lot more than he was admitting to.

A feeling she would keep to herself.

For now...

50: Getting Organised

Exhausted by the events of the past twenty-four hours, the extended Watkins family relaxed in the front sitting room at Kenny and Sally-Ann's, watching the TV; the New Year's Day action film helping to take their mind off things. Not only had the little birthday party for Kenny been a great catalyst to pull everyone together, but it had also given them some quality time to try and make sense out of the madness.

One by one, the children began falling asleep in the arms of whomever they were snuggled up with; a reminder that sleeping arrangements had yet to be sorted out. Sally-Ann exaggerated a yawn to initiate the conversation.

'Well, it looks like the kids are all tuckered out. Maybe we should figure out where everyone's going to sleep tonight, seeing as how you can't go back to your place.'

The yawn and the mere mention of sleep instigated a chain reaction around them all.

Kenny stretched, causing Lou-Lou to wriggle on his lap.

'And not only that, you folks need to go clothes shopping tomorrow. Good job the January sales will have started, he teased, knowing how much his father hated shopping at the best of times, let alone the crowded sales.'

'Oh, gawd, no! Please don't send me into town wi'ya mother to go clothes shopping!' laughed Dennis. 'Just the thought of being dragged around M & S gives me the heeby-jeebies!'

'You coward, Dennis Watkins!' Irene gave her husband a playful slap. 'I'm sure you'll get your revenge by dragging me around Burton's.'

'Children! Children!' chided Claire, holding up her hands in jest. 'I've got an idea – how about I take Irene shopping tomorrow, and Barry can take his dad and Mick to Burton's? After all, Mick also needs some new clothes. Would it be okay to leave Nick here with the girls while we go?'

Feeling forced into a corner like an old mother hen, Sally-Ann feigned a smile and nodded that it would be okay. And with the same feigned smile, she cunningly organised the sleeping arrangements. The girls would bunk together in Becca's room, so that Irene and Dennis could sleep in Lou-Lou's room for a few days, until they could find some temporary accommodation. This meant that Mick would have to stay at Baz and Claire's, in their spare room.

Let them play host to the criminal.

51: A Marked Man

'Hi, Dad.' Sally-Ann bustled into the kitchen, her arms laden. 'Here's all the stuff that Dennis and Irene borrowed from you. It's been washed, dried, and ironed, and they asked me to pass on their grateful thanks.' She placed the pile of neatly laundered clothes onto the Formica table, together with the Kays catalogue.

'Wow – you do a better job of the laundry than yer mam!' he teased. But then added with a wink and a chuckle, 'But don't tell her I said so...'

Sally-Ann chuckled. 'Your secret's safe wi'me, Dad. Irene has ordered a few bits from the catalogue as well. I've put the list inside.'

Mr Clarke tickled his two young granddaughters, happy to see them, then made some babbling noises to baby Josephine, who reacted with a huge grin, her little hands flailing in joy.

'Sit down, lass, and I'll make us a cuppa. Yer mam's just popped up t'shop. She won't be long.' Mr Clarke fussed around with the kettle and tea-bags, then rummaged to find some biscuits for the girls. 'Anyway, how's it going for your in-laws since the fire? Are they managing to get stuff sorted out with the insurance company, and the like?'

'Aye, the insurance company has been great. No hassles. One of Dennis's friends – Mr Brook, the local builder – has offered to come with his lads and help with the rebuilding work. Not only that, but Sage's Decorators have said they will redecorate the hallway free of charge. I think everyone just feels so sorry for Dennis and Irene, especially as Dennis is still in post-recovery from the heart attack. They've also managed to cut a deal at the Castle Ridge Hotel so that they can stay there for a few weeks until their place has been sorted out.'

Mr Clarke poured the now-boiling water into the teapot and stirred it. He paused for a moment, suddenly becoming lost in thought.

'There's a strong community spirit in Castle Ridge, that's for sure. Remember how everyone rallied round our family when we lost the little 'un? I don't think our Alan and Sue would have gotten through it without all the support they got.' He surreptitiously wiped away a tear, the pain of losing his little grandson still raw.

'It's funny you should mention that, Dad. Since all this business with the fire, and Mick being arrested for possession of drugs, I can't help but wonder if he was involved with all that stolen booze back then. I think he's hiding a lot more than he's letting on to the police.'

Although Sally-Ann had a deep-seated suspicion about Mick's criminal activity, she remained mindful not to say too much because of the imminent sting operation, which he had helped to set up with the police. She could at least respect him for that.

Mr Clarke came and sat at the kitchen table, bringing the teapot and two mugs with him.

'Well, I'll tell you one thing, lass – if our Alan ever finds out who was behind that – even if it was Mick – he'll tear him limb from limb. And rightfully so. There's no pain worse than having to bury your own kid.'

Their conversation was interrupted by the clatter of the front door, followed by the delighted shrieks of Becca and Lou-Lou, happy to intercept their gran as she returned from the local shop.

'Help! Help! I'm being attacked by unicorn princesses,' she joked, as she came into the kitchen with a granddaughter clinging to each hand, making it almost impossible to carry the shopping bags as well. She dumped the bags on the floor so that she could hug all her girls properly.

After putting the shopping away and settling down with a cuppa, Mrs Clarke was brought up-to-date with the Watson's house-fire situation, and Mick's involvement being classed as a "revenge attack" by other dealers.

'Aye, they were just talking about it up at the shop. Rumours are flying around the estate that he's involved in a lot of shady shi... stuff. That yellow car of his was often seen cruising around at night. I know they can't pin the glue-death on him, but they reckon it was Mick who'd been selling dope to the lad.'

She lifted baby Josephine from Sally-Ann's arms so that she could cuddle her and kiss her little button nose. 'There's other talk on the estate, an'all,' she continued. 'People are starting to put two and two together and reckon that he's behind a lot of the local burglaries. Some are even saying that it was most likely some of his stolen booze which killed our Alan's little 'un on the Jubilee weekend.'

Sally-Ann's thoughts drifted off as she absorbed the gossip that her mother was relaying. So, she was not the only one to think the worst of

Mick – others were of the same mind. Suspicions which she had harboured for years, starting with the post-honeymoon burglary at their own home. And what about the Jubilee weekend burglary at the NCB offices where Irene worked? Two burglaries connected to the family, and yet the police had drawn a blank on both occasions. Something just didn't add up.

Mr Clarke nodded sagely. Old wounds were being opened, not just for him, but for his family. As much as they didn't want to believe that someone so close to them could have been responsible, there seemed to be too many coincidences with Mick's recent activity and rumours from the past. He had a gut feeling that this could take a sinister turn for the worse.

He knew his boys and what they were capable of. He'd seen them mete out their own brand of justice at the race-track if someone had tried to pull a cheating move on them.

If their suspicions came close to any kind of truth, this could blow an irreparable divide between the Clarkes and the Watkins.

Relieved to have finished work for the day, Mick headed out the shop door, zipping up his coat against the early January chill. His head buzzed after spending the day explaining to each customer that his family was okay after the fire. He knew they were just showing their genuine concern; the Watkinses were fairly well-known in Castle Ridge. But having to repeat the same story over and over had become monotonous as the day wore on.

Not only that, but he'd had to explain to the owners of the butcher's shop about his drug bust with the police when he went in to give voluntary information. Naturally, they were shocked. He'd been given a verbal warning that should he bring any police issues to their doorstep, then he would be out on his ear and on a fast-track to the Job Centre, which was fair enough. The butcher's shop was a long-established family firm in Castle Ridge, much like his father's damp-proofing and repairs company. He knew what it meant to keep a good reputation, even if it was difficult for *him* to adhere to this social norm.

As he crossed the car park towards his yellow Mexico, he realised that there was a black BMW parked next to it, and that the doors were opening. He knew who it belonged to, and they'd obviously seen him. He muttered expletives under his breath.

Mick reset his mind to make sure he didn't give anything away about tonight's planned sting operation. He couldn't wait to be rid of this black cloud; this millstone that had been chained to him all these years. That thought alone gave him a much-needed surge of courage.

Time to start play-acting.

He approached the car, his swagger cocky. The two goons stepped out, then one opened the door to the back seat.

'Hop in, Micky. The boss would like a word...'

Alistair was sitting in the back, having deigned to bring himself out of his ivory tower and into Castle Ridge. Mick knew the meeting had to be important.

He heard the car doors lock – *CLICK* – trapping him inside.

'Happy New Year, Michael. I'm so glad to see that your family is okay after the little fire at your house the other evening.' Alistair sneered, feeling all-powerful. 'I do hope you realise that was just a little warning of what to expect if you try to turn tail on us. I'm sure you now realise where your loyalties lie, eh, Michael? You belong to me...'

Mick looked his half-brother in the eye, his gaze hard.

'Of course I do! And that's why I let the cops bust me for the dope. I told them that the fire was just a turf-war thing, end of story. No names. Nothing. And nothing to connect the burglaries and the electrical stuff. My parents are a bit suspicious, but I've reassured them that it was 'cos of the drugs. Probably connected to the glue-kid.'

'Good to hear, Micky. I've worked hard to get this far up the chain, and I don't want a little prick like you messing things up for me. I know you think that your blood-tie will give you some kind of immunity, but believe me, I'll sell your soul to the Devil if I have to.'

'Don't worry, I left no trail back to you. But just to be on the safe side, I think it's best that I lay low for a week or two. Let this blow over. We can't take a chance that I'm being watched.' Mick let the words sink in; he knew that Alistair wouldn't want to risk getting caught.

'But what about tonight? We've got a delivery coming in that needs weighing and bagging for sale.'

Mick shook his head. 'I can't risk it. Like I said, you need to cut me some slack for the time being.'

As much as Alistair hated to admit that Mick was right, he knew that he had a valid point. The risk of being followed to his place was too great. He gave his goons the nod to unlock the doors so that Mick could get out.

As he made the move to exit the car, Alistair grabbed Mick's coat sleeve, his warning clear.

'Lay low. Keep quiet. We'll be in touch.'

A nod between the two half-brothers sanctioned their agreement and ended the meeting.

Mick got into his own car. His hands were shaking with a mix of stress, nerves, and excitement as he turned the ignition. He watched as the black BMW drove away, and smiled.

Once he was safely home, he called his contact within the Drug Department at the police station to confirm the time and place for the bust.

This was it. Game on!

52: Judas

The raid was executed swiftly and efficiently; the police taking down Alistair and his cronies with the maximum of goods on the table. Their arrest would no doubt send a ripple warning throughout their underworld community. No one was immune from the "knock at the door". It could come at any time.

And it certainly wasn't the start to 1985 which Alistair had expected.

As much as Mick tried to relax on the sofa at Barry's house, he remained alert. If the raid went wrong, or Alistair got spooked in any way, he would no doubt suspect that Mick was behind the tip-off. That was a scenario that Mick couldn't even bear thinking about. He'd already brought enough shame and heartache to his family and the wider community, if he was being totally honest with himself. But he knew that he'd made the right decision in exposing Alistair's criminal activities to the police.

'Penny for 'em...'

Suddenly aware that Barry was setting a tumbler of Jack Daniels in his hand, he looked up and nodded a thanks to his brother. Since being offered the spare room at Barry's house after the fire, he'd felt secure in their small family life. Little Nicky had been a great distraction, though it gave him a pang of jealousy that Barry was raising him with Claire. These were alien feelings to Mick, but maybe this was what real life felt like when you didn't have the criminal fraternity breathing down your neck. Perhaps one day he would be a father, but until then, this was as close as he could get.

He looked at his watch without really registering what time it was.

'I was just wondering how everything was going with the police operation. Whether I will come out of this unscathed. You never know how far these people will...'

Without getting a chance to finish his sentence, his pager, which he'd set on the coffee table, vibrated with a message. Mick looked at his brother, then back at the pager. He picked it up, his hands visibly shaking.

It simply said *Judas.*

Barry passed the Polaroid camera to Mick, who quickly took a photo of the pager message as pictorial evidence – just in case.

'Is it from them?' asked Barry.

Mick nodded. 'Yep. I guess the sting is going down. The message is from Alistair – apparently I'm a Judas!'

The pager buzzed again.

You bastard

Mick quickly snapped another photo, only for the message to be replaced by another one.

You're dead

The Polaroid camera flashed again, capturing the threatening message.

Mick put the camera down on the coffee table and took a steadying gulp of his Jack Daniels. Uncontrollable sobs suddenly choked his body as he let out all his emotions.

Barry came and put his arm over his brother's shoulder, and held him until his tears subsided. For all that had happened between them, they were still connected, no matter how twisted the bond. Barry poured another slug of JD for each of them, this time to be savoured. They clinked their glasses together before each took a sip of the golden bourbon.

After settling Nick off to sleep, Claire came and joined them in the sitting room. She poured a glass for herself, then sat in the cosy armchair, tucking her feet up under her legs.

It was a strange moment devoid of noise.

A moment where words were not needed.

A moment where *nothing* was enough.

The pager was now similarly silent. Mick guessed that Alistair and Co were safely bound in handcuffs in the back of a police van, and were on their way to the nick. He was sorely tempted to smash the pager to smithereens, but knew it was best to wait. This was the only link that could serve as evidence, should any more messages come in.

'So what happens now?' asked Claire in a low voice, not wanting to disturb the moment, but curious for an update.

'I gave the police this number, so they'll call me here as soon as there's any more news. Presumably, once they've charged them with possession with the intent to supply, and whatever else they can make stick. They had a warrant to do a full search of the premises. Shit, this is going to be big...'

Claire looked at him, her eyes full of compassion. This shift in his persona had changed her feelings about him. He was just one of life's lost boys, for whom fate had dealt a shitty hand. The runt of the litter; the underdog. She could think of a million other metaphors to describe Mick.

'Don't worry, we've got your back,' she reassured him. 'Meanwhile, I'll go and find something to put those Polaroids in, and keep them safe.'

Just as she stood up, the phone rang. They all looked at each other and froze momentarily. Mick took a deep breath, then went through into the hallway to take the call.

He returned a short while later, his eyes filled with tears.

'That was the police. It's over... They just confirmed that Alistair and his two sidekicks are in custody. I let them know about the pager threats and that we have photos.' He looked towards the Polaroids lying on the coffee table. 'I know that they're on their way behind bars, but it just feels good to have some kind of insurance. I still don't trust that Alistair won't get some other shithead to clean up his mess.'

Relieved by the good news, Barry and Claire came to give Mick a hug, making him feel secure for the first time in many years.

'I'd better go and phone our Kenny, and let Mum and Dad know.'

Once he had notified the rest of the family, Mick felt the desperate need for some fresh air and a walk to burn off the pent-up tension.

Up until the police's confirmation that everything had gone ahead as planned and the targets secured, Mick had been nervous to the point of throwing up.

What if Alistair had been aware that he was being double-crossed and had evaded capture? He shuddered involuntarily at the thought and glanced around quickly, scanning the shadows. Mercifully, this hadn't been the case. He felt free to walk around without the need to watch his back.

He pondered his life. Would he have followed the same path, knowing then what he knew now? He had to admit that the buzz of getting in and out of somewhere unseen was like a drug. Would he have been tempted to go into this line of "work" after meeting Alistair? Definitely not. The man was an arrogant prick and thought only of himself.

But everything else that followed?

The misery and heartache that he'd caused those closest to him. And yet here they were, supporting him in his darkest hour. That's what you call family.

Real family.

Real family wasn't always cemented by blood ties.

It was *unconditional love* that bound a family together.

In his heart of hearts, he knew he'd done the right thing; the Devil sitting on his shoulder had lost this fight.

53: Lightning Strikes Twice

Hail and sleet rattled relentlessly on the kitchen window, casting a grey hue over both the morning and Claire's mood. January seemed to drag on forever. As she looked at the darkening clouds, she thought of Barry out there at this very moment and shuddered involuntarily. It was impossible not to feel a sense of compassion and solidarity for the men who were standing out on the picket lines in all weathers; day after day, week after week, month after month.

The battle had been raging for ten months now, with still no resolution. Though coal mining was hard and dirty, the men were not only loyal to their work but loyal to the cause, that was for sure. She sighed, hating all that it was doing to divide not only local communities, but the country as a whole.

Mick came into the kitchen, being playfully led by Nicky, who was pretending to have captured a big, hungry dinosaur.

'Mam! Mam! Can you feed this T. rex – he keeps trying to eat me!' laughed Nick, while Mick roared and clawed at the little boy's head.

The Cretaceous distraction was just what Claire needed to break the suction on her melancholic mood.

'I think that's a very wise idea,' she laughed. 'Uncle Mick brought bacon and sausages from the butcher's, if you and the T. rex would like some?'

Mick's eyes lit up at the mention of bacon, and he quickly stopped trying to eat Nicky. On the other hand, Nick said he would rather just have some Ready Brek and a banana, and asked if he could take it into the sitting room and watch the Saturday morning cartoons.

After settling Nick down with his breakfast and snuggling him up in a cosy blanket to watch TV, Claire came back into the kitchen to find that Mick had already started cooking for them. She smiled, impressed at this new and improved version of her brother-in-law.

A flush rose to his cheeks when he turned around and noticed her smiling at him.

'What? Have you never seen a man cooking before?' he teased.

'Well, I've never seen *you* cooking before!' she retorted. 'It's nice to see this domestic side of you. You'll be baking sponge cakes for us next!'

'Hey, take it easy! Let's see if I can cook this lot without burning it, first!'

While Mick plated up the perfectly cooked bacon, eggs, and sausage, Claire busied herself with making a pot of tea and some toast. It was a moment of homely togetherness which they'd never really shared before.

It was during their relaxed conversation about the progress of building work at his parents' house and Nick's upcoming sixth birthday party on Valentine's Day, Mick not only felt but *knew* the time had come to speak about the past.

He took a deep breath to mentally prepare himself.

'I've never really thanked you guys for taking me in after the fire at mi'mam and dad's place. I'm really grateful. I like being a part of Nick's life.' He looked at her from under coy eyelashes before looking at her fully. 'I wish things could have turned out differently for me. For us.'

Claire was taken aback by this last statement.

'For us? What do you mean?' she asked, not sure if she really wanted to hear the answer. After all, it had been years since "the incident".

'Ever since I first met you – when you and Sally came for Sunday lunch – I just fell for you. Well, more than that – I fell *in love* with you right there and then. And nothing has ever changed. I still feel the same way...'

He paused and looked down at his plate, embarrassed at having confessed so much all in one go. 'And then when our Kenny and Sally-Ann got married, and I got drunk, well, it was the only way that I could find the courage to let you know how I felt. Except, it came out all wrong. And what I asked you to do was wrong. But I just wanted to be close to you. I wanted what I couldn't have.'

Unable to stop them from forming, tears filled the corners of his eyes. 'Do you know that's the only time I've been with a girl? You're the only girl I've made love to. Ironic that it resulted in our Nicky. What are the odds, eh?'

'Shhhhh! Keep your voice down,' Claire hissed. 'Nick's getting to an age where he's starting to understand these things. I... I'm sorry, Mick. I never realised that you felt this way about me. And all these years...' She felt at a loss for words. Did she really want to hear more?

'D'ya know, mi'mam even asked me whether I'm gay,' Mick continued. 'Just cause I've never had a girlfriend. And she thinks it's weird that I still live at home, at my age!' He rolled his eyes, more in jest than in seriousness, in an attempt to lighten the moment. 'I would seriously wait for you and Nick until the end of time. I'm sorry if this has come as a shock, and maybe not what you wanna hear – but I just had to say it. I can't hold it in any longer, not while I'm staying here, and being this close to you every day. I'll leave if you want me to. If this makes you feel uncomfortable.' He put his hand on hers, fully expecting her to pull it away.

But she didn't. She left her hand underneath his, then met him eye-to-eye.

'I admit that I've recently suspected you have feelings for me. Real feelings. I can see a longing behind the eyes,' she confessed.

Claire's breathing became deep, laboured, as her pulse raced. She slowly pulled her hand away, then entwined her fingers in his, causing him to catch his breath.

Was he misreading the signs she was giving?

'There have been times,' she continued, 'when I've had the same feelings. Ever since that night at the wedding – it left me feeling confused. Like maybe I was with the wrong brother... But I felt like it was too late to change. I was already seeing Barry, and it would have seemed strange to swap. So that's who I made my life with.'

She looked at Mick to try and gauge his reaction before resuming her confession.

'As characters, you're both very different. He can be very fiery behind closed doors. Well, I know that you've witnessed the force of his temper. Don't get me wrong, he's never hit me or anything like that. But, well, I... I can't even explain it... You're different.'

In the heat of the moment, Mick took her in his arms, and they embraced each other tightly. Each could feel their own heart banging with nervous passion; a feeling of right and wrong in conflict.

'I wonder what fate is doing to us now?' he whispered to her, as he nuzzled into her neck.

Claire breathed in deeply, confused by her emotions. She knew she should push him away, that she should stop what was happening before it went any further. 'Let's not tempt it again...' she murmured, looking into his hazel green eyes. But she could feel Mick already growing hard against her, igniting her own flame.

They backed up against the kitchen door to ensure that Nick couldn't walk in, and resumed what they had started all those years ago, first with an all-consuming urgency, before taking each other again with more gentleness and passion, neither of them giving a thought beyond that very intimate moment.

54: Home is Where the Heart is

Irene stood in the kitchen – *her* kitchen – and looked around at the freshly scrubbed units and painted walls. It was good to be home!

The past six weeks had been, without doubt, surreal and memorable, albeit for the wrong reasons. She certainly hoped that they had turned the metaphorical corner, and that their share of bad luck had been used up for the year. And if nothing else, today was a day for celebration; the family had come together to help them settle in with a housewarming party. Not only that, it was Valentine's Day, and Nicky's sixth birthday. Her heart felt like bursting with warmth, love, and gratitude.

She was genuinely thankful to the team of tradesmen who had carried out the repairs to the fire-damaged hallway. Brook's Builders, aided by Dennis and Kenny, had stripped out the old staircase and plasterwork. Then the electricians and plumbers came to do their first fixes, in readiness for the new staircase to be fitted and the walls replastered. Second fixes were carried out, Sage's redecorated where necessary, then Castle Ridge Carpets came and laid some new Axminster. Not only that, but she had a new front door, and the blackened stonework had been sandblasted clean.

It was more than she could have hoped for in such a short time. Staying in a hotel is nice when you're on holiday, but very strange to live in one for six weeks. And the strangest thing of all? Having to take down the Christmas decorations, which were still up in the Lounge/Diner! The tree was certainly a bald, sorry mess by the time she'd stripped it and put everything away.

'Right then, young man – I think it's time to get you home before your tummy bursts! How many slices of birthday cake did you have?' teased Barry, ruffling Nicky's hair.

'Aww, I don't want to go home. I like it here at Gramma's new house. The new carpet is so bouncy, and I want to stay and play with Becca and Lou-Lou.' Nicky pouted, then playfully ran away to hide.

'Sorry, mister,' laughed Sally-Ann, 'but the girls have got to go home, too. You've all got school tomorrow. C'mon, time to get our coats on.'

A chorus of reluctant 'Awws' came from the kids as they dragged their heels and headed into the hallway to get their coats, shepherded by their respective parents.

'You can come again at the weekend,' said an exhausted Dennis. As much as he loved having his grandchildren come to visit, this evening had been a full-on sugar high of cakes, fizzy drinks, and excitement for them.

Barry grabbed a Wrangler jacket from off the coat hooks, only to realise that he'd picked up Mick's instead of his own by mistake. Apart from it being one size too small, he inadvertently pulled out a packet of condoms from the breast pocket when he went to get out his car keys.

His eyes widened in merriment.

'Hoho! And how long has this been going on?' he chuckled.

A blush rose to Mick's face as he made a grab for the condom packet, and was about to splutter some excuse, when Barry continued the teasing.

'Look at this,' he winked. 'Our Barry has *finally* got a girlfriend! And being sensible about it...'

'A girlfriend! Really? Since when?' chimed in Irene, happy that her youngest son had started seeing someone.

While the family was giving Mick a congratulatory slap on the back for his amorous subterfuge, Sally-Ann noticed that Claire also had a slight blush to her cheeks while animatedly trying to button up Nick's coat, thus avoiding making eye contact with anyone. Sally-Ann smiled to herself. Was she misreading the signs? Had something been going on between Mick and Claire while he'd been staying there? Surely not, after all that had happened in the past. Maybe old wounds were being touched on, giving Claire the guilty flush?

Kenny broke into her train of thought as he ushered his family towards the door.

'Bloody 'ell, it's pitch dark out 'ere. You want to be careful you don't fall over and hurt yourselves, especially at your ages...' he teased his parents.

Irene rolled her eyes and lunged to give him a play-slap.

'Cheeky bugger! Aye, that's one thing that the electricians forgot to do – they didn't put up any new outside lights. It needs one by the front door, and one over the kitchen door. They put in all the wiring and the switches, just not the light fittings.'

'Tell you what, Mam,' chipped in Mick. 'Why don't you choose summat from the Argos catalogue, and then I can go into Chesterfield on Saturday and pick up a couple of lights for you?'

'And I can come and fit them for you, no problem. Teamwork, eh!' added Barry.

'Well, I guess that makes me redundant,' laughed Dennis. 'I'll just drink tea and supervise, then!'

As Barry put on his own Wrangler, he stole a look at Mick and Claire. Based on the evidence of the used and knotted condoms which he'd recently found at the bottom of the bathroom waste bin, and the pack of condoms which had just "fallen" out of Mick's jacket pocket, all things pointed to an affair. And to top it all off, he'd found a pregnancy test kit in the dustbin. That said, Mick *could* have been bringing a girl back while they were out, but his gut instinct somehow told him otherwise. Should he just watch and wait, and let fate take its course? Or should he intervene? He gritted his teeth.

It felt like one more kick in his useless balls.

But it was a kick that motivated malicious thoughts.

After going out to the garage with Kenny to see which tools he would need to fit the lights, a plan began to formulate in his mind...

55: Hammer to Fall

Grateful for having been allowed to stay at Barry and Claire's while the repairs were being carried out at his parents' house, Mick wanted to buy them both something nice as a thank-you. Plus, it would be Claire's birthday next week, so he decided to kill two birds with one stone and pop into Chesterfield. That was the nice thing about half-day closing on Wednesdays; it broke up the working week and gave him a little free time, rather than having to cram everything into the weekend.

His brother had been talking about updating the CD player for the stack system, so that seemed like the ideal gift. And perhaps a disc or two for Claire, for her birthday. He mentally tried to remember which bands were her current favourites.

Inspired by the thoughts of music, Mick decided to put on some sounds. While trying to drive one-handed and keep an eye on the road, he rummaged in the centre console, selecting Queen's *The Works*. He slipped it into the CD player and cranked up the volume, before heading down the A632 of Colliery Hill, towards town.

As he drummed along to *Radio Ga Ga* on the steering wheel, the sudden sight of a dog running out into the road instinctively caused

Mick to swerve and pump the brakes. He pulled sharply to one side as he endeavoured to manoeuvre the car out of harm's way. Like many people, he often found himself driving on autopilot, wondering how one absently got from A-B. But with the February weather being so shitty and visibility reduced by the sleet, Mick was grateful for having stayed focused; otherwise, he could have hit and injured the dog! His heart hammered with relief at the near miss.

Yet it was this focused state of mind that told him something was not right with his vehicle. As the car veered to one side, he became aware that the steering had become lighter and wasn't going in the direction he wanted. Mick fought with the car, stamping on the brakes to try and regain control, but the car lost traction and hurtled towards the kerb and bus shelter on the opposite side of the road. As the passenger side front wheel connected with the solid objects, the impact served to flip the car into the air, arcing over into a series of rolls –

One...

Two...

Three.

The Mexico landed on its side, with a now-unconscious Mick at the helm; his head having been smashed from side to side with each subsequent roll and impact. Sliding uncontrollably along the road on the driver's side, the car hurtled to a bone-crunching stop into the small crowd of strikers and policemen on the picket line of the colliery, the front-liners bearing the brunt of the collision.

For a brief moment, the world stopped until the dust had settled, barring a sharp whistling sound filling the ears of those gathered.

The screams of men began rising through the eerie silence of the aftermath.

Men screaming in pain, their bodies shattered.

Men screaming for their nearby buddy to check whether they were still alive.

And some men were silenced, their voices no longer to be heard by their families.

'Do you mind if I close the window? I'm all for a bit of fresh air, but it's getting a tad chilly in here.'

Without waiting for her office colleague to reply, Irene walked over to the panoramic office windows to close the top opener. She stood for a moment, idly fussing with one of the plants on the ledge before looking out across the car park towards the colliery gates. The winter sky hung heavy; a dark indigo hue, punctuated by sinister, battle-grey clouds, each one laden with unshed sleet.

'Look at those poor men out there in all this bad weather. That's dedication to the cause, eh? Stood out in the cold and wet. I'll be glad when this strike's over. Shall I put the kettle on?'

As she busied herself in the little kitchenette, a series of distant dull thuds caused her to look upwards. She stopped what she was doing to focus on the noise.

'Did you hear that? It sounded like a rumble of thunder. I hope we're not in for a storm.' Irene began counting under her breath, waiting for a flash of lightning, but nothing came. Realising her mistake, she rolled her eyes and shook her head. 'Silly me! It's lightning first, *then* the thunder... Maybe it was an empty lorry, or something?'

Now equally curious, her colleague went over to the window to take a look.

'It was something on the picket line, by the look of things. I can see the men running towards the gates.'

Irene came over to the window to join her colleague. She hopped from foot to foot, straining to get a better view.

'Well, whatever's happened, it must be something big. Men are running in all directions,' she said, her curiosity piqued.

Another of Irene's work colleagues came and stood with them to see what all the commotion was about, particularly now that sirens could be heard screaming down Colliery Hill, their growing intensity indicating that they were getting closer.

'Ooh, I wonder if something's happened on the picket line? Maybe it's a clash between the police and pickets again. Isn't it time for a shift change? Perhaps the, ahem, scabs are trying to cross the lines?'

'Nah, this seems a bit more than a picket-line skirmish. The local fire brigade and a police car have just arrived. Look...'

'I can hear sirens coming from the other direction, too. I bet that's the ambulance coming from the hospital.'

The three women turned around sharply, each giving a small shriek as the office door burst open, followed by the breathless entrance of two men, one of whom Irene recognised as her neighbour from over the road. His face was ashen with shock, his eyes wide.

'It's... It's your lad,' he gasped. 'The one with the yellow car. There's been an accident, Irene... The men... The men are badly injured.'

The two men reached Irene just in time to catch her by the arms as she collapsed, her knees buckling from under her. They eased her down into a nearby chair.

'Michael? Michael has a yellow car. Is he okay? Is he injured?'

'We can't tell at the moment, lass. The firemen are on the scene now. But his car hit a lot of the men. It's carnage out there...'

Irene screamed as her shaking hand shot to her mouth.

Barry was also out there...

'Fuuuuck! Noooo!'

When her pregnancy suspicions had been aroused, Claire's mind had gone into overdrive. Although it had been almost seven years since she'd last experienced these symptoms – the queasy stomach, tender breasts, and missed period, a woman never forgets – she instinctively knows.

The blue colour on the *Colorstick Pregnancy Test* confirmed all she needed to know. She looked heavenwards, then closed her eyes and breathed deeply while she processed the information. Just to be on the safe side, she had bought two test kits. The first one had shown positive when her period was newly overdue. Yet somehow she was hoping for a different result today. An involuntary scream escaped as she flung the test across the bathroom.

She knew exactly when and who. And it wasn't Barry. What was that about lightning never striking twice in the same place? Argh! They thought they had been so careful.

Karma – it was fuckin' Karma!

To avoid any local gossip or nosy guesswork, she had even gone into Chesterfield to get the pregnancy test kits rather than use the local chemist in Castle Ridge. And at that, she'd gone to the little out-of-the-way chemist of Dent's down on Saltergate, rather than Boots in the town centre. Anything to avoid being seen. Yet what did that matter now? The results were still positive. There would soon be enough gossip once it started to show. Plus, there would be a shitload of family conflict.

She and Mick would be outcasts.

Her tormented mind began to picture scenario after scenario as to how this would all unfold; none of them good. Could she even take the ultimate step of telling *no one* about the pregnancy and going for a termination – the secret being hers alone?

Claire unconsciously fiddled with her wedding ring, the symbol of eternal love. Of love that was unbroken and whole.

With her head devoid of solutions, she reluctantly picked up the pregnancy test stick and headed downstairs to bury it in the dustbin alongside the other one, well out of sight.

As she reached the bottom step, the ringing of the telephone jarred her back to the present moment. Who could be ringing at this time of day? Maybe it was Barry checking up on her? After all, he knew that she hadn't gone into work today because she'd been feeling unwell.

She reluctantly picked up the phone, ready to fake sounding ill.

It wasn't Barry. It was Irene. A very distraught Irene, who was struggling to speak between choking sobs.

'Oh, God, Claire. There's been an accident! I tried to call you at work, but they said you were at home, sick. It's the boys. Here at work. Mick... His car went off the road. And the miners, the picket line... Oh, God, it's carnage. Barry's out there, too. I don't know if my boys are alive. They won't tell me anything...'

Claire's knees buckled as she took in the news from her mother-in-law, almost dropping the phone.

A car accident? Mick? How? What had this got to do with the picket line? Barry!

Her mind raced as she sat on the floor, looking at the telephone receiver in disbelief. She could just hear Irene's voice faintly calling her name.

'Claire? Claire? Are you still there?'

'Y...Yes, I'm still here. What happened, exactly? An accident, you say?'

She could hear Irene blowing her nose before she spoke.

'From what they can tell, our Mick's car must have lost control near the bottom of Colliery Hill and flipped over a few times. But the car skidded into all the men on the picket line at the gates. That's as much as they'll tell me about the accident itself.'

Claire's stomach lurched as she heard the news, and her hand shot to her mouth, much like Irene when she was initially told by the first responders.

'Luckily, there were a couple of St. John's lads on hand to help until all the emergency services got there. They set up a triage so that they could help those most in need. The fire service is just trying to cut Mick out of the car, and there are some men trapped underneath the wreckage, but I don't know any more than that. Oh, Claire! It's terrible, just terrible.'

'What about Dennis? Does he know?' asked Claire. She could hear a cacophony of voices in the background as news of the accident had begun to spread, and families were being directed into the offices to await news. The faint sounds of sirens could be heard in the distance. Goosebumps rose on her arms, and her scalp prickled.

'Yes. I spoke to Sally-Ann, and she knew where they were working today. She managed to get in touch with them, so Den and Kenny are on their way to me now, here at the pit offices.'

'Do you want me to come to you, too?'

'No, it's okay, love. You stay there and wait for Nick to finish school. I'll call you as soon as I have any more news. Talk to you later.'

Claire set the telephone handset back in the cradle, her mind in shock and disbelief at the news Irene had just delivered. A car accident at the pit – Mick's car had crashed into the picket line, and Barry was on picket duty...

She stared at the pregnancy test on the floor beside her.

Fate was in a bitchy, vengeful mood today!

Irene disconnected her call to Claire, then wiped her eyes and nose with a handful of tissues. She looked around the offices, now thronging with those similarly affected. Since news of the accident had been relayed to the men's immediate families, they had been asked to convene at the offices. It was somewhere warm for them to wait and to support each other until more was known.

As a way of keeping busy, Irene went to help her colleagues make some pots of tea and find some biscuits, before bringing them through to the offices on a trolley.

Everyone looked up as two policemen came into the reception area, their faces grim-set, and helmets removed as a mark of respect. One held a clipboard under his arm. First-aiders and Red Cross volunteers followed behind, ready to assist.

The offices fell deathly silent until one by one, heart-rending sobs tore through the air as the news was delivered to all those waiting for word of their loved ones.

Some received more tragic news than others.

Irene included.

Sally-Ann took a few moments to absorb Irene's news about the accident before calling Kenny at the job site where he and Dennis were working.

This was bad.

Really bad.

The next number that she dialled was her dad.

And the number after that was to Alan, one of her brothers.

She asked them both the same question –

'Did you do anything to Mick's car?'

Even when people are incarcerated, the underworld has its own line of communication, and messages can be exchanged in and out when the need arises.

Alistair smiled when he received his most recent message.

56: A Town in Mourning

The depressing greyness of February had eased into March, with Castle Ridge still under a cloud of mourning. The mood of the congregation in St Mary's Parish Church was subdued, as two more of the town's young men were laid to rest. The only sounds punctuating the solemn silence were those of Irene's uncontrollable sobbing, snuffled coughs, and the shuffle of feet on the stone floor.

As the local vicar delivered the sermon, and eulogies were given in honour of Barry and Michael, family and friends listened and remembered them. Some had heads hung low, some stared towards the two coffins at the front, their eyes drained of emotion, while others gazed at the stained glass windows, taking solace in the ornately crafted images.

Sadly, it was a scene that had been repeated a few times over the past week, with four other men having lost their lives in the accident. At least seven others had been injured, two of whom seriously, and were still in the hospital. The lucky ones had sustained nothing more than a few bumps and bruises as they'd been quicker to react and move out of the way, perhaps dragging a colleague to safety with them.

Ironically, the miners' strike had been called off just the day before the funeral; almost a year to the day after the long and bitter fight had begun, and work was resuming today. As a token symbol to the heroes of the fight, carnations were being handed out to the men as they entered the gates to Castle Ridge colliery by the wives who had supported them. A wreath of carnations was also laid at the crash site to honour the memory of those who wouldn't be returning, and one was sent to be laid on Barry's coffin.

Now that the church service and interment were over, the distraught Watkins family, together with their in-law families and grandchildren, were joined by the other mourners for a wake at the Sports Bar and Grill.

A finger buffet had been set out in the upstairs reception room, allowing people to eat and mingle as they felt able, all ensuring that they spent some time talking with Dennis, Irene, Kenny, and Claire.

Kenny came and sat beside his mother, bringing her a fresh cup of tea and a few sandwiches. He gave her a wan smile and held her hand.

'Here, you should try to eat summat. What a day, eh?' he said, leaning back in his chair and exhaling deeply.

'I know. It just doesn't seem the right order of things. It should be you young 'uns burying us oldies. We should be the first to go,' snuffled Irene.

'Aye. But I guess that's the problem with accidents. There's no age discrimination. Talking of accidents, is there any news from the police investigation? Did they find owt wrong with the car, or connect owt to the road conditions?' he asked, toying with a sandwich, his own appetite equally lacking.

Irene shook her head.

'The police forensics team was hoping to get a report out this week. They've been going over the wreckage with a fine-toothed comb. I'm just grateful that the toxicology report on Mick came back clear. At least I know he wasn't to blame in any way. I can sleep a bit easier knowing that.'

Dennis came and sat with them after chatting with Claire and her mother.

'How's Claire holding up?' Irene asked. 'She looks pale. Uff – to think the poor girl should have been celebrating her birthday with her family last week, and instead she was helping to organise funeral arrangements. Where's the justice, eh!'

'Her mum's taking good care of her and Nicky,' acknowledged Dennis. 'She's going to take 'em both to Whitby for the weekend, and book into a hotel. The sea air will do 'em good.'

'D'you know, that's not such a bad idea, Den. Maybe we should book a little break somewhere? I think it'll do us good to get away after all that we've been through.' Irene was momentarily interrupted while someone came to pay their condolences.

Dennis looked at her, his eyes tired, and his demeanour exhausted.

'Aye, I couldn't agree more, lass.' He took hold of her hand and kissed it. 'I think we've more than earned a little holiday. It'll give us summat to look forward to.'

Irene grimaced as she took a sip of her now-cold tea and pushed the cup away.

'Why us, eh? What have we done to deserve all this? Life just isn't fair...'

They looked at each other with a shared understanding of the grief they were both experiencing.

Seeing Claire walking towards them, Kenny stood up to give her a perfunctory hug and offered her his seat. He kissed his mother on the top of the head and gave his father's shoulder a gentle squeeze.

'I'd better go and check in with Sally-Ann and her lot. I'll see you later, eh.'

'Aye, see ya later, Ken. You're a good lad,' said Dennis, trying his best to be stoic.

Claire hugged her in-laws before sitting down, prompting Irene to take hold of her hand. It somehow felt symbolic; a way of uniting her with Barry.

'Dennis was just telling me that you're going away with your mum for a few days. It's such a great idea. We've decided to do the same thing, too. My God, we need a rest after all this. We need something to look forward to...'

'I couldn't agree more. It'll be good to get a bit of sea air.' Claire paused, then blushed a little, knowing what she was going to say next. 'I know this is neither the time nor the place, but, well, I just needed to share a bit of good news with you both...'

Irene's brows furrowed together in puzzlement, almost as if good news couldn't exist in her world at the present moment.

Claire continued her explanation, keeping her voice low so that others couldn't hear.

'I'm pregnant. And before you ask, yes, the baby's Mick's.'

Dennis and Irene stared at her, stunned and speechless.

'It's not what you think, though,' she added. 'It was done to give Nicky a blood sibling.'

With her mind still in disarray at the news she'd just been given, Irene looked at Claire, unconvinced.

'Really? After all the heartache that it caused last time?' she asked, her tone terse and sceptical.

Having rehearsed this conversation in her mind, Claire gave a prepared and feasible explanation.

'We did it in a non-sexual way,' she lied, knowing there was no one alive to dispute otherwise. 'We didn't want to say anything until we knew for sure, but then, well, fate intervened, and took them from us. They never knew that they were going to be "dads".'

Her in-laws remained silent, both still unsure of what to say.

'Well, I'm lost for words, Claire. That's quite some news,' said Dennis, after uncomfortable moments of wary hesitation.

'It certainly is,' concurred Irene, still feeling overwhelmed by this unexpected news, and today, of all days...

Claire sighed inwardly, relieved that the pregnancy news had gone as well as expected, given the circumstances. After all, the explanation did sound logical.

'I haven't told Nick or anyone else yet. You're the first to know. I was going to wait until after my first doctor's appointment before I announced it, but I felt like we needed something positive today. I haven't even told my mum, so can you keep it to yourselves for now?' she asked.

'Of course. How far along are you?' asked Irene, her maternal instincts slowly warming to the idea that another little piece of Mick will live on.

'It's still early days – about six weeks, something like that,' said Claire, laying her hand gently across her stomach.

'Well, your secret's safe with us, Claire,' whispered Dennis, just as Nick came across and jumped onto his grandad's knee.

As the wake started coming to a close, people began to come over and shake their hands goodbye. Irene perceptively noticed that neither Sally-Ann nor members of her family had been very noticeable at the gathering, but had rather kept themselves to themselves. It almost felt as though the Clarkes were closing ranks. Maybe being at a funeral for young people had touched a raw nerve with them, particularly as it was something they too had sadly experienced.

Strange how people react around death. Sally-Ann was usually one of the first to roll up her sleeves and help out with any kind of situation. That said, she had been busy with three grouchy kids who'd had to endure a cold church and a long service. At least she'd had the good sense not to take them up to the cemetery for the interments. But the Clarkes were all courteous enough to come and say goodbye to Irene, Dennis, and Claire, and once again offer their condolences.

As Kenny, Sally-Ann, and the Clarke family exited the function room, the noise and chatter of them leaving caused the two plain-clothes detectives in the Bar-Lounge area to glance over at them. Calculating that they must be some of the last people to leave, one surreptitiously nodded to make a move.

The detectives stood up and headed in their direction. As the family group walked past them, the officers stopped and bowed their heads out of courtesy and gave a solemn nod of condolence.

On entering the function room, the officers could see that Dennis, Irene, and Claire were saying goodbye to the stragglers, so they politely waited to one side, hands clasped in front of them.

Once it was clear to go and speak to the Watkins', they went over to introduce themselves and offer their deepest sympathy.

Puzzled and flustered as to why the police would be in attendance at a funeral wake, Irene was curt and sharp with them.

'I've just buried two of my sons! Couldn't this have waited?' she hissed.

'That's why we're here, Mrs Watkins.' The detective's voice was calm and soothing, much like a doctor's "bedside manner" voice. 'We have some news about the accident for the three of you. Yes, sorry, it's probably not the most appropriate place, but here we are. Can we go and sit down?' He ushered them over towards the corner where some comfy armchairs were located.

Once seated, the other detective took up the thread.

'As you know from the traffic report, there was nothing to suggest that Michael lost control because of the road conditions. Yes, it was sleeting, but the roads weren't icy, and his tyres were in good condition. Anyway, we now have the forensic results back from the detailed investigation on Michael's car. It would appear that he lost control due to a mechanical failure.'

'But how can that be?' asked Dennis, his eyebrows raised in surprise. 'Our Mick always took good care of his car. It was always clean and well-maintained.'

'Well, that's the thing. The investigator could see that the car had been well-maintained, which is why these flaws rang alarm bells. It appears that a couple of wheel nuts had been cracked loose on the front driver's side, plus some bolts on the steering arm and track-rod, causing the vehicle to lose control. And with devastating consequences.'

The three Watkins sat in stunned silence while they absorbed the explanatory news.

Dennis looked puzzled.

'But wouldn't that mean sabotage? That someone had deliberately done this to Mick's car?' he asked.

The detectives both nodded their heads sagely in acknowledgement.

'Sadly, yes,' concurred the detective who had just been explaining the defects to the car.

Irene closed her eyes, squeezing out the tears that had been building up. She took hold of Dennis's hand, quelling the urge to scream.

'I know Mick had made some enemies in his time, but who could have such a life-threatening grudge? To play with someone's life? And not only that, risk the lives of others. Who could do such a thing?'

In her mind's eye, she pictured Alistair's two henchmen – those two had no scruples when it came to revenge.

The detectives looked at each other, knowing that they were about to deliver the final blow. The most senior of the two spoke up.

'As you said, Michael took care of his car and always kept it clean. This meant that our investigators were able to lift some clear prints off the front wing, plus a clear handprint and fingerprints from the front bumper. We're sorry to say that the prints belonged to Barry, the other son, whom you lost in the accident.'

The detective looked at Claire apologetically, knowing that it had been her husband, Mick's own brother, who had, in all likelihood, caused the tragic accident.

For a few brief moments, time stood still, save for the muffled bustle in the background of the staff clearing away the tables and going in and out of the kitchen.

As the officer's words sank in, Irene let out a howling guttural sob and screamed heavenwards.

'Noooo! It cannot be...'

Dennis stared at the two detectives, shocked into silence. He reached for Irene and held her in his arms in a bid to console her.

Claire broke the silence first, her voice small and fragile.

'But why? Why would Barry do this to his own brother?'

Her mind raced for answers. Had Barry found out about her and Mick sleeping together? Did he know or suspect that she was pregnant? Would Barry really have gone this far? She put her hand to her stomach, an involuntary wave of guilt making her feel queasy.

'Well, you tell us. Any information would be helpful.' The detective looked at her pointedly, almost as though he was trying to scare an answer out of her.

She took a deep breath before replying, knowing that she would need to give some kind of plausible reason why. But exactly how much should she reveal?

'My little boy is actually Mick's biological son. We had a one-time-only drunken fling, which resulted in me getting pregnant. However, it never even occurred to me that it was Mick's baby. Anyway, a few years later, Barry and I decided to go for some fertility testing. That's when his infertility came to light, and we discovered that Nick wasn't his kid, but Mick's. It caused a hell of a rumpus...'

The two detectives were listening, wide-eyed, to the story that was unfolding about the two brothers.

'I can well imagine,' said the senior detective. 'And was there still any friction between them? Anything that could have pushed Barry to do something like this?'

Claire cleared her throat before continuing. Here's where she needed to keep the facts hidden and remember the story she'd created around this latest pregnancy.

'After the recent house fire at Dennis and Irene's, Mick came to stay with us for a few weeks. For some reason, the three of us agreed that it would be good for Nick to have a biological sibling and not be an only child. We'd always wanted another baby, so... So, we...' she blushed slightly, as she tried to describe the "conception process". 'We used a non-sexual method to try and get me pregnant. With one of those turkey-baster things to, you know, shoot his stuff up inside of me a few times.' Claire wanted to crawl under the chair and die of embarrassment.

One of the detectives made a point of jotting down notes as Claire spoke, adding to her nervousness. She noticed that Irene and Dennis were blushing at the "non-sexual" conception.

She gave a weak smile, then sighed before continuing, as if fishing for sympathy.

'But the sad irony is, I've just found out that I'm pregnant, and neither Barry nor Mick ever got to know. They won't get to meet Nicky's sibling.' She wiped away the few tears that had now conveniently formed.

'Well, that's quite a story!' exclaimed the senior of the two detectives. 'So, do you think there could have been some kind of brotherly jealousy behind his act of sabotage? A random moment of madness?'

Claire suspected that the detectives didn't seem convinced by her explanation. She needed to give the story more foundation.

'When we found out about Nicky's true paternity, Barry smashed up Mick's Capri with a cricket bat in a pique of anger. So yes, maybe something had flipped in Barry's mind. Maybe he regretted what we'd started. I don't know. I guess we'll never know the real reason.'

Irene winced as she recalled the day when Barry went on the rampage and totally destroyed Mick's car. It was the catalyst for all that was to follow.

'But when could he have sabotaged Mick's car this time around?' she asked. 'Unless... Oh, no! He must have done it when he came to fit the outside lights that evening. He borrowed some of your tools out of the garage, remember?'

Irene looked at Den, her heart broken by the thought of Barry's calculated plans for revenge. If only he had stopped to think about the potential consequences, which had been all too sadly realised.

Dennis rubbed his face with both hands and wiped away the tears that were beginning to spill over.

'So what happens now?' he asked, looking at the two detectives.

'A formal report will be issued, based on accidental death; in essence, nothing can be proven, even though that's what the evidence *suggests*. We've bagged up all of Michael's belongings, and they can be collected and signed for down at the station on Beetwell Street.'

'And the car?'

'We'll just send it to be crushed, if that's what you want?'

Dennis nodded his approval.

'I never want to see that car again...' And with that, he broke down in tears, sobbing uncontrollably. Irene and Claire both went to his side, their own emotions also getting the better of them.

The two detectives stood up, ready to leave. Irene nodded towards them and mouthed a silent *thank-you* while she consoled Dennis. They reciprocated with a polite smile and a small finger salute to the forehead.

Claire also gave them a wan smile of thanks, grateful in the knowledge that only she alone knew the real story behind the child's conception; there was no one alive who could prove otherwise.

57: The Final Dominoes Fall

In the wake of the recent tragedy, the family had agreed to come together and support each other, particularly as today would be Irene's first Mother's Day without two of her boys. Not only would it help keep her busy, but they could all mourn the day together.

The three Watkins women were in the kitchen, standing around a pot of home-made chicken stew, stirring, tasting, and adding some dumplings when Dennis and Kenny came in, the grandchildren hot on their heels. Their arms were laden with Mother's Day gifts and bunches of roses.

Kenny couldn't help but laugh when he saw them huddled together over the stew pot.

'My God, "Double, double toil and trouble" – it's the three witches from Macbeth! Does the stew have an "eye of newt, and toe of frog"?'

'No, just "wool of bat and tongue of dog", you cheeky git,' replied Sally-Ann dryly.

'Wow! Somebody knows their Shakespeare,' teased Claire.

'Ah, it's just 'cos my class had some project to do in English when I was at school,' Kenny explained. 'We had to split into groups, and each group was given a well-known scene from one of Shakespeare's plays and had to act it out. I was one of the witches. It was a lot of fun, actually.'

Sally-Ann looked at him, her face bearing a puzzled look.

'Where's Josephine?'

Kenny's eyes fell open wide with shock.

'Josephine? Shit! I left her out on the Castle Parks...' he teased, but seeing the genuine look of worry on his wife's face caused him to quickly retract his statement. 'She's fast asleep, so we left her outside in her pram.'

Sally-Ann flicked the tea-towel at him in response, catching him on the forearm as it cracked sharply.

'Ouch!'

'Serves you right,' she laughed.

'How was your walk? Did you all have a good time?' asked Irene, trying her best to be cheerful, as she put the lid onto the stew pot.

'It was really good,' said Becca. 'We played lots of chase games, and now I'm so hungry!' she complained.

'Well, lunch is almost ready, we've just got to wait for the dumplings to fluff up. Why don't you go and wash your hands while you're waiting?'

'Ah, but first, you lovely ladies,' said Dennis, 'Happy Mother's Day. We know it's not easy for you, but, well...' He looked into his wife's eyes and gave her a compassionate hug.

The grandchildren joined in wishing them a Happy Mother's Day before they gave them the roses, gifts, and kisses.

While Irene took the children upstairs to wash their hands before lunch, Claire and Sally-Ann went through to the dining area to start laying the table. Claire noticed that her friend was looking at her, her eyes downcast and down in the mouth.

'Is everything okay, Sal?' she enquired.

'It's just, well... I owe you a big apology. I never said how sorry I was when you lost Barry. You must have been devastated, and I feel like I wasn't there for you when you needed someone.'

Claire stopped what she was doing and looked at Sally-Ann, eye-to-eye.

'It's been a rough few weeks,' admitted Claire. 'And yes, I noticed that both you and Kenny seem to have been a little bit cold towards me recently. It feels like I've lost my best friend...'

This last comment jarred Sally-Ann and caused a blush to rise.

'Sorry! But, well, you know how I felt about Mick,' she replied, lowering her voice so that only the two of them could hear. 'I still think he was responsible for the burglary at our house, and the death of our Alan's little 'un. To be honest, the rest of my family feels the same way. We're still convinced that the hidden stash of booze was from one of Mick's burglaries. Maybe that's why we couldn't grieve with you at the funerals. It was tough for us, too.'

'Yeah, I can understand that,' Claire said, her voice equally hushed. 'Mick certainly did ruffle a lot of feathers with those around him.'

'I have to confess something else to you as well.' Sally-Ann held her eyes downcast, the feeling of guilt too strong. 'Don't hate me for saying this – but I even asked my dad and our Alan whether they had anything to do with the damage to Mick's car. That's just how much I know they hated him.'

Claire blinked at her friend in disbelief, her eyebrows raised in shock.

'Seriously! Wow! That said, I was similarly shocked when we found out that it was Barry who had sabotaged the Mexico. Or, at least, that's what the police are assuming. His fingerprints were all over the front of it.'

'But how do they know they were Barry's prints?' asked Sally-Ann, putting the soup bowls in place around the table.

'His fingerprints are in the police database from when he was arrested on the picket line, that day when the flying pickets came up to Castle Ridge Colliery.'

'Ahh, yes. But why would Bar...'

Their low-voiced chat was interrupted by Irene and the kids returning with clean hands, just as Dennis came through from the kitchen with the pot of stew and some bread rolls. Kenny followed behind with the now-awake Josephine.

'Perfect timing!' said Sally-Ann, realising that it was time to change the topic of conversation. 'The table's all ready – and I'm starving hungry. Who else is hungry?' she teased, her voice drowned out by a chorus of *me!*

After everyone had finished their lunch of chicken stew, followed by the now traditional dessert of Arctic Roll, Claire prompted Nicky to go and get her handbag, as they had something special for Granny.

Happy to oblige, he retrieved the handbag and, with his mother's permission, took out the beautifully wrapped gift to give to Irene.

'Happy big birthday, Granny!' trilled Nicky. 'These are some dragon tears for you,' he laughed.

'Dragon tears? I didn't know dragons could cry! Well now, I'm really curious...'

Irene carefully unwrapped the package to reveal a beautiful set of teardrop earrings and a matching pendant in glossy black Whitby Jet. Her eyes sparkled with joy.

'Nick chose them for you while we were away in Whitby with my mum last weekend,' said Claire.

Irene gave Nick a huge hug and kiss on the forehead, prompting him to wriggle away from all the kissy-stuff.

'Well, I think you've got very good taste, young man! Thank you, they're beautiful. I'll treasure them, always.'

'You're welcome, Granny. Can we go upstairs and play with the toys in the spare room now?' he asked, now bored with the grown-ups.

Irene gave his hand a little squeeze.

'Of course you can, my love. But don't go into Uncle Mick's old room. Just the spare room...'

'Okie dokie.' He gave her his best boyish grin, then shot off upstairs with Becca and Lou-Lou stomping eagerly behind him.

Once the grandchildren were out of earshot, Irene looked around at the remainder of her family, her eyes wet with brewing tears.

'I still don't have the heart to go into Mick's bedroom and sort out his things. It just feels too soon. Maybe once we get back from holiday...'

'Same here,' said Claire. 'I'm nowhere near ready to move on, either. I can still smell Barry on his clothes. It gives me a strange kind of comfort.'

An uncomfortable silence enveloped the family as their thoughts drifted off towards Barry and Mick.

Realising that the conversation had taken a maudlin turn, Irene tried to lift the mood with a dose of over-acted cheerfulness.

'My goodness, I can't believe that I'll be fifty next week!'

'And off to the city of love, eh! Paris in springtime...' Kenny gave her a nudge and a wink. 'Talking of which, what time do you want me to take you guys to Manchester tomorrow, to the airport?'

'Anytime around nine, something like that,' confirmed Dennis. He paused and took a breath, his face clouding over with sadness. 'It will certainly be a welcome break after all that we've been through, eh, lass.' He took Irene's hand and squeezed it.

'That it will,' she concurred. 'We need a bit of positivity. Talking of positivity, you have some good news to announce, don't you, Claire?'

Claire blanched and froze at having been put on the spot by Irene.

'Erm, yes... News. I'm er, I'm pregnant. I'm having a baby,' she stammered, knowing full well that there would be an immediate inquisition by Kenny and Sally-Ann.

They both looked at her; Sally-Ann's face was a picture of speechless shock, while Kenny remained passive and difficult to read.

'And yes, before you ask,' continued Claire, 'the baby is Mick's – just as is Nicky. But this was done with Barry's blessing. He wanted Nick to have a sibling – a blood sibling.' A flush of colour rose to her cheeks as she endeavoured to describe the process. 'I can see what you're thinking. We used a non-sexual method to conceive.' She was almost beginning to believe the story herself, covering up the lie of her short but passionate affair with Mick while Barry was out of the house.

'Wow, that is big news! Well, congratulations,' said Sally-Ann, not quite sure what else to say. 'And how does Nick feel about being a big brother? Have you told him yet?'

'Yes, he knows a baby is growing in his mummy's tummy, and he seems happy and excited. It's just a shame that neither Barry nor Mick knew about the baby before the accident, but at least they're leaving a legacy for the future.'

Kenny narrowed his eyes, his face disbelieving. He began clapping sarcastically.

'And the award for Best Actress goes to... Claire Watkins! Legacy – don't make me laugh!' he snorted. 'Actually, Barry suspected that you were pregnant with Mick's kid.'

Seeing the aghast, speechless reactions of Claire and the family, he continued his tirade. They needed to hear the truth, not Claire's airy-fairy "story".

'Wha... What are you talking about?' she stammered, unsure whether or not she'd heard right.

'Baz knew. He found some used condoms in the bathroom bin. And he found one of those pregnancy sticks showing "positive". It doesn't take much of a genius to put two and two together. You and Mick were at it behind his back, weren't you! There was never any "sibling agreement".'

The dining room now fell silent, all eyes on Claire. She could feel her heart hammering in her chest and the heat rising in her face.

'But how do you know? When did he tell you all this?' Claire's mind was racing, shocked at having been found out.

'The night we all came here for Nick's birthday party and Valentine's. That's when Baz told me. He deliberately planted that packet of condoms in Mick's Wrangler pocket. That way, he could make them fall out when he put on the wrong jacket "by mistake". He was watching for your reactions. Then, when Baz agreed to put up the outside lights for Mum, I went out to the garage with him to see what tools he would need to do the job. That's when he told me about his suspicions. He wondered if you'd said owt to Sally-Ann – any hint of what was going on. He was well pissed off!'

Kenny banged on the table for emphasis, making everyone jump, though no one dared to interrupt. He pointed a finger at Claire.

'You broke that man's heart not once, but twice! *You* made him go to those lengths!' His voice began to crack with emotion. 'I admit I was just as shocked as anyone else when the police report came through. I would have taken a guess at Alistair and his cronies, not Barry. That just goes to show how hurt and angry he was...'

'But why did you keep this to yourself, Ken?' Sally-Ann asked. 'This is a *BIG* secret to keep, all things considered...'

'Because he asked me to keep quiet. That he would deal with the matter when the time was right. He must have tampered with the car when he came to fit the lights. Ideal opportunity. Besides, I was curious to see how fate would play this one out – what kind of truth it would reveal.' Kenny glowered at Claire, making her shrink back into her chair. 'And it revealed a conniving liar!'

Irene looked at her daughter-in-law, her eyes full of tears. She could barely speak, her voice just a shocked whisper.

'Is this true, Claire? Is this how the baby really happened? Was it worth it to mess with the lives of two of my sons? And now I've lost them both.' She broke down in tears.

Dennis put his arms around his wife in a bid to offer her some comfort and solace while she cried without control into his chest. He glared at Claire, his face hard.

'I think you'd better leave. You've caused more than enough heartache for this family, with all your shenanigans.'

'But… But Mick and I… Barry, we…'

'You heard Dad,' snarled Kenny. 'Just go! And take your bastard cuckoos wi'ya!'

Claire stood up to leave. Her legs felt weak, making walking difficult. As she left the room to go and get Nicky, she could hear everyone sobbing around the dining table, even Kenny.

She was now persona non grata in the eyes of the Watkins.

During the drive home, she did her best not to cry, so as not to alert Nick that there was anything wrong. He'd accepted his mother's explanation that she didn't feel too well, and that's why they were leaving the family gathering early.

Her mind jumped around with all the accusations that had been flung her way this evening.

So Barry knew!

Or, at least, he had made assumptions and come up with the correct result. But why hadn't he said anything? He hadn't shown any ill will towards either of them in the days preceding the accident. Was he just trying to get Mick out of their lives once and for all? These were all questions to which she would never have the answers.

And now here she was, pregnant, and an outcast from the Watkins clan. She was pretty sure that this would also include Sally-Ann, someone with whom she had been friends since infant school.

Her mind made a warped family connection – just like the McCormicks, Nick's true paternal bloodline – she'd gambled and lost everything.

She looked in the rearview mirror to take a look at her son, her eyes barely able to focus. He saw her reflection and gave her a big smile, then yawned.

'I love you, Mam. Are we nearly home yet...?'

'I love you, too. Yes, almost. We're just going past the old-age home and allotment gardens. Won't be long.'

Nicky's hand suddenly shot to his mouth as he started to heave.

'I think I ate too much, I... I feel sick...'

'Hang on! Hang on! We're nearly there! Try not to be sick in the car.'

She sped up a little, whilst rummaging in her handbag on the passenger seat for some tissues, hoping to try and make it home before Nick threw up.

With her eyes momentarily off the road and her mind distracted from driving, Claire hadn't noticed the large, slow-moving Massey Ferguson tractor with a muck-spreading tanker on the back looming ahead of them. Like a shadowy spectre, it was partially cloaked in wispy ribbons of evening spring mist, the farmer's day of work just coming to a close now that the sun had gone down.

Without enough time to either brake or take avoiding action, the grinding screech and thud of metal colliding with metal filled the air, the impact too much for the little Renault 5 against the solid tanker.

The car, which had once borne the miracle of life coming into this world, now carried its occupants towards their untimely demise.

Epilogue

'The past few weeks since the death of my daughter and grandson have been unbearable. Not only that, she took her unborn child with her. I think both myself and the Watkins family have suffered more than our fair share of tragedy this year. We can only assume that it was a tragic accident – the poor, innocent farmer was just in the wrong place at the wrong time. He's absolutely traumatised, as you can well imagine. Life can be so unfair...

The circumstances surrounding both of Claire's pregnancies, and the resulting deaths of Barry and Mick meant that none of the Watkins came to the funeral – not even to honour their little grandson being laid to rest. Yes, he might have been fathered by Mick, but the little lamb was still a Watkins at heart. He knew nothing of his true parentage or McCormick heritage. To deny Claire was to deny Nicky.

I tried to make contact with them regarding the funeral arrangements – I would have really liked for Claire and Nick to have been laid to rest with Barry and Mick. Despite everything, Barry was Claire's husband and Mick was Nick's biological father. Sadly, they absolutely refused for them to be buried together. But at least Claire and Nicky have a lovely little plot near some cherry-blossom trees.

The funeral was only a small affair. Just my closest family, and some of Claire's work colleagues. I don't know how I would have gotten through it without my brother, Ted. He's been my rock. I'm pretty sure that I saw Sally-Ann at the back of the church, and someone recently left an anonymous bouquet of flowers on their grave. I can only assume that it was Sally-Ann. Despite everything, the girls had been friends since childhood, so I hope that she has a little forgiveness in her heart.

As a young couple, I doubt that Barry and Claire had made any kind of Will. Well, when you're young, you don't think death is just around the corner, do you? So I suppose the next battle that I'll have to deal with will be the sale of Barry and Claire's house. No doubt the Watkins will want to get involved with that. But then again, I'm sure they have all the right business and legal connections, so we'll get the best advice possible.

Claire told me all about the fertility issues which she and Barry had been experiencing, which, in essence, led to the opening of Pandora's Box. It certainly brought to light the shocking discovery of Irene's infidelity. I always said that woman was "all fur coat and no knickers". She likes to put on a show of having class and wealth, but she's no better than anyone else. Dignity and respect are earned, not bought. And yet she judges Claire!

We never know what life is going to throw at us. My advice – just be honest and true. Secrets and lies very rarely stay buried.

Twists of fate will always make sure of that...'

Thanks and Acknowledgements

Thanks!

To my boys, Diddi, Róbert, and Daníel – thank you for all your love, support, and patience. It means the world to me. And thanks for giving me a mechanic's perspective on steering failure!

To Russ C – thanks for giving me the seeds of an idea for this novel. Also, for your insights into colliery life.

To Pam A – it warms my heart to know that I inspired you to start a degree course later in life. You're never too old to learn! I wish you luck with your future writing projects.

To my beta-readers – Russ C, Pam A, Kev B, and Carolyn B – with grateful thanks to you all for taking the time to read the first draft, and give me your critical feedback.

To my wonderful friend and multi-award-winning photographer, Heather Burns, of *Heather Burns Photography*. Thanks once again for creating an awesome cover for my book. Your creative talent for photographic artistry knows no bounds!

To my friend and fellow author, Matt Ferraz – many thanks for your wise words and advice, "Why use ten words when four words will do!".

To the good people of *Old Bolsover Pics* Facebook group – thank you for your information and memories in connection with Bolsover Castle, and the 1977 Silver Jubilee celebrations.

Thanks to photographer Gabriel Rutenberg for my author portrait – yes, one day I will get a new portrait done, but at least with this one I will never look any older!

And finally, to our darling Roma – Rest in Peace, sweet girl. Thank you for every day that we shared together. You will forever be in our hearts and thoughts. Sending all our love to doggie heaven xxxx.

Acknowledgements:

Shakespeare W: (1623) The Tragedie of Macbeth
Disney W: (1937) Snow White And The Seven Dwarfs
Homer: The Iliad

Paternity Testing:
https://easydna.co.uk/knowledge-base/paternity-testing-using-hla-typing-and-pcr-polymerase-chain-reaction/

Coal Not Dole (Channel 4)
https://www.youtube.com/watch?v=ZQsRQaGF02Q

1977 British Grand Prix (Summary)
https://www.youtube.com/watch?v=wL2UCGv4TFU

A small favour to ask...

Dear Reader

I hope that you enjoyed reading *Twists of Fate*.

If you have five minutes to spare, I would be extremely grateful if you would leave a small review (for example, on Goodreads or Amazon). Why? Not only is it a great way to raise the profile of indie authors like myself, but reviews also make our work feel appreciated.

Should you wish to read any of my other books, here's the QR code to take you to my website, and a selection of **PURCHASE LINKS**

Thanks for your support!

Ann Thorsson

For more information about Ann Thorsson:

Like & Follow on social media:

@ann.thorsson.author

Facebook:

https://www.facebook.com/ann.thorsson.author/

Instagram:

https://www.instagram.com/ann.thorsson.author/

Printed in Dunstable, United Kingdom

69162136R00205